The crash of the bedroom door opening caused Polydektos to jump from his dream. He sat up on one elbow and wiped the tears from his eyes as Talaemenes came rushing into his room unannounced.

"They are all dead, all of them...," the young man was shouting wildly at the top of his lungs. Then he stopped and almost fell over. He clutched at a pedestal to steady himself, but in doing so knocked the marble bust of Hypnos the God of Sleep on top of it to the floor. He just pointed, his mouth wide open in a silent scream that would not come from his airless throat. Polydektos blinked, sniffed and turned to see what the boy was pointing at. To the end of his days, he wished he hadn't.

His beautiful wife Kephissa lay next to him, but she was not whole or in the land of the living, nor sleep.

THE ATHENS ATROCITIES

BY ALEXANDER ARROWSMITH

For Tasha & Andrew

Chapter 1

Athens 432 BC

Polydektos lay on the far right of the large bed he had bought for her, watching. Sometimes, it was all he could manage at this time of night. He rubbed at his oiled pot belly, wondering when it had got so big and when he had stopped looking after himself. He was forty-six years old, he still had a good head of hair, and his arms and legs were still strong, but his once proud soldier's torso was going to seed.

His former brothers-in-arms still called him 'General' on the streets of Athens, and he always had time for his men; he was glad to share a cup, or usually a jug, of wine with them and recall the glory days. But that's all they were, glories of battles past; there were no more campaigns for Polydektos, for even his old friend Perikles feared to send such an old drunk onto the battlefield again. Not out of worry that he might not lead his men to victory; more of pity to him, lest he'd die short of breath with a spear through his innards.

He had been a good leader, a strong tactician, and a brave warrior on the battlefield. He lost count of the number of Persian and Spartan heads that he'd cleaved from their shoulders. Now he was a ghost of the fine Athenian man he had once been. He was just a fat, drunk citizen who liked to go down to the law courts of a morning and vote everyone guilty, even the plainly innocent, to get his thrills. He drank, ate, and fornicated (when he could manage it) too much, even for his own liking, but he couldn't stop.

He felt he had little else to live for.

Three years ago, his only son had died in battle, killed by a stray spear.

An Athenian spear. The cruellest way for such a fine young man to die, at the hands of his own army. Some overeager peltast or scared soldier, or maybe even a mortally wounded man letting off a dying throw, had sent that fateful spear. It didn't matter in the end; all that mattered was that his beautiful heir was dead and his life and house were in ruins. He had a daughter, yes, but that was a small crumb of comfort to him. Losing Sokos did not just mean the death of his only son; it meant the demise of his family tree. A whole legacy of valour-at-arms for hundreds of years lost to one stray spear that the Fates cruelly sent thudding into his son's back. A little way left or right, and he would have lived, but no.

Polydektos drained his cup and looked across the vibrating bed as the two young figures copulated hard, sweat and oil mixing with the tang of the incense sticks burning on the low table nearby. Talaemenes was his young companion and had been for two years. Polydektos had wooed him, as he reminded him of his lost son at that age. He was seventeen, making love to their hetaira girl by the name of Gala. She had been taken into slavery so young that even she did not know the country of her birth. Somewhere to the northwest, Polydektos thought, as her skin had a creamy white complexion and her hair was dirty blonde.

She was a beauty, a jewel among girls, and Polydektos paid for her to live here and take no other men to her bed than Talaemenes and him. The rest of the time was spent learning the ways of society life, weaving fabrics, and learning to play the harp. She had the most wonderful laugh; it could melt the storm clouds that followed over Polydektos's head every day. A night with her was worth a thousand with his wife.

He had joined in at first as they made love in the Kerberos position. *Making the beast with three heads*, Talaemenes would joke. It made Polydektos feel alive for a time. But now he let them have their fun, raising a toast to youth and lust, as he drained another cup of wine. It was late, he knew, and his wife would already be asleep in the large, cold bed that they shared.

Polydektos felt tiredness overcome him, and he lay his head down as Talaemenes and Gala climaxed.

They parted, and Talaemenes took a swig of wine to quench his post-coital thirst. Gala moved over to kiss Polydektos, and they cuddled up while Talaemenes spooned her from behind.

He felt her soft kisses on his lips as he drifted off into his wine-induced sleep.

Chapter 2

Polydektos awoke to find it was still dark outside. Talaemenes was hurriedly dressing next to the bed.

"We fell asleep, Polydektos! Your beloved wife will have our guts for bowstrings. I deem it is but two hours before the cock crows on a new morning."

"Gods dammit, it will take a field of flowers and a mine filled with gold to appease her this time." The older man sat up but nearly fell back on the bed next to the sleeping hetaira, his head spun so much.

"A little too much wine, perhaps?"

"Far too much, I would say," Polydektos replied as the room stopped spinning at last. Rising naked, he walked over to pour water into a bowl to splash on his sleepy face and let it run down his spine to wake up his body.

"Here, let me help you," Talaemenes said, now fully dressed. He walked around the bed to stand before Polydektos. The fit young man set about dressing his older consort from head to toe. Polydektos just closed his eyes, liking the feel of the handsome young man's soft, cool hands as he dressed the former general. He knew he'd been lucky to gain the boy's attention two years ago; now the lad practically kept him going like a wounded soldier's crutch. After losing his only son, Polydektos relied on the boy more and more with each passing week—reminding him to buy flowers for his wife and daughter, what religious festival was up next, where he should be when he'd once again imbued too much vintage grape.

Polydektos felt his belt being tightened and opened his eyes to find that he was fully dressed. His head hurt a little, but he wasn't swaying about anymore.

"Fit for purpose now," Talaemenes said in a cheery proud voice.

"Fit for the dung-heap more like," Polydektos replied, turning around to look at the naked soft lines of Gala as she slept. "Shall I wake her to say farewell?"

"I've put her monthly remunerations on the side under the bowl," Talaemenes said. "Let the girl sleep—she has done a goddess's work tonight."

"Sssh. The gods do not sleep like us mortals. Best remember that, boy," Polydektos warned as he adjusted his belt and reached down for his himation.

"But you yourself are often heard to curse the gods," Talaemenes said, putting on his outer clothing.

"Yes, but I am past caring and getting old," Polydektos replied, pushing the youth towards the door. "You have battle and adventures to look forward too. I have only the slow death of ages every man must endure."

"Don't say that, Polydektos! My life would be nothing without you," the youth replied with heartfelt earnest, pulling his older lover into a tight bear-hug.

"And my life won't be worth living if we are not home before dawn. Now let's hasten like Hermes, home." Polydektos kissed Talaemenes soft bare cheek, then headed for the door.

They went outside into the night, across a wooden balcony and down a set of steps to the courtyard and through the arched rear exit of the shared house. They left the House of Javelins, a humorous nickname a hetaira girl had come up with years ago to describe the deeds of men and their personal weapons inside the plush whorehouse. Many a Greek housewife would ask where their husbands and adult sons were off to, and *'to javelin practice'* would be their reply.

The streets of Athens were dark, and few people were abroad. The torches lit that night had mostly burned away so no one would notice the two men unless they were right in each other's faces. The way home was a twenty-minute walk for Polydektos, but someone young like Talaemenes could easily run there in less than ten. They walked as fast as Polydektos could manage in his unfit state, through the narrow streets, until they came out past a row of trees onto the Panathenaic Way. The road was wide, and only a few people passed them by. Two men came past pushing a cart full of pots; Polydektos didn't know the young man on the cart handles, but the older, white-bearded man next to him carrying a torch was Trekhos of Krete, a merchant of his acquaintance who had settled in the Polis.

"Up before dawn again, eh, Trekhos?" Polydektos hailed the old man as they passed on the wide road.

"As ever, my friend," the older man replied. "It looks like I am up before you have felt the duck feathers against your head again, Polydektos."

Polydektos laughed. "The Kretans are always known for their sharp eyes, my friend! I go to my pillow now." Trekhos laughed back throatily, and the four men went their separate ways on the road that led up to the Akropolis.

They saw no one else as they climbed the hill. The main road was well-lit by torches, but when they turned left onto a cart-rutted dirt road, the night soon closed in around them. They were bathed in darkness, as no moon shone in the heavens tonight. A certain thrill always passed through Polydektos as he walked along in the enclosing darkness. It took him back to old wars and night raids on enemy camps. He could hear the swish and creak of Talaemenes's clothes as he walked to his left. The old nervous excitement made the hairs on his legs and arms twitch—or was it just the cool night air? The Tettix were making their usual pre-dawn racket as they clung to the olive and lemon trees, rubbing their legs so the night was filled with their song.

The dirt track lessened in width as the numbers of villas on either side dwindled. Polydektos's home was situated on a small rise off the one-lane dirt track, away from the heart of the city. The hill and the Akropolis dominated the view from the rear garden of his home, while the polis lay stretched out before him like the model in the city works building. There was a paved set of steps cut into the front of the hill for a steep but safe ascent fifteen feet up to the entrance of the villa. Yet the two men took the tradesmen's path, a dirt track that wound gently up the side of the slope. They knew from experience that the quietest way back into the house was around the side of the property, not through the large creaking front doors. There was an array of potted plants and vases lined up along the walls of the entranceway. Both men coming in drunk had fallen foul of these womanly traps before, and had soon changed their tack.

Polydektos found himself pressing down on the top of his knees to get his body up the incline, something he would have run up without a care on younger legs with war-trained muscles. The slope evened out to a gentle rise and turned left around the back of the walled villa. Around the rear were a few outbuildings and a small stable for the horses and the goats to sleep in. A small grove of lemon and olive trees backed onto the property, with three lines of cultivated grapevines on the slope of the hillside. There were tended gardens for fruit, herbs, and vegetables, which his daughter Kyra had planted.

The two men had no need to go around to the single rear gate of the villa, as this would be locked tight at night. Their goal was an old, wizened olive tree that grew on the right-hand side of the villa. Its thick branches overlooking the open court-yard would be their silent way in. They only used it on rare occasions, like this, when they were very late in coming home. Yet Polydektos knew he had to make it back to his own bed before dawn. It was the one rule his generous wife insisted on. Staying out all night had cost him many bumps to the cranium and the cost of the thrown vases aimed at his head. He always tried to make it home before dawn out of respect for her—but also for his sore head's sake.

Polydektos went first, frowning and puffing so hard that his young companion had to push his meaty behind up onto the first bough of the tree. The climb was much easier after that, and the old general was soon dangling over the wall inside his own courtyard.

Has it come to this? he thought as he let go of the overhang-ing branch with both hands. *The great General Polydektos having to break into his own villa at night because he's become an old drunken whoremonger.* His sandals hit the tiled mosaic court floor hard. He went down onto his bent knees, but at least he managed to steady himself with his hands so he did not suffer the indignity of falling on his arse.

Talaemenes jumped down beside him without making a sound. His young ward had the agility of a monkey and the silence of a stalking lion. They clapped each other on the shoulders, they hurried to the stairs, delighted that they had not woken the servants or slaves so far. They took off their sandals at the top of the stairs and made their way along the balcony overlooking the pastas, courtyard, and ground floor rooftops below. They passed the guest bedroom to the small bedroom that Talaemenes slept in. They kissed goodnight, leaving Polydektos all alone on the dark balcony. Only the glow of the fires from then kitchens showed any light in his dark villa.

He took a deep breath, then made his way around the L-shaped balcony, past his late son's room, then his daughters', to his own. His skin was still goose-bumped, his hairs still on end for some reason, but he put it down to the wine. He loved the silence of the house at this time of night. He slipped into his dark bedroom. The shutters on the windows had been closed tight, and there was a faint smell of incense in the air. It wasn't one he remembered his wife Kephissa using before. Maybe one of the servants had picked it up at the market. It reminded his tired, wine-dulled mind of the travels of his youth. Perhaps it was the gift of some Egyptian merchants. They did not always share a bed, his wife and Polydektos. In fact, it was a rarity these days, and he regularly found himself sleeping in the downstairs Room for Men, or sometimes in his dead son's bed. Yet he thought it proper this night to at least make the effort of showing his love for his wife.

Fatigue made his last steps up the raised dais to his bed feel like he was wading in the sea. He near-collapsed on his side of the bed and was asleep in seconds.

CHAPTER 3

Polydektos was dreaming of his son again. Of hot-blooded battle and the day he fell—even though he had not been there to witness it. But his mind was full of such battle scenes; his imagination took those images easily from his memory. He saw the faces of the men beside his son who saw him fall, his body silhouetted against a red dusk sky. Polydektos had questioned each one over and over again to find out what happened on that fateful day. All who witnessed it came back with the same story of brutal fate, whereby the gods had abandoned his family. The battle was almost won and the day was fading to dusk, when the cruellest of deaths that can happen to a soldier happened to his only son. A stray Greek spear had fallen short of its target and speared his son through the back and half out his front. He fell forwards, the spear sticking into the earth and stopping his body from falling. He was dead before they could reach him—so had said all his fellow soldiers. The man who threw that fateful spear was either dead or never found; such is the vagueness of war.

He son was hailed a hero and given a grand funeral that even Perikles attended. "Sokos, son of General Polydektos, has died in battle, but like a true Athenian, he has not fallen," the great man had said before the funeral pyre.

The crash of the bedroom door opening caused Polydektos to jump from his dream. He sat up on one elbow and wiped the tears from his eyes as Talaemenes came rushing into his room unannounced.

"They are all dead, all of them…," the young man was shouting wildly at the top of his lungs. Then he stopped and almost fell over. He clutched at a pedestal to steady himself, but in doing so knocked the marble bust of Hypnos, the God of Sleep, to the floor. He just pointed, his mouth wide open in a silent scream that would not come from his airless throat. Polydektos blinked, sniffed, and turned to see what the boy was pointing at. To the end of his days, he wished he hadn't.

His beautiful wife Kephissa lay next to him, but she was not in the land of the living, nor the realm of sleep…nor was she whole.

Polydektos scrambled from his bed, still dressed in the clothes he'd put on the morrow before. He felt his throat tighten at the ghastly sight that befell his tear-filled eyes. His wife lay naked with no sheets covering her. Her head had been cleanly severed at the neck and lay on the pillows, three fingers' breadth from her neck. Her arms and legs had also been cut from her torso and placed a similar gap away.

Talaemenes rushed over to catch Polydektos before he could fall. The light from the shutters and the doorway showed the horror-filled bed and his dismembered wife of twenty-seven years. Yet it seemed to both men that she was carved from marble, so white was her flesh. Yet that was not the oddest thing about her murder.

"She is like Kyra, there is no blood," Talaemenes managed to speak at last.

Polydektos looked up at Talaemenes and suddenly found the strength to stand, turn in his arms and run for his daughter's bedroom. "KYRA!" he yelled as he charged along the walkway and into his daughter's bedroom.

Talaemenes sank to his knees and buried his tear-streaked face in his hands. He knew what Polydektos would find, because it had already broken his young heart.

Polydektos could not later recall running from his villa, or how he got onto the main road, or how much of his hair he had pulled from his head during this madness. The Scythian Rod Bearers were called and took him back to his villa, where a small crowd had gathered on the hill before the road running up to his open front doors. There they found Talaemenes sobbing, his body prostrate, and his face buried in the dust.

The Rod Bearers parted the small crowd and lifted the sobbing youth to his feet, which were bare and stained with dried blood.

"What has happened here?" asked the Scythian Captain.

"They are all...dead." Was all they could get from Talaemenes over and over again. Polydektos, on the other hand, stood—held up between two Rod Bearers, as he wavered if left to stand alone. His eyes were blank. The Scythian officer had seen this look before, but only on the battlefield after it had been won. The Thousand Pous Stare, some called it. It was the look a soldier got when he had seen too much death for a single man's mind to comprehend.

The officer of the Rod Bearers was tall and had to stoop to get into Polydektos's eye line. He cupped the bearded chin of the dazed man and lifted it until their very different eyes met. "What have you witnessed?"

But Polydektos's eyes did not even register the tall, lean slave. The Captain of the Rod Bearers let go of the man's chin before the drool from the side of his mouth ran down and touched his skin.

"Do you know these men?" the officer asked the small crowd of onlookers.

"Yes," answered an older, thin man with bandy legs and a long white beard. "That is General Polydektos and his ward, Talaemenes. I am one of their neighbours. They live up there in that very villa." The old man had to turn his entire stiff-limbed body to point upwards to the villa on the hill. The Akropolis rose up on the large hill behind the red roof tiles of the villa.

Suddenly a black-bearded man came into view on the brow of the hill, by the stone steps leading down to where the throng stood. He cupped his hands over his mouth and shouted down to the Rod Bearers. "Come quick, there has been a massacre here!"

"That's what I've been trying to tell you," Talaemenes pleaded with the slave guards. "Someone has killed Kyra, her mother, and all the slaves and servants inside."

"Come on," the officer of the Rod Bearers ordered, as he led the way up the steep stone steps that were cut into the hillside. A path led to the steps before the front doors of the house, both of which were wide open. The officer noted more than one set of bloody foot and sandal prints leading up the steps and into the large villa.

"Who are you?" the officer asked the bearded man when they reached him standing halfway along the path.

Just then, a young man of maybe seventeen years ran out of the house. He was thin, with dark curly hair and a smooth, almost ladylike chin that had yet to see its first beard.

"She won't leave her bedside, father," the youth said to the dark-bearded man on the path. The young man looked pale of face, and the Scythian officer thought he was close to vomiting.

"Who are you people and what are you doing in this man's house?" The Rod Bearer officer turned to point to where his guards were holding up the dazed Polydektos.

"I am Eretmenos, and this is my son Euneas," the bearded man spoke, but was interrupted by his son being sick on the scrub grass beside the path. He patted his bent-double son's back and then returned his attention to the Rod Bearer Captain. "My wife Dexamene is sister to Polydektos's wife, Kephissa. We live just down the hill from here. One of our metic gardeners saw Polydektos run off, while Talaemenes was left sobbing on the road, saying all were dead. Our gardener ran to fetch us at once. He should be inside somewhere searching for any survivors."

"Survivors, you say?" the Rod Bearer Captain repeated, eyeing up the entrance to the villa. "And have you found any survivors?"

"None so far." Eretmenos shook his head. "The whole place reeks of death. The slaves are all dead, but I see no wounds on their bodies. The metics, though, have had their throats cut, and there is blood everywhere."

"What about the wife and daughter?"

Eretmenos suddenly put his hands on his knees and bent forwards, breathing hard through his large nose. He did this for a few seconds, then straightened his back again and breathed heavily through his mouth several times. He was not helped by his son heaving up more of his breakfast not far behind him.

"I've never seen anything like this before, not even during my life in service to the city in time of war. I think it is easier if you come and see, though you will wish you hadn't." Eretmenos gulped and turned to lead the way back into the house.

The officer pointed and gave orders to his men. He sent one back to fetch more Rod Bearers. One he posted on the steep steps, another at the entrance to the villa to keep nosy people out. He sent another around the rear to search the outbuildings and to guard the back gate to the property. That left two men to follow the officer inside.

"I will stay here and tend to Polydektos," Talaemenes said as the Rod Bearers let him go. The youth caught the falling man and cradled his unblinking mentor in his arms as he knelt.

"Keep an eye on my son too," Eretmenos said to Talaemenes. "Don't let him enter the house again."

Talaemenes nodded in reply. Eretmenos nodded back his thanks, turned, and took a deep breath before leading the Scythians into the charnel house. The entrance led through a passage lined with pot plants, vases, and busts of gods and ancestors. It opened into a courtyard with an old, overhanging olive tree giving shade to the altar of Zeus Herkeios, god of boundaries. There was a faint odour about the open courtyard, but the Rod Bearer officer could not place it.

"Where did you find the dead slaves and servants?"

"The slaves are just in there," Eretmenos pointed with his left hand to a closed door just next to the entrance hall and the pastas that ran the length of the building.

The Rod Bearer officer moved closer to the slaves' small quarters and then turned back to his bearded guide. "And the servants of the house?"

"Over there," Eretmenos pointed across the courtyard to an open doorway next to the stairs. The only other room on the ground floor with a doorway was the storeroom, between the living room and the room for men.

The Captain pointed for one of his men to go and check the servants' room. Only the slaves like himself were locked away out of sight when company came to stay or dine. He opened the wooden door to the small slaves' quarters, and he was nearly overcome by a sickly-sweet tang to the air inside, one that made his eyes water slightly. The light from the courtyard showed the slumped, unmoving bodies of four adults and two children. The Captain put his hand over his mouth and touched the bare ankle of the girl child nearest the doorway: it was stone cold. He said a silent prayer to his gods and stepped hurriedly out of the room again. He left the door open to let the morning air in and the fumes of death out. He and his other guard moved away from the foul, corrupted smell and into the centre of the courtyard.

The other guard he sent returned from the servants' room, shaking his head and making a cutting motion across his neck with his right forefinger.

"I told you," Eretmenos said, growing visibly annoyed with the Scythians. He was no doubt impatient to go upstairs and get his wife out of this place, away from so much wanton murder. "Can we proceed upstairs now?"

The Captain nodded, then whispered to the man next to him, "Take a look around, just in case the murderers are still hiding down here."

The guard nodded and headed over to search the kitchen, while the Captain and the guard who had searched the servants' room followed Eretmenos upstairs. They strode after him along the balcony, past three open, empty bedrooms. The next bedroom had a modesty curtain drawn across it, and the far bedroom had a wooden door.

"We found my niece in here," Eretmenos said, pointing to the curtain. Then his wavering finger pointed to the open doorway of the last bedroom. "And my wife's sister in the main bedroom."

The Captain nodded to his guard to look inside the daughter's bedroom, while he followed the bearded man to the open main bedroom door. Below, the Captain could see his other man leave the kitchen, munching on some food he found there, before he disappeared from sight under the balcony to search the living room. He wiped at his lips, trying to get the sickly-sweet taste from the slaves' room from them. He entered the main bedroom and saw that a weeping woman was kneeling beside the sheet covers of the large double bed. Her arm was across the top of the bed, and her head pushed into it as she cried. Also, he thought, to keep her eyes from the atrocity that had happened to the wife of this great house.

He didn't want to, but his feet propelled him forwards to the end of the bed. The shutters were open, and sunlight streamed across the dismembered corpse of Kephissa that lay on the right-hand side of the bed. Her once beautiful head had been severed from her neck, and her arms and legs had been cut off. Yet there was hardly even a drop of blood anywhere on the bed to be seen. The officer made a secret sign of his religion and looked upon the woman with wide eyes.

"Only the foul Thanatos could have done such a thing," Eretmenos murmured as he hurried over to try and pull his distraught wife away from the bed.

The Scythian Captain nodded, even though the Greek gods were not his gods. Only an evil deity could have done this and not leave a drop of blood behind. No mortal could accomplish such a thing and slay the entire household without the alarm being raised. His thoughts went then to Polydektos and Talaemenes, and his suspicious mind wondered how they had escaped the slaughter. Yet he was only a guard and no enforcer of the peace. Any deductions and questions of his own were irrelevant.

Eretmenos tried to tug and pull his wife from where she had collapsed by the side of the bed. This just made her wail and tear at her own hair in despair. Just then one of his guards entered, looking pale and ill.

"By all that is unholy, the daughter and the mother have been slain in the same way. I have never seen such a thing in all my life. What else but an angry Titan or monster could do such a thing? Surely the gods deserted this house last night." The guard was glad of his spear to lean on.

"Nor I," the Scythian Captain replied. "We need to leave this accursed house now."

His last words were louder and directed at Eretmenos and his spouse. He wanted to go over and pull the weeping woman from the house so he could get back to his barracks. Yet to touch the wife of a Citizen would bring more trouble than just hearing her pitiful wails of woe.

"Let us go and see if the others have found anything." The other guard nodded and followed his leader back around the upper balcony. The other bedrooms upstairs were empty and showed no signs of a struggle. It was only when they returned to the courtyard that two of his other guards called out to him. They held rags over their mouths and were using their free hands to drag an unconscious male from a secure storeroom. The smell from the small, enclosed room was even sweeter than that in the slaves' quarters had been. The officer peered inside. The place was full of stores, jars, and pots of food. The sickly thick air inside made the officer's head swoon, and he quickly ducked outside again.

"Is he alive?" he said, pointing to the man.

"Yes sir—but dead asleep—like the goddess Nyx had kissed him."

"Take him out into the fresh air and find out who he is?" the officer ordered and then cleared his throat. He took one look around the courtyard and exited the villa. He had had enough of the foul breath of death and evil that tainted the dwelling. He remembered a tale his grandmother had spoken to him long ago and far away, before his capture and new life in Athens. She spoke of a worm that had the head of a lion and the wings of a mighty eagle. This creature's breath was like vapours from a poison bottle. It would fly to a village at night and breathe its foul breath like a mist until the whole place was covered. None ever woke from their nightly slumber and the creature would take only gold and silver and leave the village and fly off to the mountains to sleep for a hundred years. It was said if people found the dead villagers all they noticed was a thin mist and the sweet smell of figs.

Euneas, the son of Eretmenos and Dexamene, ran over to the man the Rod Bearers brought out into the morning sunlight. He began to sob over the unconscious man and slapped at his cheeks, trying to revive him.

"You know this man?" The officer moved over to stand so his imposing, muscular frame made a shadow over the boys' heads.

"He is Borilos, our gardener. He entered the house with us to help with the search," Euneas replied with tears in his red-ringed eyes. "Will he recover?"

The officer shrugged; he was no healer, only a warden of the law courts. As soon as all his men had returned from their searches of the grounds, he would return to his barracks, make a report, and then drink as much wine as needed to forget what he had seen this morning. He looked from one set of sobbing men to another, and it irked his warrior nature. Tears were for the womenfolk, not for men.

He slit his eyes against the glare of the bright morning sun and looked at where Talaemenes was comforting the distraught Polydektos. He saw the closeness between them and wondered once again how they had survived the slaughter. More wailing and sobbing from the entrance to the villa made him exhale with simmering resentment. It was Eretmenos and his hysterical wife. He was glad to see the rest of his men returning from searching around the rear of the property. The tight knot in his shoulders eased a little at the knowledge that he could make a swift, forced-march exit from this wailing place of death.

But he didn't get away that easy. Dexamene came staggering up to him, her hair a wild mess, looking like she had been dragged through a hedge. Her eyes were red with tears that soaked her flushed cheeks. He grabbed at his sword belt as she screeched up into his recoiling face. "I want you to arrest Polydektos and Talaemenes for the murder of my sisters and niece!"

"Citizen," the Rod Bearer officer called over to Eretmenos, "control your wife."

Eretmenos and his son hurried over to drag her away from the tall Scythian. Yet still, she cried and shouted for Polydektos and Talaemenes' arrest.

"Be quiet in your grief, wife," Eretmenos grabbed her face in his hands as the guards and people around the hill looked on. "Know your place," he warned her.

"I know I am just a woman, but I have been gravely wronged by those two men," she pointed a shaking finger at Polydektos again, who barely knew what was going on around him, such was the deep well that his grief had taken him. The world around him seemed too loud and too bright. He just wanted to close his eyes and let Hades take his cursed soul.

"Mother, be quiet please," Euneas pleaded. He looked from Borilos' prone body back to his mother, held between him and his father. He was feeling distraught about his pretty cousin Kyra, whom he had one day hoped to wed. He just wanted to get his mother and Borilos home and seek out a healer for the gardener.

"Euneas, you are a man now. You can do this for me, like any good son would. Accuse them for me, please—think of my sister and poor Kyra, dismembered on her virgin bed."

Euneas looked into his mother's eyes and all his resolve melted away. He had always been so close to her and never went against her will. He looked at Borilos lying unconscious for reasons unknown, then back to his mother's pleading face. He thought of beautiful, gentle Kyra, whose lips he would never kiss... whom he would never take as his wife. Love of his mother and confused, raging anger welled up in him. He stood up straight and his parents backed away from him.

"Euneas, what are you doing?" his father asked with concern.

"Before the gods and the citizens of Athens, I accused Polydektos and Talaemenes of Athens of the murder of my Aunt Kephissa and my cousin Kyra. I do this as a citizen of Athens, as is my right." Euneas raised his arms wide to the small crowd around him and then up into the blue morning sky.

"What are you doing?" His angry father stormed over to him and cuffed him around the back of the head. "Retract this accusation now, boy."

"Is he old enough?" asked the Scythian officer, looking from mother to father to son.

"No he's just a lad, full of grief. Pay him no mind," Eretmenos pleaded softly with the Rod Bearer captain.

"No, you are wrong, husband—he registered with the Deme only last week," Dexamene corrected her husband.

"You are an Epheboi?" the Scythian asked the youth.

Euneas nodded. "Yes, I start my service next month." The

rage in his broken heart was cooling. He looked over where Talaemenes was staring daggers at him. His uncle was just sitting in the dust, staring at his feet and not taking in his surroundings. Euneas suddenly wondered what in Hades his mother had gotten him into.

"Then let the Law Courts decide their fate," the Scythian officer shouted, so everyone could hear. He clicked his fingers and marched away down the hill, with his men following him. He was glad that he could get away from that accursed hill and the wretched family drama which was playing out up there. A cool barracks and a jug or two of wine were all he wanted. The crying, shouting, pleading, and raised voices were soon a distant memory as he and his men marched down the hill again. The images of the slain would take a lot longer to forget.

CHAPTER 4

Neither Gala nor Talaemenes could get a word out of the grief-stricken Polydektos. News of the awful, near-supernatural murders had spread throughout the city, as had the accusations of Euneas. Talaemenes had taken the dumbstruck general down to the House of Javelins to get him out of the public eye.

Eretmenos visited them that evening to apologise for the rash actions of his son and wife. He had no clue who had killed Kephissa, Kyra, and the rest of the household, but he did not think Polydektos capable of such atrocities. He did not go far enough to say that Talaemenes wasn't involved, though. He came to say his peace, convey his sorrow, and tell them that Dexamene had laid out the two corpses as best she was able. Tomorrow would be the day of mourning, and he would keep his wife out of the way in the afternoon if Polydektos felt up to visiting the bodies. Kephissa and Kyra would have separate pyres in the Kerameikos cemetery. Perikles himself sent word that he would attend the ekphora procession and cremation. Perikles's personal message to his old friend expressed his sorrow and grief for Polydektos's loss. What he did not do was visit Polydektos himself, just in case the murder accusations were proven in the law courts to be true. He was a true friend, but a politician after all. It would not be good for his image to be seen in the House of Javelins consorting with murderers.

Eretmenos went on to say that the metics and slaves had been taken from the house to be cleansed and would be buried tomorrow. Seeing that Polydektos was in no fit state to reply, Eretmenos apologised again and left him to his grief. Gala and

Talaemenes did their best to look after Polydektos. He would take no wine, only water, and would let no food pass his silent lips. They put him to bed early and took to the balcony off the bedroom to give him some peace and quiet.

The sun was setting over the city, and Talaemenes wondered how things could change in the blink of a Cyclops's eye. Yesterday night had been full of love, lust, wine, and merriment. Now, less than a day on, he and Polydektos were strangers in their own home and accused of mass murder. He turned to Gala, who sensed his mood and took him into her perfumed arms. He had been so strong for his Polydektos all day, but now his grief for Kyra sprang from his eyes like spears of water.

Sleep would be hard to come by for all three of them that night. Polydektos lay in numb, open-eyed silence; Talaemenes was open with his grief for the whole world to see. Gala comforted them both through the hours of darkness.

When Talaemenes awoke the next morning, he was still tired. His head and jawline ached with grief, not only for his own loss but in empathy for the loss that Polydektos was suffering. Surely his lover had been cursed by the gods. He sat up in the bed next to the still sleeping form of Gala. She shifted slightly as he moved, but did not wake.

Polydektos was up—that is, if he ever went to sleep in the first place. He sat in a chair next to the shuttered window, completely naked. His eyes were dark-ringed and his stare hollow and vacant. His face was still rugged and handsome, though grey hairs were taking over his once-impressive clipped beard. His chest was still broad and strong, but his hairy belly was round like the side of a vase. There were folds of fat weighing down on his groin, and his legs had lost the sharp veined lustre of his younger years.

Talaemenes, also nude, climbed carefully out of bed, so not to wake Gala. He poured some wine into a cup from a nearby table and walked over to his mentor to offer it. Polydektos made his young companion start as he deftly knocked the cup aside.

"Water," the former proud Athenian general croaked.

Talaemenes hurried to pick up the spilled cup. He turned

to head for the nearby bedside chest that the water jug was on, but he found the now woken Gala hurriedly filling a cup for Polydektos. Her red see-through chiton, cut from her left shoulder to her waist, exposed her left breast. Usually, the sight of her exotic body would cause stirrings in the youth, but not today: the day of mourning. She smiled as she handed it up to him and he thanked her with a nod. He slowly walked over to Polydektos and held the cup up to his mentor's lips to drink. He downed the whole cup but refused any offers of food.

It took ages to try and dress Polydektos, as he would not help himself. They put him in a simple white tunic and placed sandals on his feet. He refused any oils for his hair or body and simply sat there, waiting for the morning to wane a little.

"It is time to pay our respects to the dead, Polydektos," Talaemenes said from a standing position directly in front of the great man. Gala stood just behind to the young man's left, a black himation covering her modesty. When the General did not reply or move, Talaemenes and Gala moved forwards and took an arm each. He let himself be lifted and guided out of the room, but he moved like a hollow tree eaten away by disease from within. They took him out through the rear balcony, down some steps, and into the small, shadowy courtyard of the House of Javelins. There were bowls, water troughs, and tables around the yard for the women to wash outdoors and unseen. In the centre of the earth yard was a fountain. To the left of it was a large cold pot that they used sometimes to dye and clean clothing. The firepit under it was unlit, and layers of grey ash were piled up inside a ring of stones.

Polydektos made his first independent movement of the day, leaving his young companions behind as he rushed over and threw himself down in front of the cold firepit. He frantically scooped up mounds of ash in his hands. He rubbed the grey ash into his hair and then his beard, then covered his cheeks with it. His companions did not stop him, as this was the first show of grieving, they had seen from him since yesterday. They waited until there was no more ash to grab before moving forwards to lift Polydektos up by his armpits. They helped him to the alley that led into the street beyond. Gala kissed his ashen lips, then retreated back under the archway that led back to the rear courtyard. She, as a hetaira, knew her place and could not have accompanied them even if Polydektos wished it. It would not be proper to take their lover to mourn over Polydektos's murdered wife and daughter.

Gala pulled her himation over her head like a cloak as a mark of respect for Polydektos's loss. She waited for them to be out of sight before turning the other way down the street. Then she took the back streets and ways to the temple of Artemis to pray for the dead.

It took longer than expected to reach the hill on which Polydektos's villa stood. Eretmenos was waiting outside the front entrance next to a large bowl of water. He was wringing his hands when the two mourners approached, his face etched with worry.

"Polydektos, please believe me that I am sorry for the trouble my wife and insolent son have caused you in this time of deep grieving." Eretmenos approached to put his hands on the ash-stained shoulders of his brother by marriage, but Polydektos just waved him away and entered the cooler confines of his house.

Talaemenes shrugged and placed a gentle hand on Eretmenos's shoulder. "I think it best if you wait outside."

"I think you are right," Eretmenos nodded, glad that he wouldn't have to enter the house of death again. He walked over to a bent over olive tree and tried his best to sit in the narrow shade it provided from the noonday sun.

Talaemenes watched him go, wondering what fate awaited them in court at Dexamene's doing. Those thoughts evaporated as he entered the pastas and made his way over to where Polydektos was standing in the courtyard. Talaemenes had never been in the villa in such silence before, not during the day. Even after late night festivals, the place used to be buzzing with slaves and metics going about their daily routines while their masters slept. It did not feel like a place you could call home anymore: it reeked of death, a terrible lingering vengeance of the gods or Titans.

Talaemenes moved next to Polydektos. Before them, in

front of the court's altar, were two biers side by side. Kephissa and Kyra each lay wrapped in many layers of white cotton shrouds—wrapped tightly to keep together their dismembered body parts, so only their painted faces were visible. Garlands of flowers lay across their necks to hide the severing wounds that befouled their murdered corpses. Scented oils covered up the smell of the bodies and the strange sweet taste that lingered around the villa. All the windows and doors had been opened by Eretmenos, but still a trace of the sickly funk clung to the corners and materials of the home.

They stood looking at the two dead women for an hour. Talaemenes's mind, by then, had begun to wander from his initial grief to what would become of him and Polydektos. Surely the household had already been murdered by the time he and Polydektos had climbed into the courtyard, over the overhanging olive tree? Yet they had been so worse for wine, he could understand why they had not noticed anything in the darkness. Wine always blocked his nose after the first three cups. It took a good breakfast and a lot of snorting to free them up again the next morning. He wondered about the trial and what he could possibly say to get them out of this mess. He was thinking all this when Polydektos turned on his heel and walked out of the house. Talaemenes gave one more silent prayer to Kyra's remains and hurried out after him. He rushed outside to find Polydektos cleansing himself from head to toe with the clean water by the front entrance. The youth waited for him to finish, then did the same in the now ash-muddied waters.

Polydektos turned towards his young companion as Eretmenos got up from under the olive tree and wandered over. "I need to be alone for a time."

Then he was off at a pace down the hill, past the bemused Eretmenos. The older man watched Polydektos go, and then gathered up his clothes and walked up to Talaemenes. "Where is he going?"

"I have no idea. He said he wanted time to be alone," Talaemenes replied, watching as his lover marched down the hill.

"I fear this is too much for him. He never really got over the loss of Sokos," Eretmenos commented. His hand was at his eyebrows as he also watched Polydektos disappear down the hill. "Maybe he is going to one of the temples to pray?"

"Or maybe he's going somewhere to end his misery," Eretmenos said, giving a darker, more worrying suggestion.

Talaemenes wanted to sprint after his mentor, but he would not interfere in Polydektos's wishes. He just hoped that vengeance for his lost family would soon kick in and give the former general a reason to live.

Talaemenes rubbed his chin, exhaled, and turned to go back inside the house.

"Is it wise to go back in there alone?" Eretmenos asked the youth. The place stank of Hades and other foul gods' work. He did not like being alone in there at all.

"I need clothes for myself and Polydektos for the funeral tomorrow. Don't worry, I won't linger inside there any longer than is needed."

Eretmenos watched the tall, strong youth go back inside the house. He frowned at a thought that crossed his mind. Shaking it from his head, he went around to the rear of the property to fetch some more clean water for the purification bowl. When he returned with a high, clay-baked urn that had been stored in the shade at the rear of the villa, he saw that Talaemenes was already leaving. The youth was nearly out of Eretmenos's eye line, as Talaemenes was going down the path on the front of the slight hill. The young friend of Polydektos was carrying a large bundle over his shoulder, wrapped in a white cloak. The older man set down his urn of water by the front entrance and wiped the beads of sweat from his brow and upper lip. He watched as Talaemenes came into sight again, going down the dust track towards the Panathenaic Way. He wondered what the youth was carrying in the bundle.

Eretmenos watched until he lost sight of Talaemenes, and then bent down to empty the purification bowl around the side of the villa. He filled it up again with clear water purified at the temple of Athene earlier this morning. He tried to get the bowl as much in the shade of the entrance of the house as he could. He used what was left in the urn to have a drink to cool himself down. He wondered what the young man had brought out of the house. He could go inside and check, but the thought gave him cold shivers, even on such a warm day. Instead, he wandered down to the shade of the tree again, laid his head and back against the trunk, and nodded off until his wife returned.

CHAPTER 5

It took Gala and Talaemenes until dusk to locate Polydektos. After separate fruitless searches of the city, they found him together, in the Kerameikos cemetery. He was sitting under the shadows of some fig trees, watching the men build two large funeral pyres side by side: one for Kephissa and one for Kyra. He was dusty and unkempt, but at least sober. He'd watched the men work all afternoon until the pyres were ready. The men had eventually left, leaving him alone in the vast cemetery.

Talaemenes looked over to the dark corner where both his parents were buried. He had a sudden yearning to visit their graves but knew getting Polydektos back to the House of Javelins was his only mission as night fell. Maybe after the double funeral tomorrow, he could spare some time to visit their grave *steles* and share a moment of calm remembrance. They had been in their forties when they had him, having all but given up on the blessing of having children. His father had died of a liver complaint when he was ten, his mother of loss and despair two years later. An elderly aunt had taken him in so he could continue his education. Then he had met Polydektos at the Gymnasium when he was fifteen. He would listen to the general sit and tell of his war stories and exploits on foreign soil. Talaemenes had made sure he would always be there to listen to the former general. He used to run naked up and down the *dromas* practice running track near to where Polydektos sat. It had taken months for Polydektos to notice him, such was the grief of the man for his lost son. Yet when he did, a little light seemed to return to his sunken eyes. He sent gifts, weapons, and food treats nearly every day to Talaemenes' aunt's house.

Talaemenes had played hard to get at first, until Polydektos had introduced him to Gala. Then he had given in to the kinds of pleasures both she and Polydektos could offer. He had fallen in love with the stubborn old man. He left his aunt's and moved into Polydektos's home. Kephissa treated him well enough, but Kyra took him as a replacement for her dead brother and a warm kinship arose between them—not a sexual one, but more of a sibling's love. To Kyra, he could speak of anything. Of his worries, his delights, his plans, and what meaning the gods and Fates had for them. Kephissa wanted Kyra to marry her cousin Euneas, while Polydektos favoured Talaemenes as his new son and heir.

Such plans were like the dust they walked on back to the Dipylon Gate. Kephissa and the innocent Kyra would be nothing but dust tomorrow, and nothing would ever be the same again. Talaemenes had to get Polydektos through the funeral first and then the trial. Things looked bleak for both of them, to say the least.

Polydektos hadn't spoken during the walk back to the House of Javelins, where Gala and Talaemenes bathed him. Then Gala cut his hair and trimmed his beard, while Talaemenes oiled his naked body, ready for tomorrow. They ate a small meal of cheese, bread, and fruits, but no wine passed their lips. They spoke little, and Polydektos went to bed early that night. Gala and Talaemenes bathed together after she cut his hair.

"So are you worried about the trial?" Gala asked from her side of the small bath. It was in an open communal room below her bedroom in the courtyard, yet the rest of the woman there had known about the greats losses Polydektos had suffered and kept their distance out of respect and fear. They heard the gods had cursed the home of Polydektos, and they worried that being near him could contaminate them.

Talaemenes was rubbing at the sole of her right foot, which was out of the water and resting on his taut stomach. He had been trying to concentrate on the funeral first, then worry about the trial. The water in the bath suddenly felt cold against his back as fear crept up on him. Polydektos had been a great Athenian general in his time and a friend to Perikles, while he was a young nobody. Out of the two of them, he knew which one even he would find guilty first. He could lose everything. They could take away his citizenship, and he would have to leave Polydektos, Gala, and Athens behind. Worse than that, he could lose his life.

"Now I am," he replied letting go of her foot as it slipped back under the water.

"I'm sorry," she said, pulling back so her chest rose out of the water. "At least you have me to rely on. You and Polydektos were both here until the early hours, and I can say that to the court."

"Yes, but you were asleep when we left," Talaemenes replied, flicking his fingers at the surface of the water.

"But *they* do not know this." Gala tilted her head sidewards as she spoke.

Talaemenes could see a ghost of a smile on her lips in the light from the brasier to heat the water. "I would not have you lie for us, Gala. We have lost so many people dear to us already."

"I would do anything for you and Polydektos, you know that." Gala pushed herself forwards across the bath to press her body against Talaemenes's chest. "Anything for you."

"You are kind Gala, but all I and the gods require is that you tell the truth when or if you are asked for it. Only the truth will save Polydektos and me." Talaemenes hugged the girl close, his arms around her back. Even though he had spoken the words, he was not sure he truly believed them.

The clouds had rolled in overnight, hiding the sun behind a white cotton blanket. All three of them had slept fitfully and so were up early, an hour after the dawn. They washed and dressed in silence. Gala dressed in black again, pulling her himation up over her head to cover her features. She would be there at the funeral, but would not accompany the men on the funeral procession from their home. Talaemenes wore a simple, long white tunic and a green himation that Kyra had given him as a gift.

Polydektos was dressed up in his war finery. He had sandals and polished bronze greaves on his lower legs. His thick, firm thighs were bare. He wore a pristine white tunic with a pleated skirt, on top of which he wore linen armour, as he has gotten too fat for his old breastplate. Gala had freshly oiled his trimmed beard and dyed the grey hair black with berries. On his head, Talaemenes placed his polished bronze helmet, with white and red plumes running from front to back on the top. Apart from his bulging stomach, he still looked the imposing general he had once been. Talaemenes handed him his sword belt, but Polydektos shook his head. They left it on the bed as the three of them walked down the stairs to the alleyway out of the courtyard.

Polydektos was glad at least of the cloudy skies, as he was in armour. Yet was it a sign of ill omen from the gods at what had befallen his wife and daughter while he slept off his wine? Gala wished them well as she headed off towards the Dipylon Gate. She would pay her respects from a respectable distance at the rear of the congregation, while Polydektos and Talaemenes headed for the Panathenaic Way, which would take them up the hill to the villa. Today was the *ekphora*, the carrying out, and Polydektos would do his womenfolk proud on this day at least. He held a gold coin in each of his palms, his hands both hard, tight fists, so the coins were digging into his skin by the time he made it halfway up the road to his home. Even though his mind was blinded by sorrow, it did not escape his notice as he passed that the Agora was full of people today. Many stopped their shopping and conversations as Polydektos and Talaemenes walked past, up the hill. The former general in his battle regalia had only tunnel vision for the road. Putting one foot after the other was effort enough, knowing what awaited him at his villa. Every step closer to home was heavier than the last. It was like he was pushing an invisible wall in front of him, and with every step, some Titan would add an extra brick on top.

Talaemenes could hear the words of the people they passed as he stout-heartedly walked beside his mentor. Some of the older women were dressed in black and were saying prayers for the dead women. Others were saying what a terrible loss it was, and how Polydektos must be somehow cursed by the gods of Olympos. Others, though, had less than kind words for the former general. Some whispered about the murders, while other critics threw openly hostile accusations at them both as they walked past. Most were directed at Polydektos himself. He was a man of fame, while Talaemenes had not yet proved his worth on the battlefield. If Dexamene and Euneas had their way, he never would as a citizen of Athens.

Eventually, they passed the Mint, and the hustle and bustle of the Agora and its market stalls were left behind. They turned off the paved road onto the dusty track leading up to the villa. This, too, was lined with people, but they were neighbours and family and had only kind words for the passing Polydektos. A freshly painted black waggon with gold trim was stationed on the path up to the side of the villa. It was to be pulled by two horses, one white and one black, oiled and set with red and white plumes on the heads of their polished leather bridles. A one-armed man sat on the front seat of the waggon, waiting for the bodies to be loaded on. He was a former soldier under Polydektos's command, and the general had lent him the money to start up a fish stall after his army days were obviously over. The proud man left the reins on his knees and saluted his general. Polydektos grimly nodded back in recognition of the gesture.

As the two men reached the crest of the small hill before the villa's entrance, Polydektos noticed a group of twenty men in uniforms much like his. They were middle-aged to old men, dressed up in their finery as best it would still fit—men he had fought with under his command in faraway lands. Images popped into his mind of their younger faces, and of battles far away on foreign soil against the fiercest of terrifying foes. Thunder rumbled somewhere behind the Akropolis. He looked up at the cloudy skies and prayed to Zeus and the gods of the four winds to blow any rain clouds away. Not for his mortal sake, but the sake of his innocently slain womenfolk. Images of war went from his mind for the time being. Yet even with his mind full of devastating sorrow and loss, something from his war days nagged unheard at the back of his skull. He passed a few distant relatives and cousins as he entered his home. He shook their arms and took in their words of condolence, but hurried in as fast as he could along the pastas and into the courtyard.

Eretmenos was there, next to his son Euneas and his wife Dexamene. She was on her knees before the litters where her sister and niece lay. She had the look of a woman who had not seen sleep in a week. Her eyes were bloodshot through crying, her hair a tangled mess under the black himation that covered only half her head. She had scratch marks on her cheeks, and clumps of her dark hair were missing. She was wailing loudly, only drowned out slightly by the awful playing of hired flutists. Behind her were three old hags like the Stygian sisters, dressed in black and beating at their sunken breasts for all their two obols' worth. Hired mourners always left a bitter taste in Polydektos's mouth. There were enough people present to do that for real, yet he let Dexamene have her moment. She had lost a beloved sister and niece, even though she thought of him as the malefactor.

Eretmenos walked over and grabbed Polydektos's arm, and they shook. "The saddest of days," he said, with a bowed head.

Polydektos nodded his thanks at the kind words offered, as he was sure he would receive none from the rest of Eretmenos's family. He was right. Euneas kept his eyes to the floor, out of embarrassment or fright at his armoured uncle. As he approached the gap between the two litters, Dexamene looked up briefly from her loud mourning to shoot him a look of daggers. He ignored her and concentrated on the painted faces of his beloved wife and daughter. Even the act of leaning down to kiss them was robbed of him, in case it disturbed their severed heads. Instead, he went to his wife and placed the gold obol coin from his left hand in her mouth. Then he turned his head and did the same with the coin in his right palm, between his daughters slightly parted lips. He wondered what pain they had endured during their savage and strangely orchestrated deaths, and hoped they would soon be in eternal peace.

He stepped back next to Talaemenes, who hung back away from the corpses. The youth was avoiding looking at them at all costs, and was glad when Dexamene stood up and covered their faces with festal white linen. His heart sank to his feet then, knowing he would never see Kyra's face in this life ever again. He let out a sob and tears rolled down his smooth young cheeks. He had to be strong and control himself for Polydektos's sake. He and the other men had an important job to do.

Taking Kephissa's body first, Polydektos and Eretmenos took the front of the litter, with Talaemenes and Euneas at the rear. They lifted it up as one to their shoulders and slowly carried Kephissa out of her home for the last time, at a slow marching pace. Dexamene and her entourage stayed with Kyra's body. The men outside bowed their heads and took off their helms as the litter was carried out to the waiting waggon. The womenfolk all cried loudly, some wailing to the heavens for justice. The clouds above were less grey now, showing more blotches of white in them, the thunder and threat of rain not repeated. The four men went back inside again to bear poor young innocent Kyra out of the only home she had ever known, out and around to be placed on the black waggon next to her mother.

Polydektos managed to hold back the tears until then. Thinking of his beloved daughter suddenly let the dams burst. She never would have the chance to leave the villa and forge a new home with a suitable husband. She would never know the joy of having children and raising them to be soldiers, or poets, or great men of honour. She would stay forever young in his mind, like her late brother. They would never know the pain of getting old and losing everything they held dear.

A younger, distant cousin hastened forward, bearing a silver tray on which was placed two honey cakes. Dexamene placed each near the tightly wrapped right hands of the two dead women: an offering to fling to Kerberos in the afterlife that guarded the entrance to Hades. Then they were ready to set off. Polydektos and, much to Dexamene's annoyance, Talaemenes led the funeral procession. They walked six feet in front of the black and white horses. Dexamene, Eretmenos, and Euneas followed the rear of the waggon. After them came the rest of the friends, relatives, and neighbours, followed by Polydektos's former colleagues, the hired mourners, and the flute players. Polydektos was glad the racket-making flute players were at the rear, or there would be more than just two funerals today.

Some of the neighbours lined the side of the road, letting the procession pass before joining at the rear. The walk down the Panathenaic Way was much different than the lonely walk up it. A group of soldiers out marching to their posts stopped beside the road and removed their helms. People stood and paid their silent respects as the waggon went down the way, past the Agora, which came to a stop to watch. Whether they thought Polydektos was victim or criminal did not matter for the moment; everyone's thoughts were of the murdered mother and daughter.

On the funeral procession went, past the Altar of the Twelve Gods, then between the Royal and Painted Stoa covered walk-ways on either side of the road. The funeral procession seemed to take an age to Polydektos. He endured it as best the soldier part of his mind could manage, but when they passed through the Dipylon Gate, he could not remember much about it. It seemed to him like the world had dimmed and he had one foot in the dark underworld already. They moved through the cemetery of Kerameikos, towards the two huge funeral pyres that began to dominate his vision. A crowd of funeral attendees stood around the pyres in a C-shape, three rows deep. Standing on the left-hand side of the path, leading to the twin pyres of oil-soaked cedar, were four lines of ten, a phalanx of Athenian spearmen. At their head as Polydektos and Talaemenes approached was the imposing bearded figure of his old friend, Perikles.

"Lead the waggon in," Polydektos whispered to Talaemenes.

The youth was overwhelmed with honour, while his mentor walked over to clasp Perikles's offered arm. They gripped each other's arms tightly, then embraced like the brothers-in-arms they were.

"I did not expect you to come, my old friend. The honour you bestow on my poor wife and daughter is most welcome."

"You are my friend, and such is your grievous loss, how could I not attend?" Perikles smiled grimly, taking off his helm as the funeral waggon and procession moved behind them.

"You are a true friend, Perikles, and welcome here today as my brother. Yet next week at the law courts, do not come!" Polydektos said earnestly.

"Why? I would speak for you, defend you. I do have a little sway around here, you know."

"It would be political suicide if I were to be convicted. I could not have that hanging over me as well as the loss of all my kin. Stay home, please, my friend." Polydektos embraced the *de facto* ruler of Athens. He turned before the great man could argue him out of his decision. He made his way over to the waggon to help carry Kephissa and Kyra in turn to their separate pyres. He, Talaemenes, Eretmenos, and a sheepish-looking Euneas bore Kephissa first. Then they did the same for Kyra. Polydektos's legs felt like they would buckle any second under the weight of his grief, even though his daughter felt so light. Only his well-drilled soldier's body kept him upright when all he wanted to do was fall to the dirt and curl into a ball to be left to die.

He was wracked with guilt for being with Gala when he and Talaemenes could have been more use at home. The grisly murder of his entire household had surely been done before he and his young ward had returned so late. Even if he could not have stopped whatever shadowy intruders had invaded his villa, at least he would have died with their victims. At least his mortal suffering would have been over. By the will of the gods, they would have been together again in the Elysian Fields, his son Sokos once more by his side.

Polydektos's daydream of the afterlife faded away as he looked up and saw that the C-shape of mourners had closed to a circle around the two funeral pyres. He looked up at the wrapped bodies on each bier, wondering who could have done such a thing to them. Had it been some cult, or thieves, or truly the wrath of the gods upon his household for some past misdemeanour?

Yet all thoughts of the reasons for their inhumane murders disappeared from his mind as Talaemenes came up to Polydektos, holding a flaming pine torch. He had to put it into his mentor's shaking right hand before he stepped back into the mourner's circle. Polydektos could feel the extra heat of the burning link against the side of his neck. He wiped at his tear-clouded eyes and stepped towards the twin pyres. He moved into a position between them both and held the flaming torch to the sky. He wondered if he could jump onto one of the pyres before anyone could stop him, to end his mortal misery.

Just then, the sun found a gap in the cloud to shine a single ray of light onto a nearby eucalyptus tree, just outside the circle of mourners to Polydektos's left. The sudden illumination caused two nesting owls to cry out and take flight into the mostly cloud-covered sky. He and the gathered crowd let out a breath of relief; this was a good omen from the gods. Without further hesitation, he thrust the burning pine torch into his daughter's pyre and then his wife's.

The two owls flew back and circled over the crackling pyres, then flew out and away from the cemetery and up towards the Akropolis. Talaemenes and Eretmenos rushed up and pulled him from between the two pyres as the flames caught and began to burn high. Polydektos watched the two owls as long as he was able, but they soon disappeared from sight behind the walls of the city. Only then did he turn to look at the burning bodies of his wife and youngest child.

He watched the flames, and all thoughts and reason left him. His eyes were consumed by the flames, like his family's bodies. He had nothing left to give the gods and had no idea what they wanted of him. He was a husband, father, and general no more. What use was he as a citizen now, what purpose had he but to join his family swiftly in death?

He did not blink nor look away, but watched on, blank of thought as the wood and the bodies slowly gave way unto ash. Only when the pyres had buried down to the ground did Talaemenes and some of the younger men present pour water and wine over the red and orange embers. Yet the ground was still too hot for another half an hour after this dousing. Some of the younger male cousins came forwards to test it was cool enough to approach. Eretmenos brought forward two large urns, giving one to Polydektos.

The former general of Athens moved through his wife's ashes, picking up her blackened bones and skull, before placing them with some of the ash into the pottered urn. He then swapped urns with Eretmenos and did the same with his daughter's remains. He choked as was near to paralysing grief when he found the twisted remnants of a bracelet he had given her on her fourteenth birthday. It took all his will to place it in the urn.

He and Eretmenos carried them over to their prepared graves, just beyond the tree the owls had flown from. Their markers were stone, with carvings of Kephissa with a babe in her arms and a boy by her side. Kyra's mark was of her as a beautiful woman holding flowers in both her hands. The graves lay to the right of Sokos's gravestone. Polydektos, covered in their ash, placed each one in turn into the graves, with a kiss on the side of the warm urns. Dexamene came forwards as he stepped back from the graves to place clothes in each, along with a favourite brush in her sister's grave and some half-finished sewing in her niece's. Only then were they covered over. Polydektos sat down in the gap between the two graves and looked around the mourners as they brought food and wine to toast the lives of the departed. He could no longer see Perikles in the crowd of mourners, and he was glad his old friend had taken his advice and left the funeral early. It would do him no good to been seen to stay longer than expected, as Polydektos was accused of multiple murder.

He took a little water, but no food into his hollow body. He closed his eyes and the tunes of the flutists and the wailing of the hired women melted away into nothing. He lived in a world of emptiness. He was grateful that the trial was set for next week; he only wanted death, even though he was innocent.

CHAPTER 6

Talaemenes was worried about Polydektos after the double funeral. He would drink juice or water but ate little food. He had not uttered a word since the cremations and burials of his wife and daughter. They stayed with Gala, who took care of Polydektos. Worried that the villa was left empty, Talaemenes had spoken with some of Polydektos's former soldiers. He paid some of the ones who had fallen on hard times to guard the house and grounds day and night. Some refused to take any payment for it, such was their devotion to their former general.

Talaemenes took it upon himself to clear up the house, but he could find no metics that could be hired to go near the place. They thought it was an evil place where the fiends of Hades dwelt. He thought of buying more slaves, as the murderers had touched none of the wealth hidden around the house. Yet he couldn't get Polydektos to reply to his requests about this. He did not want to buy slaves when next week his head could be on a spear outside the city walls, or whatever they did to murderers. He had not given it much thought before, but it occupied most of his thoughts now. He never liked the law courts like Polydektos; he wasn't one for confrontation and oratory, another thing that worried him about the impending trial. If Polydektos refused to speak in their defence, it would be down to him. Yet he was no one, barely a citizen himself. He had no social bearing like the former general of Athens had, no high-ranking political friends. He was alone in the world with a mute, grief-stricken Polydektos. Even Gala, he had since learnt, could not confirm their alibi, as she was both a foreigner and a woman, and so banned from the law courts.

So he left his mentor in Gala's care and went to clean up Polydektos's house as best he could. Some of the braver old soldiers helped him carry the tainted pots of food from the storeroom. Some of the food inside had a blue-green colour to it. Talaemenes paid for a cart to take it, and the bed clothes and mattresses, as far outside the city as they wanted and burn it all. He lit scented oils in the bedrooms, store cupboard, and slave's quarters to banish the stench of death. He himself scrubbed the floors over and over again, like some common slave. The scrubbing also helped the heavy weight of guilt he felt for the deaths of the two women of the house. If by some miracle they were not found guilty, executed, or banished with their citizenship revoked, they would need somewhere new to live. Maybe they would have Gala live with them, to tend to Polydektos.

Three days after the funeral, he and Gala bathed Polydektos, then dressed him in simple attire. They bought wine and food from the market stalls at the Agora and went down to the cemetery again. Dexamene and Euneas were already at the graves, and left when they neared without a word being spoken between them, not that Polydektos had a word to say to anyone at that time. Eretmenos had work commitments today, or so he had told Talaemenes at the villa the day before. Talaemenes wasn't sure if that was true. It was more likely he felt the guilt of his wife and son accusing them of murder and could not face them.

Polydektos ate no food. He took a sip of the wine Gala gave him, and then poured half of the remaining red liquid onto the dirt of each grave. They stayed for an hour, enough time to pay their respects to the recent dead. Talaemenes stared morbidly at the gravestones. He no longer felt the loss of Kyra as much as he should, as he was worried about his own youthful mortality. Polydektos had lived a good life and done deeds of renown to have his name remembered years after his death. Yet he had done nothing, seen nothing of the world. It seemed to him that Polydektos was resigned to his fate, or even welcomed it. Even with Gala's warm body next to him at night, hugging him close, he still felt alone and frightened. He visited his parents' graves for a brief while, but this only made him feel more morbid and alone.

They stood Polydektos up, led him back to the House of Javelins, and put him to bed. While Talaemenes sat on Gala's small balcony overlooking the inner courtyard, he wondered what evidence or witnesses he could produce in four days' time to save his life. The whole of Athens seemed to be stacked against him and Polydektos. He hoped Perikles might speak in defence of his old friend, but they could not count on it. They had no real evidence to show that they did commit the crime, yet he hoped that Euneas, speaking for his mother, had no proof that they did. Yet even without the arguments of both sides, they were found in a house full of dead bodies with the women of the house dismembered in their own beds. There were no other suspects, no obvious enemy with a grudge against them, or the people they murdered.

Talaemenes sat on the balcony watching the sunset until Gala came out and called him inside to have the nightly meal. They sat in silence around Gala's small table, Polydektos drinking a little water, but eating and saying nothing. Already his healthy face was taking on a hollow, drained look.

Once more Talaemenes left Polydektos in Gala's tender care. The trial was only two days hence, and things were not going well for the defence. Gala, the one person that could really help them, was unable to speak by law. So Talaemenes strode purposefully up the Panathenaic Way, back up to the empty villa. It was a sizzling hot day in Athens, and his legs, in particular, were running with sweat by the time he made it up the hill.

One of the old soldiers he had hired was sitting inside the entrance of the glare of the morning sun. He sat on the cool floor, dipping his breakfast bread into a bowl of wine. A knife and two whole figs lay next to the bowl. The man started and went for his short sword as Talaemenes entered. Seeing who it was he relaxed, but still went to rise.

"No, sit, my friend, and finish your food. I was just making sure everything was quiet and undisturbed inside."

"Not heard a peep all night," the man said, chewing his bread. "Everyone shuns this place."

"But you are not afraid to sit inside?"

"Aha, not during the day, no. But at night with no moon, well that's a different matter, young man. I hang around by the olive tree outside or wander the gardens looking for tasty morsels. I've seen worse in my soldiering days—just ask Polydektos about what atrocities we witnessed in the village of Acrohaeom." The old soldier's face took on a grim look.

"Polydektos is stricken by a grief beyond compare. I do not think he will ever speak again, until we are both forced to drink the hemlock of guilt." Talaemenes leant against the cold wall of the entrance to the house, forcing himself not to cry in front of the old soldier he hardly knew.

"Things go that ill?" The man, named Alkmaion, rubbed his hands together before he stood up.

"I am completely lost without Polydektos' guiding hand. The only witnesses to our movements that fateful night were a woman and a foreigner. I have no clue as to what happened here that night. We were so drunk and tired when he got back, we would not have noticed a herd of war elephants in the courtyard. I have no enemies at all. Polydektos may, but why would they go to such vile lengths to murder his womenfolk in such a barbaric manner? All I can do is go door-to-door to our neighbour's houses, ask if they witnessed anything that night, and hope by the gods that they are true citizens of Athens." Talaemenes turned, as there were tears forming in his eyes. He waved back at the old soldier and left the villa to visit the house opposite and down the little hill. It also gave him time to compose himself again.

He looked at the endless blue sky and the Akropolis on the hill high behind him. It shone in the dry heat, simmering like it was underwater. He wiped his eyes, trying not to dwell on the fact that his death could be in only two days hence. It took another ten minutes before he could pull himself together and knock on his first door.

Talaemenes returned to the House of Javelins two hours after lunch, hungry, sweaty, and mentally exhausted. Polydektos was sitting on his chair on the small, courtyard-facing balcony, staring into the distance. Talaemenes cast off his clothes and collapsed backwards onto the large bed. He put his arms over his eyes to shut out the sunlight coming in from the balcony. His efforts had been fruitless. No one had seen or heard anything that night, let alone a gang of men intent on mass murder. He had no more tears of youth to cry, and no evidence to prove his innocence. His only thought was this might be the work of the gods. They could be cruel and vindictive at the best of times. It was the only defence that might save them; surely they could be convicted of such a supernatural crime? The jurors would have to see only the gods were capable of such an act of killing without the loss of blood.

A cool, slightly damp hand touched his toned torso and ran up to his bare chest. He opened his eyes to see Gala leaning over him. Beautiful Gala, who gave everything and asked for nothing in return.

"I've readied a bath for you, to cool you down," she smiled down at him. Her long curled hair hung down off her face to tickle his chest.

"You are always here for Polydektos and me, Gala. I can't tell you what that means to us, to me, at this time."

"Then show me," she purred and slipped off her simple dress to show off her naked womanly form.

"What about the bath?" He asked as she joined him on the bed.

"It can wait," she said, straddling him.

"And Polydektos," he whispered, as he was only just outside.

"Hasn't moved an inch in two hours," she said, then kissed him softly. Her lips tasted of figs and honey. He put his arms around her and drew her to him.

By the time he finally got into his bath, with Gala in tow, he was starving. She brought some nuts and fruits along for him to nibble, and some wine. Talaemenes chose to leave the wine, as their love-making, the heat, and his lack of food today already left him feeling light-headed. He devoured the food, leaving little for Gala.

Seeing he was still very hungry, she left the bath and set about grilling them some fish.

"You are the perfect woman, Gala," he called over to her as she pulled on an old tunic over her lithe wet body. She smiled at him as she cooked, and twisted her long hair in both hands to wring the water out.

She left the fish to grill and walked back across the courtyard to the bath. "A woman you could love?"

"Yes," he answered quickly with a nod. He might have only two days yet to live, but there was no point in hurting Gala's feelings. Smiling from ear to ear she kissed him passionately, and then went back to cooking the fish.

Polydektos ate none of the fish, and only drank some water. Talaemenes polished off his friend's fish (as he was still hungry), while Gala took Polydektos to bed. Talaemenes had seen his maudlin side before. When they had met, Polydektos was just getting over the tragic death of his only son, Sokos. Talaemenes had been a boy then. Polydektos had taught him so much about the world that they lived in, about the great city and how it was such an honour to serve her. He helped him eat the right things and do the right types of exercise at the gymnasium. He had introduced him to the crafts of warfare and the art of love-making.

Talaemenes was an orphan and Polydektos had wooed him and taken him into the bosom of his home. Talaemenes had hoped one day to be worthy enough to marry Kyra and be a son in the eyes of the law, and to him, also. Thoughts of the demise of the virgin Kyra made his heart sink once more. What hope had he now? The trial was even closer, and he had little to show for his efforts to keep him and his mentor alive.

Gala came out onto the balcony again where they ate. She sat on his lap and nuzzled her head into his neck. Her hair smelt like almond oil. They stayed like that in silence, holding each other close as the sun slowly set over the city. Either's thoughts were their own, but of the same thing: the trial. It seemed like a huge boulder had fallen into their road of life, and they were sprinting too fast towards it, unable to stop.

As the sun set, Gala fell asleep in his arms.

Talaemenes sat for another hour, until his arms and legs

went numb in places from holding her. Then he carried her inside and laid her next to the sleeping Polydektos. Talaemenes's mind was racing with facts and thoughts on the murders. Sleep would not come to him for a long time that night.

Gala was up early, hanging out the washing in the courtyard, when a knocking at the front door woke Talaemenes. He rubbed his hands through his short, curly hair and threw on a tunic, before padding off to see who it was. Polydektos, woken by the knocking, turned over on his side and closed his eyes again.

"Alight, alright, I'm coming," Talaemenes yelled as he made his way down the cool stone steps to open the seldom-used front door. He yawned as he unbarred it. Tired and with lids half shut he opened the wooden door to find Eretmenos standing before him.

"Can I enter?" Eretmenos asked as he looked this way and that down the street.

Talaemenes stepped back to let the man hurry inside. He knew – Hades, everyone knew – what a formidable woman Dexamene was. If word got back to her that Eretmenos had been spotted entering the House of Javelins, his place in the marital bed would be forfeit for a few weeks.

"Do you want to go up?" Talaemenes indicated the stone steps that led up into the large building that housed many apartments.

Eretmenos looked up the steps like they might lead to Olympos. "No, we can talk here."

He then pulled a bag from the folders of his clothes and placed it in Talaemenes's hands. It was heavy and felt to the youth that it had many gold coins inside.

"What is this?" Talaemenes shook the bag of coins at the older man's face.

"Money, to get you, Polydektos, and the hetaira girl as far away from Athens as you can. They say Corinth is lovely this time of year."

"Why do this for us? Polydektos is not short of coin."

"Tomorrow you go on trial for murder. My wife and thick-headed son will not back down. You have no witnesses to call or excuses to give. You and Polydektos woke up in a house full of the dead. With his wife and daughter dismembered in some bloodless manner, while you two cavorted here most of the night. I think you are innocent. Polydektos loved his family, and I see no ill will in your young eyes. I fear for you at the trial that you will be found guilty, and both be put to death. I would not see this so; take this money and whatever other coin you have and flee the city today, before it is too late." Eretmenos words were heartfelt and tempting to the youth's ears. He knew Gala would go with them into exile like a shot, but getting Polydektos to leave would be a different thing altogether. He was a man of honour, a former general, and there was no truer citizen of Athens save Perikles himself.

Talaemenes hefted the bag of gold in his hand for a few seconds as he thought. Then he handed it back to the startled older man.

"What is this madness? You must flee the city, Talaemenes."

"I would in an instant, but Polydektos taught me better. He is a citizen of this great city and will not cheat its laws or run from terrible odds. I hope to live to become a man of Athens, and will not run from her bosom, even if my dying day is coming sooner than I hoped," Talaemenes spoke eloquently and firmly.

"Your dying day could be on the morrow, you proud fool!"

"Then so be it," Talaemenes said, reaching over to open the front door again. "I stand with Polydektos, for good or bad."

"Then I will wish you well in this life and the next," Eretmenos went through the door and back out into the busy street. "I will speak for you both tomorrow, for what good it will do you."

"Even if it does us no help, you would have spoken truthfully from the heart, and should feel guilt-free, Eretmenos."

"Then I will see you in court," Eretmenos nodded, before hurrying off down the street.

Talaemenes closed the door again, and then headed back to Gala's apartment. She came through the balcony doorway carrying a pile of folded dry clothes to put away. "Was there someone at the door?"

"Just a beggar." He kissed her cheek and then sat on the bed so he could try to rouse Polydektos.

They had no more visitors that day. Talaemenes tried to get Polydektos to speak to him about their defence at the trial, but he would not reply. He either stared ahead at something unseen in the mid-distance, or fixed the youth with such a withering look of despair that Talaemenes had to look away after only a few seconds. He felt a chill run up his arms, even though the sun was hot on his exposed skin. It was like Polydektos had been cursed by the gods he sometimes mocked, and his soul already half resided in Hades' clutches. In the end, he left him to his own devices, sitting on the inner courtyard balcony, sipping water every now and again.

"We are doomed, Gala," Talaemenes whispered as he ushered her back inside her bedroom. The youth opened his mouth, his jaws ached as he tried to fight off tears of despair in front of her. She smiled grimly and reached up to take his young face in her hands.

"There is always hope, even in the darkest of days, my young warrior. Be brave, be confident in yourself. The gods have sent this to try you, you must get through this...I could not live without you." Gala tilted her head to softly kiss his lips. "Yet there is one way you might escape the wrath of the jurors."

"I'm open to any illuminated ideas."

Gala pulled him further into her bedroom, away from the open door to the balcony. Her voice took on a low hush, losing some of the mid-Athens accent she had picked up since being a child slave. "You and Polydektos are my life, Talaemenes. His silence will doom you both, but it need not."

"I do not understand your meaning Gala?" Talaemenes took her shoulders in his hands and held her firmly.

"If Polydektos does not speak, he will surely be found guilty. You do not to have to stay to take...the blame." Gala looked up at him with her wide, shining eyes, and he finally caught her meaning. "We could all leave now and never come back."

He held her at arm's length and then let her go. His mouth was open wide in shock, but no words came out for a few moments. "You...you think we should leave Athens and admit our false guilt by not turning up tomorrow? There is no honour in that; a coward dies a thousand times before a hero, Gala."

"Polydektos is struck dumb by grief. I fear for you both. I am terrified that I will lose you both, and I can't stand that. I love you both with all my heart." Tears ran down her sweet face.

Talaemenes had never seen her cry like this before. He pulled her to his body and held her tight. "I will do everything I can to save both myself and Polydektos. I won't become half a man, a man of lies, just to save my own skin. I do not think you could love such a man as that."

"I never want tomorrow to arrive, Talaemenes," she sobbed into his chest.

Neither did he.

CHAPTER 7

The day of the trial dawned sunny and hot.

There was a buzz around the city-state, of a sort generally reserved for Games or soldiers returning from a great war victory. Everyone from the lowest slave to the highest citizen knew the murder trial of Polydektos was today. Talaemenes was on trial for the same murders, but he was mainly referred to – if at all – as *some youth*. The whole of Athens wanted to be there at the trial of General Polydektos, the great *strategos*. They had all read the writ, hung on the outside of the law courts. One thousand five hundred and one men had been called up for jury service in the largest open-air court in the city: the Council of the Areopagos. It was reserved for the prosecution of the foulest of murderers or the most famous of men: Polydektos was sadly both. Spectators had been queuing up since dawn to get a seat to witness the trial of the year, maybe even the decade. As there were to be so many jurors, many would be turned away, to crowd outside the open-air court hoping to catch some of the words of the trial inside.

Talaemenes had hired some of the former soldiers under Polydektos' command to escort them to court. He thought it a wise precaution, as he did not know how the populous felt about his and Polydektos's presumed guilt or innocence. Alkmaion, the old soldier he had spoken to the other day at the villa, was one of the four men he had hired. He set them around the House of Javelins so no nosy citizen could try to get in to see Polydektos before the trial. He had one stationed at the front door and two at the side entrance to the courtyard at the rear, while Alkmaion was in the bedroom. Talaemenes thought the sight of his old war companion would bring Polydektos back to life, yet it had not worked so far. The general had refused his armour and insisted on wearing an old greying tunic, sandals, and nothing else. His eyes were dark-ringed, and his vision seemed hollow, like his soul had already left his body for dead.

He took some water from Gala's hands only, but no food passed his lips. His face looked slack and drawn. His belly looked to Talaemenes like it had reduced a little in size. Gala kissed them both on the lips and then hurried down into the courtyard to do some washing. She did not want to see them depart, nor could she go with them to the court, as it would be impossible to bear, waiting outside for rumour and half-news. She could do nothing but keep herself busy and hope against all hope for their safe return.

It was time to depart. They went via the back alleys, hoping to get some distance toward the law courts before people realised who they were. Alkmaion put a himation over Polydektos's face and shoulders. He took the former general's left arm, and Talaemenes the right. Two of the bulkier younger men went in front to force a passage, while another brought up the rear.

"Are we ready?" Alkmaion asked the men, but he had his eyes on young Talaemenes.

Talaemenes could do nothing but nod; his throat was tight with fear. He looked over his left shoulder for one last glance at Gala, but she was inside the bathroom and out of sight.

They moved off into the street. They were soon aware that their plan of an easy route to the law courts would not happen. People lined the streets, waiting for them. Some shouted words of encouragement, while some swore and threw rotten fruit. Others called them *'murderers'* to their faces, while other just roared like a crowd watching a race or a wrestling match. Talaemenes felt fearful at times as the crowds swelled and pressed too close, jostling them. He nearly tripped twice, but he managed to keep his feet. Falling with such crowds around might be the end of him.

Polydektos kept his head bowed and said nothing at all. The old soldiers did a good job of keeping them all moving.

As they reached the Painted Stoa, where many Athenian roads met, twenty Rod Bearers marched up to clear the crowds so they could escort them to court. The crowds got larger as they made it up the road to the law courts. Talaemenes swore he saw Dexamene at the front of the baying crowd, as he, Polydektos, and their men were ushered up the steps into the law courts. Half the Rod Bearers stayed at the entrance to help keep people from sneaking in, while the others walked them down corridors filled with columns. It was good to get out of the harsh sunlight for a little while.

Their respite did not last long, however. The Scythian guards turned left and led them down three steps. Before them was the law court of the Areopagos. It opened out to a large, oblong open-air court. Each side was lined with stone steps for people to sit—and sit they did. The court was full to bursting with one thousand five hundred and one jurors, plus nearly five hundred more spectators. There was a great hum of noise, two thousand men speaking at once, making no sense, serving but to ramp up the volume.

In the centre of the dusty court floor was a round marble dais with two stone benches. Polydektos's nephew and accuser was already waiting there, sitting on a bench, looking like a lost, frightened boy without his mother to back him up. Next to him was the clerk of the court, and stationed around the slightly raised circle were four more Scythian Rod Bearers on guard.

A few people that worked for Eretmenos and his family were milling around just inside, waiting to be called as witnesses. Alkmaion and his fellow old soldiers had to wait inside the much cooler building. They wished Talaemenes and the silent Polydektos all the luck of the gods.

Talaemenes took the himation off the general's head and hugged him close. Stepping back, he kissed the older man's lips and whispered, "Come back to me—I need you."

Polydektos raised two fingers to his wet lips and rubbed them, but said nothing. Talaemenes took his left arm and walked him out into the sizzling hot open-air court. The chittering noise rose louder than ever as they walked towards the dais. Euneas glanced at them once and then looked down at his sandals with shameful eyes. The Clerk of the Court ushered them to the bench opposite. Talaemenes helped Polydektos sit down and then sat next to him. The noise from the jurors and spectators slowly dipped as they knew proceedings were about to commence.

The Clerk of the Court moved to the centre of the round dais and raised his arms for silence. Slowly the noise around the court softened to a murmur, then dipped to near silence.

"Members of the jury of the Council of the Areopagos, are you ready to swear to the Heliastic Oath before the eyes of Zeus, Apollo and Demeter as your witnesses?"

The many jurors stood up and said, "Yes," as one.

"Then repeat after me: I will cast my vote in consonance with the laws and with the decrees passed by the Assembly and by the Council, but, if there is no law, in consonance with my sense of what is most just, without favour or enmity." The Clerk paused as the jurors repeated as much of the words as they could remember him saying. Many came to the law courts day after day like Polydektos had, and knew the oath by heart.

"I will vote only on the matters raised in the charge, and I will listen impartially to accusers and defenders alike."

This shorter end of the oath was easier to recall for most of the one and a half thousand jurors selected for this celebrity trial. Talaemenes looked around the two thousand men present, as a hush came over the court.

"I, Agesilaos, citizen of Athens and Clerk of the Court of Areopagos, will now read the charges brought by Euneas, son of Eretmenos, against Polydektos, son of Praxilios, and Talaemenes, son of Auletes: that in the early hours of the day of Hermes a week ago, they both did willingly murder both Kephissa and Kyra, daughters of Athens; being the wife and daughter of one of the accused, Polydektos; as well as every slave and metic in their household." A low, cold murmur ran through the jurors and spectators as the charges were brought to bear. "We will now hear the words of Euneas to state his case for the prosecution."

The Clerk of the Court stepped back to the edge of the dais, holding out his left arm to the youth. Euneas looked at the Clerk but did not move except to swallow hard. The Clerk cleared his throat and beckoned for the nervous young man to stand. Euneas looked a frightened child tossed into a bear pit, yet he rose on shaky legs, and went to speak, but only a squeak came out. The Clerk hurried forwards, pulling a cup and jug of water from under the shade of the stone bench. He poured half a cup for the nervous youth, who greedily gulped it down.

Euneas stepped forwards to the centre of the dais, as he wiped his wet chin with the back of his hand. "Jurors of the Areopagos...,"

"Speak up boy," heckled someone from the spectators' side of the court. A few voices rang out agreeing with him.

"Citizens of Athens and jurors of the Council of the Areopagos," his voice suddenly found some life and fire, "I am here today before you at this court to lay charges of mass murder against my uncle, Polydektos, and his companion, Talaemenes. A week ago, in the dark early hours of Hermes, they did murder in unison Kephissa, Polydektos's wife, and Kyra, his daughter. And if that heinous crime was not enough, they covered their tracks by slaying every man, woman, and child in the household." Euneas, to Talaemenes's dismay, had quickly become accustomed to the sound of his own voice. The shaky qualms and nervous tones had soon ebbed away after his opening statement.

"I, Euneas, son of Eretmenos, was in love with my cousin Kyra, and thought in time-old tradition, that I was to be her betrothed. That now will sadly never happen." Euneas let this hang, like an actor giving a virtuoso performance. It got a smattering of consoling words from the lovelorn men watching. "Here are the facts: On the morning of Hermes a week since past, Polydektos came running into the Agora raving like a madman, where he was brought back to the scene of his crime by the Rod Bearers. A metic gardener under our employ by the name of Borilos raised the alarm with us. He had been heading off to the Agora early to get the best plants when he saw Polydektos running off down the hill, raving and crying. He went up the hill to the villa to find an old neighbour next to the other accused, Talaemenes." Euneas was bold enough to point at where Talaemenes sat.

"Borilos told me he heard Talaemenes say over and over that all inside were dead. So he ran back to rouse my family, and we hurried back to the villa with him. There we found no sign of Polydektos, just the weeping Talaemenes, and I heard him with my own ears saying over and over that 'they are all dead'. My father Eretmenos, my mother Dexamene, who is...was Kephissa's sister, and I ran into the villa to find out what had happened.

"What we found was beyond any massacre I've heard about. We found a stench about the place, of evil and death. All the slaves were lying as if asleep, with no obvious wounds or means of murder, but they breathed not. The metics, on the other hand, had been murdered where they slept, with vicious cuts to the front of the neck, so they could not cry out in death and wake the household. We left Borilos downstairs to search for any survivors, while my parents and I headed upstairs to the bedrooms. We found my sweet, innocent cousin Kyra, as you come to her bedroom first. She was laid out on her white sheet, looking paler in the flesh than any marble statue. Her...her head, arms, and legs had all been severed, with neat, sharp cuts, and by some means I can't fathom, there was no trace of blood on the bed at all. Nor could we find later, any place inside the villa, where such blood-letting could have occurred. My mother then rushed off to her sister's bedroom and found her on her side of the marriage bed, in the same murdered state.

"My father and I went outside to get more help when the Rod Bearers arrived, nearly dragging Polydektos with them. We re-entered the house with the Captain of the Scythians so he could bear witness to the terrible murders. We showed him the murder scenes. Then Borilos was found, overcome by it all, and we retreated out of the villa once more. The poor man still lives but has not spoken since he awoke. We keep him comfortable, but he just lies on his mat, like he has seen something too terrible for him to behold.

"So," Euneas said, walking a small circle inside the dais to get his words across to all the men present. "We found no signs of forced entry. No signs that any of the murdered fought back, suggesting that they knew their murderers. Neighbours report no sign of any strange men coming or going up the hill that night. We have many dead and only two survivors. Let us look at them. Polydektos, a former famed general, now only good for drinking and fornicating. His own son, my beloved cousin Sokos, killed in a tragic battle accident. Deep was his depression until he found solace in the backside of pretty young Talaemenes here. Polydektos neglected his wife's bed for Talaemenes and other women around Athens. My mother informed me that Kephissa was a loyal wife, and my loving aunt knew of how low to the gutter her husband's libido had stooped, but said nothing like the good woman she was. She was not happy, but what could she do? Nothing but die at her husband and his lover's hand in the vilest way, that even the gods must have looked away in shame. They were there that night but claim to have noticed nothing. Every person in the villa was murdered, but they heard nothing. Polydektos's wife was hacked to pieces, with no blood on the sheet. This act must have taken time, but they saw nothing. Kyra, Polydektos's daughter, was beheaded and de-limbed in the bedroom next to Talaemenes, but he heard nothing and saw no murderers.

"They saw no murderers and heard no one else in the house because they committed these acts of murders that are an affront to the gods of Olympos. Everyone else in the house died, yet they lived. So either one of them or both of them, as I think, killed all the slaves, metics, Kephissa, and Kyra. These are the charges I bring to bear on the two accused before you, and demand that they be put to death for their crimes." Euneas finished on a high note, pointing in turn at Polydektos and Talaemenes, before turning on the spot to eye up the jurors and spectators.

The spectators were loud in their support of Euneas's accusations, while the grand jury chatted among themselves in raised voices. It all melded into one loud cacophony that surrounded the accused men.

Talaemenes looked around the baying spectators and then back at the silent Polydektos. His mentor sat staring at his sandals, one tear running down from the centre of each eye. Talaemenes knew Polydektos was in no fit state to speak for them, so if would be up to him. He looked up to see the clerk of the court walk into the centre of the dais again.

"Members of the jury, citizens of Athens, you have heard the words of Euneas and the accusations he has laid down before you. Now it is time for the accused to speak. Polydektos, son of Praxilios, will you come to the floor to defend yourself against the charges of murder laid on you?" The Clerk pointed at the former general, who neither moved an inch nor acknowledged he had heard Agesilaos's words.

Talaemenes rose to his feet and patted Polydektos on the shoulder. "I will speak for us both, as Polydektos's grief and loss have taken away any other thought, and his power of speech."

"Then let it be recorded that Talaemenes, son of Auletes, will answer the charges laid before him and Polydektos." The Clerk of the Court swept himself back out of the way to let Talaemenes have centre stage.

The young man could feel the thousands of eyes fixed upon him as he left Polydektos behind to address the men present. He turned slowly, taking in as many faces as he could. Inside his head, he sought the words that he needed to say to save his and Polydektos's life.

"I am Talaemenes, born in Athens, and I am here on behalf of myself and the grief-stricken General Polydektos, who has given so much to keep each and every one of you safe in their beds at night. A man who has given his only son and heir to the defence of this fair city. Is this any way to treat a hero of Athens?" Talaemenes stretched out his arms on either side. A few called Polydektos's name from the spectators, but not the jury.

"You have heard the accusations against us, but it is Euneas who has the villa to gain if we are found guilty, and gives no proof of any wrongdoing by us. He has produced no evidence of our guilt or any witnesses of us committing the false crimes that we are accused of.

"This is what happened the night of these murders, that has brought so much loss to my heart. For I loved Kyra, too, and wished nothing more than for her to be my wife in the years to come. Yet Polydektos has now lost all his family. Imagine if you can the grief that lies upon his heart this day, and for the rest of his days.

"Polydektos and I were out all day and most of the night that the murders took place. We did not return to Polydektos's villa until two hours before the cock crows. It was still dark, and Trekhos of Krete, the merchant, saw us upon the Panathenaic Way as we returned home. So not to wake the sleeping household, we entered the villa via an overhanging olive tree that grows up the side of the house. If leads into the courtyard and we have used it before in the past to gain entry. We were both very much worse for wine and immediately set off for our separate bedrooms to sleep it off. The house was silent at that time, but that was normal for that late hour of the night. I went to my bed and Polydektos to his, and we knew nothing more until the morning.

"I awoke with the sun up and a need, erm...urge to relieve myself. Once done, my head was pounding like a drum. So I went to find Kyra, as she has some poultice skills beyond her age. I went inside her bedroom and found her dead. Yet not just dead—killed. Beheaded and de-limbed in such a supernatural manner that only some foul servant of Thanatos could have completed such a bloodless feat. I ran to wake Polydektos and make sure he was alive. He was sleeping soundly next to his wife, Kephissa. She, I'm afraid, had been dismembered like her daughter, with not a drop of blood spilt on the bed. I roused Polydektos, who was instantly taken insane with grief as I told him Kyra was dead also. He ran from the bedroom and then the house. I went downstairs to find a bluish mist emanating from under the door of the store cupboard. Surely the fog from hell itself, that the harpies of Hades had used to wing themselves to the villa. The evil fog made me gag, but before I left the villa, I checked the rest of the household. The metics had all had their throats cut, it seemed, as they slept. The slaves' lips were blue, and a sweet, almost sickly smell hung about their unmoving bodies. My head swam, and I ran outside into the fresh morning air. One of the neighbours had heard Polydektos screams of grief and come up the hill to aid me. Then one of Eretmenos's servants, whose name I did not then know, also came to my aid.

He went off to fetch Eretmenos and his family, while I was sick on the ground.

"Then the Rod Bearers arrived with Polydektos, like Euneas said. I believe these murders happened before Polydektos and I returned from our night out. That would give them many hours to kill everyone there. I believe everyone was already dead, hours before we stumbled into our beds. We were too drunk to carry out such precise murders. We believe an old foe from Polydektos's past did this in cowardly revenge, or that Thanatos himself sent foul creatures of the night to Polydektos's home. I do not know the reasons for their deaths, but if we had been there, even asleep, such foul murders would have woken us.

"I have little more to say, except that General Polydektos has served this city-state well in the past and was not a man to kill innocents, women, or children, let alone his own family he loved so dearly. Unless Euneas comes out from his mother's skirts and gives any real evidence, I implore you, members of the jury, to find us not guilty and let us grieve." Talaemenes throat felt as dry as a desert as he walked back to the bench to sit next to Polydektos. The former general looked old beyond his years and had not moved an inch when Talaemenes was giving their defence speech. He squeezed his mentor's hand but got no response. He looked up to see the Clerk of the Court making his way to the middle of the dais again.

"Members of the jury of the Areopagos, you have heard the presentation of the accuser, Euneas, and the defence given by Talaemenes for himself and Polydektos. We will now hear from the witnesses for the prosecution and defence. Euneas, are there any witnesses here present you wish to call upon?" The Clerk turned to the bench opposite where the defendants sat.

"Yes, I would like to call Damester, the neighbour first on the scene of the murder." Euneas stood up quickly to speak, and then sat down again.

"Call Damester to the benches," the Clerk called to the entrance to the court.

The white, thin-haired man in his sixties walked slowly into the law court. He did not look up or around but kept his gaze fixed on the dais until he stepped up onto it. The Clerk hung back, and Euneas stood and moved to within three feet of the old man.

"You are Damester, a close neighbour of the accused?"

"Yes, my humble home lies opposite Polydektos's villa, down a slope and across the road." The old man nodded every third word he spoke.

"And you have known Polydektos for many years then?" Euneas pressed, walking from side to side in front of the static witness.

"Yes, he has been a good neighbour. His wife sometimes gives fruit from their lemon trees. Or sadly, I should say, did. My wife is very upset about this whole thing," Damester said, wringing his hands.

"Good, good. So on the night the murders happened, did you see any gangs of ruffians approach the villa, or either of the accused at all that day?"

"No," the old man shook his head. "Apart from the odd slave or metic, I saw neither of the accused that day or night, until the next morning. I did not notice any strangers on the road or near our homes, either."

"When did you notice anything amiss then?" Euneas pressed.

"Well in the morning I was outside the front of my house, tending an old olive tree that grows there, when I heard a scream and saw Polydektos go running off down the hill towards the Agora. I hurried up the hill as fast as I am now able, to find his young companion who lives with him weeping, head pressed into the dirt in front of the villa."

"Talaemenes the accused," Euneas pointed to where the youth sat, watching.

"Yes, that is he. So I rushed over to comfort the young lad, wondering what had happened. He was rocking backwards and forwards, repeating the same words over and over."

"And what were these words?" Euneas asked Damester, really getting into the role of prosecutor.

"They are all dead, they are all dead," the old man stated.

"And what happened then?"

"Then Eretmenos, yourself, a servant, and Dexamene, sister

of the murdered Kephissa, arrived. You were family, so I left it in your hands. I saw you and your parents go inside, and I went back to my home. There was a small crowd of people there and the rest of my family, so I told them what had happened. A bit later the Rod Bearers came, bringing Polydektos with them; he looked in a terrible state, much like he does now. The poor fellow has lost so much I think it's unhinged his mind."

"Thank you," Euneas jumped in to stop the bandy-legged man from babbling on. "I have no further questions for you."

Talaemenes stood as his accuser sat down.

"Damester, you said you have known Polydektos for many years. Did you ever see him strike or hit his wife or daughter?" Talaemenes began. He didn't think this witness could aid or hurt his defence either way, but he felt he had to ask something.

"No, never," Damester shook his head. "He was a family man, doted on that son of his. He was devastated when Sokos was killed."

On the bench, on hearing his son's name, Polydektos blinked several times.

"So Polydektos, family man, general, and hero known throughout Greece, was a good man, you'd say?"

"Yes, I would. He liked his wine and other vices," Damester looked hard at Talaemenes. "But I always found him to be an honourable man of Athens."

"And on the night of the murders, what time after the sun set did you take to your bed?"

"Maybe only two hours on the water clock into the new day."

"So from then on until you awoke you were asleep in your bed. Which way does the window in your bedroom face?"

"East," Damester replied, a little confused.

"So from two hours into the darkness of a new day, until you came out to tend your olive tree, you can't say who came up or down the hill or visited Polydektos's home?" It was Talaemenes's time to press the witness.

"No." Damester looked down and shook his head.

"I have no further questions for this witness. Thank you, Damester," Talaemenes politely said, then went and sat down next to Polydektos again.

"You may step down off the dais, Damester." The Clerk of the Court approached him and pointed towards the way out. He waited until the bow-legged man was halfway back before he turned to Euneas. "Do you have any other witnesses to call?"

"Yes, I call Eretmenos, my father," Euneas said, in a raised, proud voice.

As great ripple of noise went around all corners of the court, as Eretmenos rose from his position in the spectators seating area and made his way down. It took several minutes, so the Clerk stopped the water clock for the time being until he arrived. When he did, the face he had for his son was one of thunderous anger. He sneered at his only son and turned his back on him, to face Polydektos and Talaemenes.

The Clerk of the Court looked a bit put out at the lack of protocol. He would have had Eretmenos waiting in the proper area to attend the court, not have him sitting with the riff-raff. He let it go, not wanting to look foolish in front of such a packed court. He unstopped the water clock and waved for Euneas to proceed. The Clerk hated the celebrity trials—they were always the hardest to control.

"You are Eretmenos, husband to Dexamene, who was sister to Kephissa and Aunt to Kyra?" Euneas began, his confidence now flowing.

"Yes I am, and I am a friend to Polydektos and an unforgiving father," Eretmenos said, turning slightly to give his son a dirty look.

"On the day the murders of my aunt and beloved cousin were discovered, we both entered the villa with Borilos, our gardener. Could you tell the court what you saw inside Polydektos's home that morning?"

"If I must. I arrived with my wife, gardener, and son at the villa. Leaving the distraught Talaemenes, we went inside. There was a strange smell about the place. Not just the stench of death, but a sweeter, cloying smell that stuck at the back of your throat. It reminded me of a slaver trip I once took many years ago to Olbia. There were purple-blue flowers in the woods there that smelled the same. It has only just come back to me.

"We found the slaves were dead, but not by any sword or

dagger. They had no wounds; I would say they were poisoned in their sleep, by some toxin I do not know of. The metics of the house had been murdered by more traditional means. Each had had their throats slit from ear to ear while they slept. We left Borilos downstairs to search for any survivors or the culprits, and made our way upstairs. We found my wife's niece and her sister murdered in a way only the gods could have managed. I shudder and feel cold inside but to think of it, even in this heat. Poor Kyra and Kephissa...their deaths must have been terrible." Eretmenos raised his left hand to his eyes and covered them while he paused.

Polydektos blinked twice and looked up from his feet. His eyes fixed on the man giving evidence before him. The former general felt like he was looking down a dark tunnel and that Eretmenos looked far away, even though he was but a prone man's length from where he sat.

"What did you see?" Euneas spoke softly to his father, moving a step closer.

"Something I wish I could unsee, child. In their separate beds, each had been decapitated, with their arms and legs severed with clean strokes of a godly blade. No mortal man could have done such a deed as this. There was not a single drop of blood staining the sheets, or anywhere in their bedrooms. I could not pull my weeping wife from her sister's deathbed, so I went outside to get some fresh air. While my son was throwing up, the Scythian Rod Bearers came up the nearby hill, carrying the distraught Polydektos. I have never seen grief take a man so. Look now at him, he could not do this to his family he loved so dear. Nor could the youth Talaemenes, who Polydektos took in as his own son after Sokos died, do such a thing. They had nothing to gain from these murders." Eretmenos beat his chest twice and then opened his arms to the jury.

Talaemenes smiled inside. Euneas calling his father to the stand had not gone well for him so far.

"Do you know of the place called the House of Javelins?" Euneas asked his father, as the crowds and jury chatted loudly among themselves.

"Hades did it!" Someone cried from deep in the throng of

spectators, bringing laughter and cheers.

"Do you?" Euneas asked again, ignoring the outburst.

"Yes," Eretmenos said, turning slowly to face his son for the first time. "Many red-blooded Greeks know the street and the house well."

"Does Polydektos rent rooms there for a certain hetaira girl, who goes by the name of Gala?"

"Yes, he does," Eretmenos nodded.

"Do Talaemenes and Polydektos visit this girl and engage in acts of debauchery, known only to the wild pigs of the pen?" Euneas said in a louder, cocky tone.

"Whatever they do together is none of my business, Euneas. Polydektos was a good husband and father. Whether he lies with slave girls has nothing to do with the love he felt for Kyra and Kephissa."

"Does Polydektos love the youth Talaemenes?"

"I would say yes. Polydektos told me that he was as close a thing to having a son, apart from the gods bringing his beloved Sokos back to life. He would in time have married Kyra and not you, my son, I think." Eretmenos face was like carven stone as he faced his son in the centre of the law court.

"Sadly we will never know, because the accused murdered them," was all Euneas could think to reply. "No further questions, father."

The Clerk looked at Talaemenes, but the youth just shook his head. Eretmenos had done his son's case no real favours, and he could not think of anything else to ask.

Eretmenos went to speak, but the Clerk of the Court moved in swiftly and ushered him away. He was fuming, but he went with the Clerk, giving his only son evil looks as he retreated from the court. When the Clerk returned, he walked over to Euneas's bench and whispered something in his ear. Straightening up, the Clerk said aloud, "Who is your next witness?"

"I call Talaemenes, son of Auletes, to the stand," Euneas shouted, with a smirk on the side of his left lip.

Talaemenes looked up in shock at the announcement. He had seen a couple of these courtroom dramas played out when he had been here before with Polydektos, so he knew he could do nothing but stand and walk to the centre of the dais. He stood in the heat, feeling the sweat run down the inside of one arm. He could feel the eyes of hundreds of citizens upon him as a reverent hush came over the court. Talaemenes stood still and waited for Euneas to rise. The other young man of Athens took his time, having the smallest sip of water before he eventually rose.

"Talaemenes," Euneas said, walking towards the witness, before stopping and putting his hands on his hips.

Talaemenes stood still and straight, his eyes fixed on Euneas.

"On the night of the murder, you claim Polydektos and yourself were in the company of a hetaira girl. Then you say you passed only Trekhos the merchant on your way back home?"

"That is correct." Talaemenes nodded slightly.

"It is very convenient that the only witnesses to your where-abouts that darkest of nights were both foreigners and unable to speak at this court." Euneas opened his palms and arms wide as he spoke.

"I would say it is inconvenient, myself," Talaemenes replied.

"Hmmm," Euneas said, sucking loudly at his bottom lip. "Let me put it another way: No true citizen of Athens saw what time you left the House of Javelins, what time of night you were on the Panathenaic Way, nor what time you returned to Polydektos's villa. You could have easily returned home in plenty of time to commit these foul murders." Euneas raised his voice and pointed at Talaemenes.

"Well, if we apply that logic, so could you have had time to commit these murders in order to inherit the villa. Or any-one seated in this courthouse could have done the same. You speak nice words, Euneas—your mother's words—but you give no proof, nor bring forth any witnesses that saw Polydektos and me commit any crime at all. I'm sure the members of the jury have far more important duties to attend to this fine day than to listen to you peddle your lies and false accusations." It was Talaemenes turn to do the pointing this time.

A cheer rose up from the jury. "I have wine that needs drinking," cried one young juror.

Euneas looked flustered but continued on anyway. "You

admit to waking up in the villa, surrounded by dead bodies, that you conveniently did not notice when you came home that night. You saw no one else in the property, and there were no signs of a forced entry. None of the murdered put up any resistance, which tells me they knew and trusted their attackers. You and Polydektos were the only ones to leave the villa alive. If no one else was seen going in or out, then surely the two people left alive were the perpetrators of these vile murders." This brought a few murmurs from the jury.

"Murderers!" someone yelled from the spectator's gallery.

"We did not, nor could we commit such vile murders. Do you not remember how Kyra and Kephissa died? No mortal man could have done such a thing without the spilling of a single drop of blood." Talaemenes voice broke a little as he replied, his mind's eye repeating the image of the beautiful Kyra laying dismembered on her bed.

"Then who did, Talaemenes? If you and Polydektos are innocent of these crimes, who did kill them all?" Euneas shot back, thinking he had the upper hand.

"I know not," Talaemenes said in a low voice.

"He knows not!" Euneas turned to the court and cried with his arms aloft. "No further questions."

Talaemenes looked back at Polydektos, feeling alone and unsure of himself. His mentor was no help at all. He returned to sit next to him, but the former general just sat silently, like a Gorgon had turned him to stone.

The Clerk swept up to the centre of the dais and raised his arms. "I deem it is time to adjourn for one hour to cool ourselves from this hot sun and take shade and refreshments. The trial of Polydektos and Talaemenes will continue after that period. Please be prompt in your return to your seats after the break, as the law waits for no man."

The spectators and hundreds of jurors seemed pleased at the interruption. They rose from their stone seats and went to seek temporary shade and sustenance. Talaemenes helped Polydektos to his feet and led him from the hot courthouse back into the cool shadows inside. Alkmaion was waiting for them. He led them to a cool, shady bench inside the stoas of the courthouse and helped his former General sit down.

"How do you think it is going?" Talaemenes asked the old soldier.

"It is hard to tell," Alkmaion shrugged. "Neither of you can produce any telling witnesses. It could go down to who speaks the best. If only Polydektos could speak for himself, then the scales of justice would be tipped in your favour, I deem."

"Look at him, though. Will the jury see his silence as grief, or as guilt?" Talaemenes sniffed, getting upset at what may happen after the jurors had cast their vote.

"I will speak up for him," Alkmaion clasped the young Talaemenes on the shoulder.

"I know, but if we had a clue who killed Kyra, Kephissa, and the rest of the household—and why—that would be helpful." Talaemenes looked down at his sandals. "We know Euneas had a slight motive, but I'm pretty sure he would not have murdered Kyra, whom he loved in such a vile, strange manner. It would be better to have killed Polydektos and me, leaving Kyra for him to marry. Nothing about these murders made any sense at all. And why were they dismembered and all their blood taken? Was it a message to Polydektos or some form of revenge?"

"I have been musing long and hard on that myself," Alkmaion said, pulling at the grey hairs of his beard. "I do recall many years ago when Polydektos led a lochos of Hoplites— myself included—to a small coastal town called Acrohaeom. It was set on a cliff, next to a temple of Dionysos overlooking the sea. A runner had been sent to the city, saying that Persian galleys had been spotted off the coast. Yet we arrived too late. The temple had been ransacked and desecrated. All the villagers that did not flee had been put to the sword. Yet in the temple of Dionysos, we found something strange. A girl, not more than fourteen summers, had been killed and placed before the statue of the god. Her head and limbs had been sliced off with single sharp strokes and laid on a marble slab before the God. She had no blood in or around her poor pale body. We assumed she had been killed elsewhere and put there as an affront to our gods."

"What happened then?"

"We caught up with them further up the coast. When they

left their ships, they became easy targets for our spears. We left none alive to question, I'm afraid. When you have seen so much death, you try and block it out, or you cannot sleep at night, my boy."

"Do you think that it could be some sort of revenge attack by the Persians, or at least hired by someone connected with the attack? A survivor perhaps?" Talaemenes spirits had lifted, as he might gain some understanding of the reasons for the attack.

"We killed all the soldiers, but two of the galleys escaped to tell the tale. But why wait for so long? This was twenty years ago now."

"Time for people to forget, or to plan revenge. It would not be easy for a Persian or people employed by him to enter the city and commit such a crime. And it would explain why Polydektos himself was not killed. What better revenge than to watch your enemy suffer the loss of his whole family? This makes some sense now." Talaemenes tapped the back of his right hand into his open left palm.

"Yet, young Talaemenes, we have no proof of this," Alkmaion reminded him.

"I know, but it is better than an invisible enemy. If we give the jury these facts, the word 'Persian' will stir them up and bring sympathy at least to my and Polydektos's case." Talaemenes looked bright and full of hope as he hugged the old soldier to his chest. "They will question your tale, though. Do you have any other witnesses?"

"Darios there," Alkmaion pointed to one of the other soldiers in their company. "He was with us that day also."

Darios nodded.

"Acrohaeom."

They all turned to see who had spoken. What they didn't expect was for the word to have come from the dry, cracked lips of Polydektos. Talaemenes knelt at his feet and clasped his hands, while Alkmaion sat down next to his former general. The other two old soldiers clustered around the great man of Athens.

"Polydektos, speak to us. Come back to us, we need you," Talaemenes begged, pawing at his mentors' hands.

"The virgin," Polydektos muttered, in a small dry voice.

"Darios, some water for the general," Alkmaion barked.

Darios pulled a water skin from over his head, handing it down to Alkmaion. The old soldier lifted it to Polydektos's lips, who split more down his front than he managed to drink.

"You recall the murdered girl in the temple at Acrohaeom?" Alkmaion pressed.

"How could I ever have forgotten her?" Polydektos's blank eyes at last looked up at his former comrade-in-arms.

"Such sights we must try and forget, lest our nightmare take over our days, my general," Alkmaion said grimly.

"Truly spoken, my old friend." Polydektos turned to Talaemenes. "How fares our defence, my young protector?"

"Not well. We have two people that saw us that night, but neither can we call to give witness. If only Trekhos was born in Athens and not Krete," Talaemenes said, shaking his head.

Polydektos rubbed at his beard. His mind was cleared from the fog of dismay. He tried to recall the drunken snatches of that night. He mainly remembered Gala, which shamed his memory of his wife and daughter. They woke up no more than two hours before the dawn and met Trekhos , the merchant along the *Way*. They talked briefly and then headed off home. Yet Trekhos wasn't on his own; he had someone with him.

Polydektos clicked his fingers thrice, trying to remember his name. "Who is the simpleton that works for Trekhos, the pottery merchant?"

"His name is Megas, my general. He used to be a fine athlete once, but a stray discus at the gymnasium hit the back of his head and weakened his mind," Darios, always the keen athlete said.

"Find him, Darios, and bring Trekhos with him if you can to keep him calm. He may be a simpleton, but he still can speak and is still a man of Athens."

"Yes," Darios nodded. "I will fetch him at once."

They watched Darios hurry off to the Agora marketplace. Polydektos refused any wine, taking only water and bread to sustain him. "Does my nephew have a good case against us?"

"In truth, I would call us even. He has no witnesses to the

murder itself, only our waking up amongst the dead might prove us guilty in the eyes of the jury."

"For only two Obols a day in pay, that is enough to find any man guilty," Polydektos said solemnly.

"Polydektos, what happened at Acrohaeom?" Talaemenes said in a soft voice. "The virgin girl, was she like..."

Polydektos just nodded in reply.

Talaemenes began to speak again, but Polydektos stopped him with his hand. "I need to think clearly, my young friend. You have taken care of me like a son would since the deaths; now I must repay your faith and take care of you."

"Come away, lad, let the general think," Alkmaion said, gripping the youth's shoulder. Talaemenes stood, and the old soldier led him across the way to the shade beneath another column. He passed Talaemenes a skin of red wine. The youth was hesitant to drink it at first, but Alkmaion urged him to take a mouthful. "You have done as well as any shield wall in there this morning, my lad. The General is back—let him speak for your lives now."

Talaemenes looked across at Polydektos, who was chewing the bread rapidly as he thought. He had to agree with Alkmaion: the trial was on a sword's edge. Surely if anyone could tip the balance their way, it would be Polydektos.

The Clerk of the Court returned much sooner than they anticipated. He was surprised but pleased to see Polydektos in finer spirits. He led them out of the cool shadows into the hot, baking sun of midday. Darios had yet to return with their only witness. Alkmaion stayed in the shadows as they went out. "I will wave to you to let you know when he returns," he said to them.

"The trial of Polydektos and Talaemenes of Athens will now continue," the Clerk cried aloud, to the people watching. "Euneas, do you have any other witnesses?"

"No," the youth said, shaking his head.

"Talaemenes, do you wish to call any witnesses for your defence?" the Clerk asked the other bench. "If not, I call the Herald to ask the jurors for their verdict."

Talaemenes threw a panicky look at Polydektos, who had

remained seated and silent since they had come back to the benches.

Polydektos chose his timing well. He rose from his bench, strode to the dead centre of the round dais, and pointed at his nephew. "I call my nephew Euneas to the stand."

The jury and spectators went from talking among themselves to instant silence. Then a low buzz rang around the open courthouse, getting louder and louder. A few cheers rang out and the odd cry of murderer, but the noise was like nothing Talaemenes had heard in a court of law before. The Clerk of the Court had to quiet the crowds down to make himself heard. Euneas was still sitting on his bench, dumfounded.

"Will you rise?" the Clerk urged the stunned looking youth. Slowly he rose on wavering legs to face his uncle at last. General Polydektos, the great leader and vanquisher of the Persians, was standing before him, and not some callow, unknown youth. Polydektos just stared at the mother's boy quaking in his sandals before him, until the Clerk prompted him.

"Euneas, son of Dexamene," Polydektos slowly began. He chose his words carefully, insulting him by giving his mother's and not his father's name. "Where were you on the night of the murders?"

Euneas eyes widened. He'd never done anything wrong in his life, and the sudden change in Polydektos had him anxious and confused. "I was tired from visiting the gymnasium. I talked to my mother and father over our evening meal. I read for a while and then went to bed early."

"When did you arise the next morning?" Polydektos asked, with a sidewards glance at the entrance to the court.

"Er...I awoke a few hours after the sun rose. I took food with my parents again, then was just around our home when Borilos our gardener came running with cries of murder and death. Then I, my father, and my mother hurried to your villa to see what you and Talaemenes had done." Euneas words started off shaky and dry, but soon rose in pitch, like a spoilt child accusing a younger sibling over who ate the last grape in the bowl.

"And you did not rise at any other time as one day turned into the next on the night in question?" Polydektos asked, playing for time.

"No...uncle," Euneas replied, with a little more grit in his voice.

"Not even to piss in a pot, perhaps?" Polydektos asked with a smile. He raised his arms, turning and playing to the crowds inside the open court—giving him a chance to glance Alkmaion's way, but only to receive an unwelcome shake of the white-bearded man's head.

"Well, yes, once—I had drunk some wine during the evening meal."

"So you've lied to the court, then, when I asked you if you had risen from one day to the next?" Polydektos smiled. Somewhere deep down he was enjoying torturing his mother's boy of a nephew with his questions.

"I just did not deem it relevant to tell the court such matters," the flustered youth replied.

"Now you, Euneas, deem what the court should know and what it should not know. Have you changed your name to Drakon, perhaps?" This brought a ripple of laughter from the spectators and jurors alike. Polydektos glanced right again, but was rewarded this time by the sight of an out-of-breath Darios holding the arm of a very confused-looking Megas. "I have no further questions for this witness," Polydektos said, and retreated a few steps back to his bench.

Euneas opened his mouth and shut it again before stumbling back to find his bench to sit upon.

"Any other witnesses relevant to the case you wish to call?" the Clerk gave a stern look under his bushy black eyebrows at Polydektos.

"Just one more," Polydektos bowed politely to the Clerk. "I call Megas, who works for Trekhos the Kretan potter, to stand and be a witness."

"What! Megas is well known for being a simpleton and a fool," Euneas stood and shouted.

"He is still a citizen of Athens, nephew," Polydektos said with a wry smile.

"I object," Euneas shouted even louder, in his whiniest voice.

"Any man of Athens can take the stand, as well you know, Euneas," the Clerk stated impatiently. "If we dismissed every witness who had half a brain, we would have very few witnesses at all.

"I call Megas, citizen of Athens, to stand and bear witness."

Polydektos turned to see Alkmaion and Darios lead the poor, scared young man into the heat and noise of the court. They stopped at the edge of the dais, and both had to urge the poor young man on to stand before Polydektos.

"Do not be afraid, Megas. You have nothing to fear here," Polydektos urged the simpleton like he would a young child. "We are all your friends here. Do you know who I am, Megas?"

"Yes—you are the great General Polydektos. I will be like you one day after I sell a few more pots for Trekhos." The poor, unfortunate young man spoke only out of the left-hand side of his face, which caused him to drool a lot. His left eye rapidly blinked every second, and he was constantly wiping his wet mouth with the arm of his tunic.

Polydektos smiled warmly back at the lad. "Now, Megas, think back. When was the last time you saw me?"

"Two days ago at the House of Javelins. I was delivering pots for my master there. I always like going there—the pretty girls always have kisses for me." Megas spoke with the high-pitched voice of a child rather than a man. His excitement about the Javelins Girls was plain for Polydektos to see.

"Well done." Polydektos nodded. "And the time before that?"

Please don't say my wife and daughter's funeral or something of that ilk, Polydektos thought.

"On the Panathenaic Way with Talaemenes. It was the night, just an hour or so before dawn. Master Trekhos always makes me get up before the dawn—the dark scares me. I carry a torch to ward off the Harpies." Megas spoke happily away to himself, not really focusing on Polydektos or anyone else in the court.

"And that was the night that my wife and daughter died?" Polydektos didn't want to ask this but had to. Just saying that they were dead caused a ball-sized lump to rise in his throat.

Tears were close to his eyes, but he fought them back.

"Yes, that was very sad. Even Megas cried for your loss. I hope they get better soon." Megas nodded three times, wiped his mouth, and looked down at his sandals.

"Thank you, Megas. You have done well today," Polydektos said to the youth before turning to face the Clerk. "I have no further questions for this witness." He went and sat down. There was a great roar of laughter as Megas, biting his nails, came and sat down next to him.

"Any questions from you, Euneas, for this witness?" the Clerk asked. He then saw that Megas was sitting next to Polydektos and waved the lad to stand up again.

Polydektos whispered for Megas to do as the Clerk of the Court commanded at all times, and the almost-bashful lad stood up again. Megas wandered over to the Clerk and stood very close to him.

Euneas, meanwhile, sat pondering whether to question the fool or not. He had known the old Megas before his discus accident. Guilt and sadness filled his young mind about the life Megas should have led. He shook his head to the Clerk. His mother had forced him into this, and his despair at losing Kyra pushed him on. But he would stoop no lower today. The dice had been rolled; it was up to the gods now to divine where they landed.

"No," he simply replied, hands on his knees, his eyes cast down to his sandaled feet.

Alkmaion and Darios hurried out and fetched Megas, who didn't want to leave.

"Any other witnesses you wish to call?" The Clerk looked from the accuser to the accused.

Polydektos leant sidewards and whispered in Talaemenes' ear. The youth nodded and whispered something back, unheard to the court. Then he rose, puffed out his chest, and spoke. "I call Polydektos, son of Praxilios, General of Athens, to bear witness to my questions."

A loud roar erupted from both the spectators and the jurors. This is what they had turned up to see.

It took a little while to calm the crowds down before the

Clerk pointed to Talaemenes. "Continue."

Talaemenes turned to watch Polydektos stand and walk boldly to the centre of the court. He looked tired, worn and aged by despair, but still every inch a brave man.

"Polydektos, do you have any words of defence for this court?" was all Talaemenes said before he backed away and sat down again.

"I do. You all know me. I've sat on many of these trials amongst you. I've waged war to save your skins and taken your sons to death with me. All for the greater good and glory of Athens. Am I a good man? That is the gods' domain. I have my strengths and my weaknesses like any other man. Some here will like me, and some hate me; such is the life of a mortal man. I can only hope the good deeds outweigh the ill when Zeus judges me on his scales. I have little to offer in defence. The facts are what Talaemenes has already stated. I slept in a drunken stupor, while all around me the people I love were dead. This guilt I will carry with me to the grave. It is up to you whether that time is on the morrow or years down the road. But I say this: I will find out who killed my family, in this life or the next, and my vengeance will echo to Mount Olympos and back. I will leave no stone unturned, no avenues unsearched for the perpetrators of this sickening crime." Polydektos raised his arms upwards, his hands pointing to the heavens. Tears were flooding down his cheeks. Euneas could see the grief in his uncle's eyes and felt like jumping up and calling a halt to the whole trial. Yet he had gone too far and was too cowardly to back down now.

"Good men of Athens," Polydektos cried aloud, "our fate is in your hands."

A roar broke through the court, like storm waves hitting a harbour. Polydektos closed his eyes and breathed out through his nose. His last battle was over. He opened his tired eyes again and walked over to sit next to Talaemenes, who embraced him.

It took a full five minutes for the clamour around the Law Court to die down.

Polydektos, Talaemenes, and Euneas could do nothing now but wait.

"Jurors of the Court, you have heard the evidence and listened to the testimony of the prosecutor and the defendants. The Heralds of the court will now come amongst you with the urns of justice. You must cast your bronze ballot into the guilty or non-guilty urn, and then the votes will be counted and the verdicts given. This will take some time this day because of the large number of jurors present on this case. Be patient—we will get to you as swiftly as we can. No one is to leave before their ballot has been placed. We will reconvene when the ballots have been all counted and the verdict is ready to be given." The Clerk of the Court lowered his raised arms and looked from one bench to the next.

"You are dismissed until the verdict is due. I caution you to stay inside the walls of this court," he said in a lower voice, "as there is a large mob waiting outside."

Polydektos and Talaemenes stood up and left the heat of the open-air law court. Both were glad to be under the shadows of the building again, with friends. They went and sat on the benches as before, nobody saying a word.

They could not see Euneas and assumed that he had found some dark rathole to climb into until the verdict was due to be announced. Talaemenes tried to stay calm, but his hands were shaking quite badly. At least Polydektos had had a great life, but his could be snuffed out before it had even begun. He tried to work out how long it would take the Heralds of the Court to go around the jurors and collect their ballots, then how long again after that it would take to count from the guilty or not-guilty urns. He figured that even if they went as swiftly as Hermes, it would take an hour of waiting at least.

Polydektos thought of nothing but his daughter and wife and how they died. Fear had left him; hope had left him. The only thing he held onto was revenge on those who killed them in such a barbaric manner. Whether that revenge would come in this life or the next was up to the court to decide. He cared little either way.

In the end, the ballot and count took nearly two hours.

The Clerk of the Court ushered them back into the bright, even warmer sunshine. An escort of four Rod Bearers followed close behind the defendants. They fanned out around the central dais again. Euneas stood on one side by his bench, Talaemenes and Polydektos next to their bench, and the Clerk in the middle.

"I, Agesilaos, Clerk of the Council of the Areopagos, will now give out the verdict of this court in the case of Euneas versus Polydektos and Talaemenes of Athens. It is the verdict of this court, as balloted by the jurors, that it finds Polydektos, son of Praxilios and Talaemenes, son of Auletes *not* guilty of the murders of Kephissa and Kyra by a vote of one thousand four hundred to a hundred and one. It is, therefore, my duty to let them walk from this law court free men, with unblemished reputations and as true citizens of Athens. Euneas, son of Eretmenos, I find you accountable for bringing this frivolous case before such a large jury at cost to the State. You will stand trial at a later date for this crime. All are free to leave."

Polydektos let Talaemenes hug him close as the youth whooped for joy at being found not guilty. Polydektos forced a thin smile, as the spectators (inside and out) and the jurors shouted down at them. Polydektos was glad he had been acquitted, but still felt much guilt for the loss of his wife and daughter. Tonight he would get drunk, and then tomorrow he would stop at nothing to find the true culprits and slay them with his own sword.

CHAPTER 8

Polydektos drank enough to be deemed sociable, as there seemed to be a festival-like air in the courtyard of the House of Javelins. Eretmenos had brought a lull to the proceedings earlier when he dragged his wife and son with him. He had made them prostrate themselves in the dust before Polydektos to beg his forgiveness.

Polydektos had said nothing, but taken both of them by the hand and helped them up off the ground, much to Talaemenes and Gala's disgust.

"I offer you these words only, and let you find what comfort in them you will. From this hour forth to my dying breath, I will not rest until I find the perpetrators who slew my beloved wife, daughter, and entire household. This I swear on my heart, for the loved ones we have all lost." Polydektos put his palm over his heart. Euneas and Dexamene wept openly and went away, knowing that their grieving action in bringing the court case had been wrong. Polydektos and Eretmenos had gripped arms and parted as brothers. No more would be said of the matter now.

"You were extremely magnanimous with Dexamene and her son," Talaemenes said a little later as he sat next to Polydektos. He was a little worse for drink, and he and Gala had slipped off earlier, Polydektos had noticed. They looked a fine couple together, but they had no life together apart from these moments they shared. Talaemenes was a young man of Athens, strong and bright, with a big future ahead of him. But man and mistress were all they could be. If they married, any children born would not be deemed citizens of Athens. They would be looked at, as was their mother, as foreigners. If you weren't a citizen, then life would be hard for you. No father would want that for their offspring.

Polydektos vowed not to sleep with her again as her lover. He had to be pure of heart and body now. He had only one reason for living: vengeance on those who killed his family and household.

"I might have done the same thing in their position. Dexamene was grieving for her sister, and Euneas for the love of my sweet Kyra that would never be. You are my heir now, Talaemenes, but I have little to offer you but a house full of death. I will leave you now and go to my bed upstairs." Polydektos stood from his chair to leave, but Talaemenes grabbed his arm to halt him leaving.

"I give thanks that you have come back to us, Polydektos. You saved my life." Talaemenes's eyes were sad and full to the brim of wine-tainted tears.

Polydektos leant down and kissed him on the lips. "Things will never be the same again, I fear, my young companion—at least not for me. I am like a shell of a man, with no comfort living inside. I will endure this mortal life only to gain vengeance, and then I will join my family in death."

The older man slipped his hand from Talaemenes's grip and headed upstairs to bed. Gala, who had been watching from across the courtyard, came over and bent down in front of her weeping lover. "What ails you this night, my love? I thought you would be happy in being found not guilty by the court."

Talaemenes wiped his youthful tears from his eyes, feeling embarrassed, as a man, to cry in her presence. "It's Polydektos. I thought he had come back to us, but now I'm not sure he ever will."

"Time might change things. Give him space to grieve, time to adjust, and help him seek out those who killed his family. Maybe he will come back to us after that. All we can do is be his family now, and help him as much as we can."

"How did a woman get so wise?" Talaemenes said, touching the end of her nose with his finger as he drank down the remains of his wine cup.

Gala laughed. "How did a man get so drunk so quickly?" she replied, pushing one hand up his bare thigh and under his garments. "Not so drunk, I see."

Talaemenes reached down and grabbed a clutch of her hair, pulling her up to kiss her cherry-tasting lips. They stayed for another hour, until most of the guests were too drunk to notice, and finally slipped off to bed hand-in-hand.

Talaemenes awoke with a dry cough, an aching head, and a full bladder. Gala was still asleep in the bed next to him. Her turned back was naked all the way down to her tailbone. Talaemenes swung his legs over the side of the bed. His head swam, and he felt like he was going to be immediately sick. He rested his elbows on his bare knees and put his head in his hands. He closed his eyes and hoped the room would stop spinning soon. He breathed in several times through his nose and waited for it to stop. His head and bladder still ached, but the dizzy sickness had left him for the moment. He stumbled around, finding a pot to piss in and a jug of water to swallow down. Then, feeling sick in his stomach, he went back to bed, even though the sun had been up for many hours already.

Polydektos, who had drunk little the night before, had been up since daybreak. He sat on his knees in the dust of the Kerameikos Cemetery, between his wife's and daughter's graves. His son's grave was the next one along. He—the oldest of the four, who had faced death in battle many times—was the only one still alive. He was dressed in a simple white tunic, covered in dirt from the ground. He had with him two things: his sword, and a small jug of wine he had purchased from a passing merchant on the way through the Dipylon Gate.

He poured half the wine on his wife's grave and half on his daughter's grave. "I hope you are all together somewhere, sipping wine and feasting," he said, tossing the jug into some nearby bushes to break.

Then he took his sword in his right hand and the blade across his left forearm. It made a red line of welling blood. Polydektos sheathed his sword and squeezed his bleeding arm over each grave in turn. "I swear to you in my life's blood, that I will live to see those who killed and defiled you perish by my sword. I swear this to all the gods. Only then will I be worthy of joining you in Elysiom."

Polydektos stood up and tore part of his tunic off to bandage his cut forearm Then he left the cemetery and headed back into the city.

When Talaemenes awoke the second time, the sun was high in the noon sky. Sometime in between, Gala had risen, dressed, and left him to sleep off his hangover. His mouth tasted like he'd licked a goat's backside and he still had an aching head. He drank some fresh water from the moved jug, which Gala must have refilled while he slept on. The sickness he'd felt earlier had gone, to be replaced by a gnawing hunger.

He got out of bed naked and stretched out his lithe body. He drank more water and went to urinate again before he washed and dressed. The small room where Polydektos had slept separately last night was empty, its bed made. Talaemenes went down into the courtyard to find Gala singing a love song to herself while sweeping up the mess from last night's festivities. She smiled across the courtyard and pointed to the small breakfast table she had set up under the shade of the staircase.

He looked at the table laden with fruit juices, figs, and bread and waved his arm over the table in eternal thanks towards her. She waved back, before continuing to sweep and sing at the same time. Talaemenes drank down the pear and apple juice while lining his stomach with oil-dipped bread, then devoured several figs. His head still ached a little, and he was glad to be out of the harsh sunlight But at least his stomach felt more settled, and the taste in his mouth was more pleasant. He left the fried canary alone, as he didn't feel up to it. Shading his eyes from the sizzling hot midday sun, he walked over to Gala.

"You breakfast brought life back to one who felt like the dead this morning," Talaemenes said, reaching out to kiss her nearest hand.

"And you slept like the dead also, while snoring like a lion," she replied with the dimpled smile he loved so much.

"Have you seen Polydektos this morning?" he asked, wishing he could get out of this burning sunshine as quickly as he could.

"No." She shook her head. "His bed was made, and he was gone before I woke."

"I wonder where he has gone so early. I hope he is all right."

"He is a grown man, Talaemenes; he can go where he wishes. But if you are asking my humble woman's opinion of where he might be, I would guess at one of the temples or the cemetery."

"The gods have gifted you with both beauty and wisdom, my fair Gala." Talaemenes took her cheeks in his hands and kissed her long on her soft, full lips.

He hurried off towards the Dipylon Gate first. The sun was beating down on his head, and he soon slowed to an ambling pace. He bought a cheap straw petasos to keep the midday sun off his aching head. It took him longer than it usually would to reach the gate. He stopped to buy a jug of water on the way, as he was constantly parched.

The cemetery had a few people milling about, and one funeral on the cheaper far side. Talaemenes stood in the shade of the large olive tree that hung over the graves of Polydektos's family. It looked like someone had been here this morning, by the disturbed sandal marks leading up to the graves. Probably Polydektos, but where had he gone?

He made a brief visit to his parent's grave to show his respect. Then, taking Gala's advice once more, he headed off back into the city and towards the various temples near the Agora first.

It proved a fruitless task, as there were many temples to many gods, and it seemed that Polydektos had not visited any of them today. After two hours, Talaemenes's hung-over body felt exhausted. He sat in the shade of a stoa in the middle of the Agora, just watching people pass by. He bought two apples to eat as he sat, hoping to glimpse Polydektos walking by due to lucky chance. He was halfway through his second apple when his friend Ibykos happened by with a male companion Talaemenes did not know.

"You're missing the show, Talaemenes—you should be down at the gym," said Ibykos's friend, who obviously knew who Talaemenes was. The trial had made him semi-famous, it seemed.

"What does he mean, Ibykos?" Talaemenes called back.

Ibykos gave his younger friend a stern look. "It's Polydektos. He's at the gymnasium, daring anyone willing to race or wrestle with him. You better go up there, my friend—he is losing every match and race and making quite the spectacle of himself."

Talaemenes wasn't sure where he got his second wind of energy from as he pushed past Ibykos's smug-looking friend and ran off across the Agora. He managed to keep his speed up until he was out of the marketplace, but then a stitch in his side and a cramp in his left leg slowed him down. The gymnasium that both he and Polydektos frequented was away from the centre of Athens. It took his fifteen minutes at his reduced, pained and shuffling walk to get there. He was pleased of the cooler shade as he ventured inside. His head was buzzing again, and his stomach was doing sickly back flips.

Talaemenes had to stop at a communal jug to ladle water into his parched mouth before he could continue. His head and stomach calmed a little as he headed around the main palaestra area. He kept to the roofed shade, looking through the columns at the naked and nearly naked men beyond. There were several wrestling, boxing, and bloody pankration matches going on, but all the fighters were younger and fitter men than Polydektos. He turned a corner to walk up the other side of the vast, open, sun-filled palaestra. He bobbed his head inside the various rooms incorporated into the building—mostly changing rooms or rooms filled with punching bags suspended from the rafters by ropes. Polydektos was in none of them.

Talaemenes's stomach cramped a little and he had to lean against a pillar for a minute, breathing hard until the pain faded. It did give him time to eye up the men in the top half of the sand-filled courtyard. Close to his side, several young men were practicing the javelin, something Talaemenes excelled at. Further across, next to the long jump pits, men were learning how to throw a sling shot. They were given a wide berth; shots at the training stage had a tendency to fly anywhere. Polydektos, it seemed, wasn't in the main palaestra.

Rubbing his side, he walked up to where the square shape of the main building was joined to the left by a long, thin covered offshoot. The dromas was a long running track, used to practice for outside races at the local stadium. Talaemenes could see the entrance to the baths from the T-junction. He wished more than anything to strip off his clothes, relax in the cool waters, and hydrate his weary, hung-over body.

An urgent roaring from a small crowd by one of the wide marble benches along the running track caught his attention. He hurried up the track to see a smiling youth with the bum-fluff beginning of a beard come running past and raise his hand in victory.

Talaemenes looked down the long track for the runner's opponent. He recognised the sweating, red-faced athlete right away. It was Polydektos—and he wasn't looking too well. He was covered in oil, dust, and sweat and had blood on his knees. He huffed and puffed to the finish line drawn in the sand and collapsed. He immediately vomited an empty, dark yellow sick from his stomach lining onto the ground. Talaemenes barely held down his own breakfast at the sight and rushed over to help his companion to his feet. Ignoring the barbed snipes and laughter, he led the older man to sit on the farthest unoccupied bench closest to the palaestra. A philosopher friend of Polydektos, a former stonemason in his late thirties, brought him lemon-scented water to cleanse his mouth.

Talaemenes nodded his thanks as the dark-bearded man stood and looked on with concern. "Drink this, you silly old fool," Talaemenes said, pressing the bowl to Polydektos's cracked and dust-covered lips. He took two large gulps until Talaemenes brought the bowl down, to stop him from filling up only to be sick again.

"He would not listen to any council this day," the philosopher friend stated. "He has run himself into the ground. Grief, I fear, has made him want to act as a youth. Back when he was bold, strong of shoulder, and had no cares or burdens upon them."

Talaemenes was young and had little time for men who stood about all day talking about things. He craved action and adventure, as do many young men. Yet that side of him had diminished over the past week. Death, mystery, and trials for one's life tended to do that.

Polydektos coughed but did not vomit. He looked at Talaemenes with sorrowful eyes. "I'm sorry you have to see me like this...a bloated-bellied spectre of the man that I once was."

"Why are you doing this to yourself—to punish yourself for not saving your family? Or are you trying to kill yourself?"

"Neither, my young friend," Polydektos said, pointing at the bowl Talaemenes held to his knees. Talaemenes moved the bowl back into Polydektos's trembling hands and helped him take more measured sips this time. The old general let the water drip off his ragged and untidy beard. A droplet of water ran between his fatty pectorals, leaving clean lines in the dust down to his groin. Polydektos closed his eyes for a few seconds and caught his breath again. "I'm trying to get fit as best and as fast as I can. I need to get fighting fit once more, for the trials ahead."

"Surely you have had enough trials this year for ten men, my friend," the stonemason-cum-philosopher said.

"Yet on I must go in this mortal toil, to find out who slew my beloved Kephissa and Kyra. And for that, I will need all my strength and wits about me."

"Would it not be better to start slow, out of the public gaze?" Talaemenes said, looking around at the people walking by and staring at them.

"I care not for the public, or anything else. Men came into my home and killed my family in the vilest way possible, and I'm still none the wiser as to why!"

"If we wish to seek the truth of all matters, we must become like a new-born child," the philosopher said, waving his hands in the air like he was swatting flies. "Start from a place where we know nothing and rule out nothing; only then can you have the capacity to learn new truths," the philosopher said, waving his hands in the air like he was swatting flies.

Polydektos nodded. "I must empty myself of all feelings, like I was a different person from another country investigating these murders. First of all, I must lose this weight around my core, and bring strength back to my flabby arms and legs.

Then I shall be ready. No stone or avenue of questioning shall I leave unturned until I learn the truth of this matter. Are you with me?"

"Always," Talaemenes said, putting his hand on Polydektos's closer knee.

The philosopher bowed at little towards his friend. "I am with you in mind, if not body. My strengths lie in thought and debate, rather than the running track."

"Sokrates, I would not expect anything less, my friend," Polydektos said with a brief laugh. "Now, Talaemenes—help my weary foolish body to the baths. I ache in places that I've not known in years."

All three men spent an hour relaxing in the baths. Polydektos and Talaemenes went to the anointing room to oil and scrape themselves clean, while Sokrates had work to be getting on with. Feeling relaxed, they dressed and had a hearty meal of goat with vegetables and fruit juices. Polydektos was very clear that no alcohol would pass his lips for the foreseeable future. Talaemenes understood his reasoning and promised to himself to try not to drink wine or anything of the like in front of his companion.

"What now?" Talaemenes asked, pushing back his empty plates of food. He was feeling much better, from head to stomach.

"Tomorrow morning I will spend at the gymnasium, and every morning until I deem myself back to fighting fitness. In the afternoon, we will go back to the villa and search every room from top to bottom, to try and find any clue as to who did this crime against us."

Talaemenes nodded in agreement. The thought of spending each morning in the gymnasium was a pleasant thought. The afternoon, in contrast, brought back to him what he, but mainly Polydektos, had lost. "Will you keep the villa, or sell it?"

"Keep it for now, but I don't think I could ever sleep there again. In time, we will find a new place to live, but until then bedding down with Gala will be good for you." Polydektos gave the youth a knowing smile. "You shall be my heir, and in two years' time, after your military service, we will find you a suitable Athenian wife."

"What will become of Gala?" Talaemenes said, feeling sorry for the loving foreign girl, but knowing Polydektos was speaking wisely.

"I will take her as my housekeeper. I will not marry or have children again, but she will be a pleasing companion and a loyal servant." Polydektos sipped at his fig and orange juice and eyed the youth. "Don't tell me that you have fallen in love with her?"

"No, no, but I care for her. I don't want her thrown out like dirty laundry when I am wed; that would not be fair."

"I would never let that happen, Talaemenes. She has been good to us, taken care of us in our time of need. She will be taken care of to the end of her days—we must both see to this."

Talaemenes nodded his agreement. With Kyra gone, Gala had been the only other woman he had cared to love. He'd had wild midnight post-coital fantasies of running away with her to Krete, or one of the smaller islands, to live out their days as husband and wife. But they were only dreams; being an Athenian meant more to him than any woman. He just hoped she realised that.

"Come then, my young friend—escort me back to my bed at the House of Javelins. My old bones and flabby muscles need their rest more than ever this day."

From an alleyway to the side of a pottery shop, a cloaked figure watched them head west, back to the centre of the city. The figure waited for them to get twenty steps ahead, then followed nimbly after.

CHAPTER 9

Polydektos kept to his word and woke Talaemenes early from his slumber next to the naked Gala. She had been very amorous the night before, keeping the young man awake to all hours. Even when he wished for sleep, the deft touch of her nails, fingertips, and lips made his body deny what his mind craved.

Yet here Polydektos was, just after dawn. The older man smiled down at him in a knowing way, the first smile Talaemenes had seen on his friend's lips for a long while. Polydektos walked round the bed to open the shutters to a new dawn and stepped out onto the balcony. Talaemenes's eyes drew as slits against the unwelcome morning glare. Gala groaned, turned over, and picked up her tunic from the floor to cover her face from the sunlight.

Groaning, the youth forced his naked frame out of bed. He drank straight from the water jug, then splashed some into his left hand to wipe over his eyes, cheeks, and neck. He peed in the pisspot and threw on yesterday's dirty tunic. He staggered outside, tired but not hung over, yawning until his jaws ached.

"Gala kept you from your sleep, I see," Polydektos said from his seat next to the small table on the balcony. The table was laden with fruits, berries, and porridge, and a jug of juice sat in the centre next to two cups. An empty chair was pushed out waiting for him. "And what I heard."

"I could have used your help last night, to share my burdens," Talaemenes said, sitting down in the chair with a bump. He picked up two grapes and popped them into his mouth.

"And I thought I was the unfit one. You have youth on your

side, Talaemenes. I see that mornings down at the gymnasium will be good for you as well as me. You will soon be joining the army and will be glad of the extra training.

"I will not indulge in such things, nor wine, until after the killer or killers of my family are caught. Then after they are dead, I will drink to honour my beloved Kyra and Kephissa." Polydektos poured himself some juice and offered some to Talaemenes's cup. The younger man picked up his cup to aid the pouring.

"We will not stop until we find out who has done this evil act."

They clinked cups and drained them.

"Now let us eat heartily, lest I have nothing to vomit up this fine morning." Polydektos picked up some figs that he had quartered open and began to eat.

Vomit he did, but not as much as the day before. With Talaemenes by his side, he did not run himself into the ground as much. The fit, lithe youth made him rest and take on water. They also moved from boxing to long jump, then to javelin and discus throwing. Only here could the older man best his youthful companion. Polydektos looked upon his young companion's toned, dust-covered body with jealousy of his fitness. The old lust for Talaemenes had dulled; he felt shame that his nights with him and Gala might have been better served at home with his wife and daughter.

Polydektos bathed and went to the massage room after to be oiled, scraped, and stretched. Then they had a pleasant lunch at a tent-covered eatery on the shady side of the Agora. It was well into the afternoon by the time they trudged up the Panathenaic Way to the villa. The sun was sizzling hot, making the road ahead shimmer like a desert mirage. The sun was relentless, and they were both tired from their exercise this morning. Yet their slow, reluctant pace was more to do with their destination, rather than their fatigue.

Outside, they met Alkmaion, who was still taking shifts to guard the place from thieves and inquisitive ghouls. Polydektos was glad to see him, and they embraced as brother soldiers.

"Is it time?"

"Yes, Alkmaion, my old friend. Time to face the horrors within." Polydektos let go of the old warrior and moved towards the shady entrance. He recalled Sokos running around on the hill as a lad, as Kephissa fed baby Kyra from her breast.

"You do not have to do this today if you don't wish," Talaemenes said from behind him.

"I've put this off for too long already." Polydektos faltered, biting his bottom lip to keep back more tears of remorse and grief. He paused to take a deep breath and then plunged into the shade of his old villa, a place he had once loved to come home to. Now only ghosts remained—ghosts of the family life he had lost.

Walking along the pastas, he felt numb, as if the villa were part of an old life he'd left behind long ago. It was just brick, straw, and mortar, nothing more than that; not without his family. He moved towards the altar of Zeus Herkeios, but did not offer up a prayer to the god of boundaries. He heard the sounds of sandaled feet behind him. He turned to see Talaemenes and Alkmaion behind him.

"We are here to help," Alkmaion said.

"So you know you are not alone in this venture."

"Thanks to you, my friends. Let us proceed, then. We will search each room in turn, all three of us, until we find something or nothing, and then move onto the next room. Unless this was the act of the gods, we must find some clue to who the murderers were," Polydektos said in a resolute voice.

"Where do we start, General?" Alkmaion said, walking towards him.

"Someone drugged or poisoned the slaves, or they would have put up a fight, I'm sure. Let us begin in the kitchen."

"And what are we looking for?" Talaemenes moved closer to the open archway, to the cold, empty kitchens that were once the heart of the home.

"I know not," Polydektos replied with a shake of his head.

The kitchen had many pots and jugs to search, but none of the men found anything untoward. They ventured into the slaves' quarters next. Someone had put dried fragrant flowers in each room to clear the smell of death that had once clung to the place.

"Not a nice place to die," Alkmaion muttered.

"No, but where is?" Talaemenes asked.

"In bed, at a very ripe old age, with your friends and family around you," Polydektos replied. That quietened down his two companions.

"So there was some sort of poison in the air, put in here, that killed the slaves whilst they slept?" Alkmaion stated, changing the subject a little.

"Yes, we believe so. Though no signs of it were found in the morning, the sickly smell was still here." Polydektos said.

"Yet the metics had their throats cut?" Talaemenes said. "Why kill each different class in a different manner? Would it not take up more time? The murderers must have been here for a couple of hours at least to commit such crimes. Had they no fear of being discovered?"

"If we discover the reason behind the three types of death inflicted that night, then maybe it will lead us closer to the per-petrators," Polydektos observed. "The vileness of the deaths increases as one moves up the class ladder."

"Which means what?" Alkmaion was a great soldier of Athens, but he gladly left all the thinking and tactics to gener-als like Polydektos.

"That the murderer or murderers had more of a connec-tion with our foreign-born slaves than anyone else in the villa. The metics were not citizens of Athens, but most were born in and around Greece itself. When they invaded the villa, the only Athenians here were my wife and daughter. The slaves had to be killed, but they were killed in the most humane way pos-sible—perhaps killed by some airborne fumes as they slept. The metics were probably gassed in their sleep too, but had their throats cut in a brutal manner. The murderers did not have to do this; they could poison them like the slaves. But they wanted to make a statement. They actually wasted time cutting their throats for no reason. Then we come to my wife and daughter. They were most vilely treated of all. What can we make of these facts?"

"That the murderers hated Greeks above all the peoples of the world," Talaemenes offered.

"Yes," Polydektos cried, slamming his right fist into his left palm. "And that the murderer or murderers had more of an affinity with slaves than the rest of the household. That they or he held them in higher regard than the Greeks in the household."

"Which proves what?" Alkmaion asked, more than a little confused.

"That the murderer or murderers were either slaves, non-Greeks, or maybe both?" Talaemenes said, feeling pleased with himself for following what Polydektos was saying.

"How could a slave find time to do such a thing as this?" Alkmaion said, drawing his grey eyebrows together in a frown.

"If they were freed slaves, escaped ones—Persians, perhaps, or even foreigners posing to be Athenian citizens?"

"Which would tie in with what we witnessed at Acrohaeom all those years ago." Alkmaion moved closer to this old general. "Do you think one of more of the Persians who fled our wrath and slaughter has bided his time until now to seek revenge on you, to take away all that you love?"

"Which means they wanted you to suffer," Talaemenes pointed out. "Which also means they could still be inside the city walls, gloating at the vengeance they lay upon you, and are watching you as you grieve?"

"Yes," Polydektos nodded looking down at his sandals. Then he pulled back his himation to reveal his sword belted around his waist underneath. "That's why we must be armed at all times, my friends. For if they are still here, silent and biding their time like before, they could hit again from the shadows at any moment."

Talaemenes felt the dagger beneath his clothes, tied to his hip. He could not help but look around the villa warily, expecting to see assassins in every corner.

"What do we do now, then?" Alkmaion asked, grasping the hilt of the short sword that he kept on show all the time.

"We continue our search in the metics' quarters," Polydektos stoutly replied, walking over to the door to their larger quarters under the stairs.

The metics' quarters were just that: a large room divided up into four smaller rooms with thin partition walls. A wave of grief nearly knocked Polydektos over as he entered the hall-way that led off into the four rooms. He had been so out of his mind with the loss of his wife and daughter this past week or so that he had not found time to mourn the loss of servants he had known for many years—like Maro from the tiny island of Kos, who had begged to fight with his army during the Persian wars. He had followed Polydektos's army until the general had given in and let him join as his cup bearer. He had become a loyal fighter, and Polydektos had brought him home all those years ago. He died in the very room the former general peered into, his wife and daughter slaughtered with him. They did not deserve to die, not for Polydektos's sake. This added to his already burning desire to find who had murdered everyone in his household.

He had been the kyrios of this kleros, the head of the house-hold, and he had let them down. He had become an old, fat, drunken letch, and they had paid the price.

They found nothing out of place in the rooms, only pools of blood that had turned to brown stains on the beds and floors. They moved on to the toilet area, the andron, and then the liv-ing room. All were devoid of any clues to finding the culprits.

Polydektos had left the long thin storeroom between the liv-ing room and men's andron to last. It being an enclosed space, it had still had enough of the poison in the air the next morning to knock out one of Eretmenos's metics. This room, unlike most of the downstairs rooms, had a door with a wooden mortis lock to keep it shut. It had no windows, but the mice always seemed to find a way in every few months or so. The storeroom had a musty smell of spoilt food as they opened the door. There were large amphorae and pithos jars stacked up in three of the cor-ners and tied sacks in the other. A couple of the jars were bro-ken and leaking olive oil onto the hard, earthen floor. Another couple of jars were also on their side, but were unbroken.

"This damage could have happened when Eretmenos's man was overcome by fumes, or when the Rod Bearers came in to rescue him," Talaemenes pointed out. "How would we know if the murderers caused any damage?"

"We will take out every jar and sack into the pastas and

empty out the contents on the floor," Polydektos said, grabbing the nearest jar to him and taking it out into the pastas. "This is the only real, out of place thing about the attack, and it does not make sense. Why put the poison gas in the storeroom?"

"Unless it was put there before the attack by someone ready for that night," Alkmaion said.

"Yes," Polydektos grunted, throwing the jar through the air to crash apart in the courtyard area. Dried figs scattered across the tiles floor. "That was my thought exactly."

"But who put it there?" Talaemenes said, going into the storeroom to fetch two jars, both with handles to make them easy to carry. He came back and threw both at once. They sailed higher than Polydektos's effort, crashing apart to send red wine all over the mosaic tiles. "One of the slaves or metics?"

"But they all died, didn't they?" Alkmaion stated.

"They could have been given coins to do it," Talaemenes said, offering his opinion.

"Let us not speak ill of the dead, as they have no recourse to recount such claims. " Polydektos always treated his servants and slaves better than any man he knew in Athens. He hoped that they had been loyal to him and his family, right up to their ends. "They could just as well have taken the poisoned jars into the storeroom unwittingly. Or maybe they were put there one night after dark by stealth. Let us search every sack and smash every jar to see what we can find."

Amphora followed pithos followed sack. Soon all three men were sweating with their efforts. Polydektos and Alkmaion were puffing out their cheeks as they carried large, heavy sacks of grain and flour into the courtyard. The place was a mess of mixed dried fruits, grain, and flour, made into a muddy mess by white and red wine, olive oil, and water. The three men were dusted with it on their hands, arms, and feet.

It took them a full hour to clear the storeroom and empty its contents on the floor. Alkmaion and Talaemenes were sifting through it all with brooms to see if there was anything hidden inside the broken jugs and pots. Polydektos had lit a torch and was wandering around the empty storeroom, checking every crevice and crack in the walls. He tipped over a broken jar of olive oil he had himself dropped on the floor when they were clearing out the storeroom. Polydektos kicked out at the large piece of the broken jar, sending it to break against the wall, and hurting two of his toes in the process. He knelt down to rub his toes, frustrated at finding nothing to point them in the direction of the killer or killers.

He looked down at the oil in the left-hand corner of the room, seeping slowly into the earth floor. He had never seen it do this so quickly, in all his years living here. The floor was hard packed earth, nearly like stone in places. Most spillages had to be mopped up by the female slaves. He pulled his short sword and dug it into the earth where the oil was sinking. The earth was looser here, just beneath the surface. He stood up and hurried to the open doorway.

"Both of you fetch me a jug or bucket of water, quickly," Polydektos urged. The two men looked at each other with quizzical looks, and then hurried off out of the door to do as he urged. Polydektos went back to where the oil was seeping in and knelt down to dig at it with his sword while he waited. The soil looked disturbed under the initial crust. He moved over to dig in other places, but found it much harder work to chip away at the solid, well-walked on, compacted soil.

Talaemenes and Alkmaion soon returned from the kitchen with both a bucket and a large jug of water. He would have found the fact that they had followed his instructions to the letter amusing, at any other time but this.

"Quickly, over here," he said, pointing to the spot where half of the remains of the oil jug were. "Pour the water slowly, one after the other, where I've been digging." Polydektos stood back a little way, holding the torch over the place he wanted the water to go.

Alkmaion went first, pouring slowly, then stopping and waiting for the water to seep into the earth before continuing. Soon they had a muddy well in the corner of the floor. Polydektos held Talaemenes back and dug into the muddy hole with his sword some more, making the side bigger and the hole deeper. He moved back on his knees, not caring how dirty he became.

"Now your bucket, Talaemenes," he urged. "A little more quickly this time."

Talaemenes poured the water into the watery brown hole at a steady pace. His bucket was nearly emptied when a large bubble burst the top of the brown water with a *plop*. Then the water began to drain away rapidly, into the hole until none remained. Polydektos moved forwards and pushed the torch into the hole. At the bottom of the muddy well, about a foot down, showed the tops of three poles lashed together.

"Talaemenes, fetch tools to dig with," Polydektos ordered. The youth ran from the room, eager to find out what was beneath the storeroom floor.

He came back only two minutes later to find the two older men digging at the hole with their swords. "Here, use these," Talaemenes said, handing out two of the three spades he had fetched from one of the outer buildings.

"Open the hole up first," Polydektos said, as they all took a side to dig. It did not take them long to open up a three-foot-wide, squarish hole. Then they began to dig down into the wet earth, flinging it into three different piles behind them. They soon unearthed a wooden lattice of twelve poles lashed together; six one way and six the other. Under the wooden structure could be seen a small tunnel and two blue pots, their wide wooden bungs sealed with wax. They had to dig away some more at the edges to finally work the wooden trapdoor free.

Talaemenes, who was the thinnest and youngest, took the torch from Polydektos and went down to investigate. He handed up the blue jars first, saying, "I think it wise we not open them here or anywhere near people."

"We can take them to my small farm holding outside of the Death Gate," Alkmaion offered.

"We can purchase a cage of canaries to test the contents on, while we cover our mouths and keep a good distance away," Polydektos suggested.

"Wish me the luck of the gods, then," Talaemenes said, before he pushed the torch ahead of him into the tight, earth-packed tunnel under the house.

Polydektos reached down and patted the youth's back as

he pushed himself along the dark tunnel, with two dead mice for company. The tunnel was tight even for the youth, and the air was sour and unpleasant-tasting. Talaemenes thought about going back to tie something over his mouth when the tunnel came to a dead end, only a body length away from the hole in the storeroom corner. He turned on his back, keeping his lips tight shut, and pushed the torch upwards. The hole went up just over a foot, ending with another trapdoor. This one had no holes in it, but was of the same size.

"There is a way to the outside," he called back down the tunnel.

"Can you get out that way?" Polydektos called down to him.

"I'll try," he called back. Leaning the flickering, oxygen-starved torch in one corner, he reached up with both hands and gave a heavy push. He heard the ripping of roots, and then the trapdoor lifted up, sending dim light into the hole. Spitting out the earth that fell onto his face, he hurriedly pushed the trap-door open and scrambled out of the tunnel. As he brushed the dirt from his face and hair, he saw that the wooden trapdoor had been covered with sods of dried yellow grass about a finger's length deep. He was on the other side of the house, with wild bushes that had grown up next to the wall of the house over the years. It was a perfect place to dig a hole, unobserved at night.

He heard one of the men inside calling to him, but he could not tell who it was, or what they were saying. Just for youthful fun, he ran around to the front of the villa, through the entrance, to come up behind his companions. Polydektos and Alkmaion were on their knees calling down the hole to him.

"Are you through yet?" Alkmaion called down the hole.

"Yes," he said simply from behind them. He smiled and leant on the doorframe, amused to have crept up on the two old soldiers and made them jump.

"Don't ever do that again," Polydektos's face flared with anger, his sword pointing towards the youth.

"It was easier and less dirty than crawling back through," Talaemenes said, and he could hear the whining of his own voice in his own ears. It must sound worse to these hardened warriors who had crawled through blood and guts spilled battlefields so many times. Alkmaion lowered Polydektos's sword with his fingertips and gave the youth a favourable grin.

"So we know how the murderers got in, and it looks like we have the foul substance that killed everyone before vile actions were brought upon the bodies. What do we do with this information? It does not lead us any closer to finding out who did this to your wife and daughter, does it, Polydektos?"

"No, but we can rule out any act of the gods in this now. This was pre-planned murder on a grand scale. I was the target, but not for death; the perpetrators wanted me to suffer a pain worse than any spear thrust. We also know that the hole was only large enough for someone thin to fit through. And these are not the acts of soldiers. A true warrior would want to face me in battle and watch me die by their own hands." Polydektos stood up and sheathed his sword.

"Poison is not the weapon of a strong man," Talaemenes said, looking down at his sandals. He was still a little stung by Polydektos's harsh words.

"No, it is the weapon of cowards, foreigners, and women," Polydektos stated.

"What shall we do now?" Alkmaion asked of his former general.

"We look upstairs," Polydektos said, leading the way.

Sadness crept over the two men of the house and only survivors of the attack as they entered Kyra's sleeping quarters. Polydektos stopped at the threshold as a wave of recent grief flowed over him. Only with the steadying hand of Talaemenes on his shoulder could he force his heavy legs to move. The three men took up positions around Kyra's deathbed.

"So you found but one drop of her blood on her sheets?" Alkmaion said, stroking his beard.

"Yes," Polydektos said, pulling back a sheet to point at the single drop of blood. It had turned from red to dried brown.

"Then she and your beloved wife were not killed in their beds, merely placed there afterwards for evil effect," Alkmaion said, looking around the room.

Polydektos just nodded in reply.

"It would take a few hours to drain even a dismembered

body of all its blood. Forgive me, but the bodies would have to be hung somewhere. We need to find out where; it cannot be far, for the murders would be in fear of being caught. We need to find the place these atrocities happened, Polydektos."

"You are right, Alkmaion. But if it were in the house, so much blood would not be easily disguised or scrubbed away in one night. A body holds much blood; we know of that from the battlefield, my friend. Someone skilled in the art of bloodletting or butchery would have such skills. "

"The Persians, I have heard told, have such butchers and tor- turers in their ranks," Talaemenes said, wanting to help.

"Only a spy or assassin skilled in hiding their identity could roam Athens unaccosted to kill at will," Alkmaion said, moving around the room. The whole house still reeked of death, and it made him jumpy.

Polydektos lowered himself down on his daughter's bed and sat in silent thought.

The other two men exchanged worried looks, hoping he wasn't slipping back into his dark, silent days of grief again.

"So who are we looking for?" Polydektos said, standing up and slapping his right thigh. "Someone who hates me beyond any other person in Greece. Someone who can walk along an Athenian street without anyone taking any notice of them. A person who has skills of alchemy and of butchery. Someone who is not afraid of blood, and can gain access to the side of my house without being noticed," Polydektos mused, rubbing at his bearded chin with thumb and forefinger.

"Nobody takes much notice of a slave," Talaemenes said, clicking his fingers.

"Or of a metic about their business," Alkmaion added.

"Or a merchant, with a cart loaded with pots," Polydektos said to himself, in barely a whisper.

"The potter, Trekhos of Krete. He was on the Panathenaic Way, with his servant, carrying pots from the way this very villa stands," Talaemenes said aloud, thumping the nearby wall with his fist.

"But his servant spoke for you at your trial." Alkmaion pointed out.

"Because he had no choice, once I remembered that Megas was a full son of Athens," Polydektos said. "And Trekhos, being from Krete, knew he would not have to give evidence at the trial. We saw them on the road, but we just assumed they were going about their early morning business. Trekhos 's shop is nowhere near there—it is over in the northern part of the city. There are no clay pits nearby, so where had he come from, and what was in those pots?"

"Blood, perhaps," Alkmaion whispered.

"Talaemenes, I want you to search the rest of the upstairs rooms, and when you are done, the grounds to try to find where this butchery of my family happened. Alkmaion, fetch a handcart, secure those two jars, and take them to the rear of the property. Let no one go near them. Then I want you to visit every alchemist in the City. Give them each a mina if they will come here three hours hence. There we will test out the poison gas from a safe distance, and see if any of the alchemists know what it could be, and where it comes from," Polydektos ordered.

"What are you going to do?" Talaemenes had a pretty good idea already.

"I will visit our Kretan friend's shop and try to speak to Megas alone, if I can. He may be innocent but complicit at the same time. Trekhos could not make it through that hidden tunnel, but I'm sure Megas could." Polydektos made for the bedroom doorway.

Talaemenes grabbed his forearm to stop him going. "One of us should accompany you, Polydektos. It could get dangerous."

"Have faith in this old soldier," Polydektos said, tapping his sword sheath. "You have your orders." He left the two men alone with their thoughts in Kyra's bedroom.

"What if he gets himself killed?" Talaemenes asked Alkmaion.

"Then that is the gods' will, and we will know the truth of the matter and avenge his death. Come, lad, we have lots to do this afternoon." Alkmaion strode from the room, to visit the bedroom where Kephissa's dismembered body was found.

CHAPTER 10

Polydektos had not felt so pumped up and full of purpose in years. He strode up the Panathenaic Way, ignoring the gripes and pains from his leg muscles. He passed the place where, in a drunken state, he and Talaemenes had met the merchant. He was unsure of any reason the Kretan would want his family dead. Maybe he was just employed by the murderer to carry away the blood? Or maybe he was just an innocent on the road late at night, and would have a valid reason for being there. Either way, Polydektos would find out the truth of the matter.

Trekhos's shop and studio were close to the walls in the 'Potters' Quarters' of the lowest city, near the Dipylon Gate. As a metic, he could not own the building where he both worked and lived, but could rent it from a friendly Athenian, probably in Megas's name. Polydektos had known the Kretan for fifteen years on and off. They had drunk wine together, and had travelled the seas on two occasions when he had taken on more secretive state missions to other Greek islands, all in the name of Athens. He had found him a gregarious companion, with the usual vices men have. He had never detected any ill feeling from the man, who could have killed him on many occasions over the years.

He wasn't convinced that Trekhos had any involvement in his family's deaths, yet he might have unwittingly become part of the plot, even without knowing it. Polydektos had to make sure first, and then proceed from there.

The streets were tighter together in this district of lower Athens. The place had fewer of the new Perikles builds here.

There was more mud, clay, and straw here than stone and marble. Polydektos stepped over a dead dog in the middle of the road. The dog had an arrow sticking out from its left eye and two flat rut marks across its crushed hind section. People had just pulled their heavy carts over it, rather than move it to the side of the road.

A turn left and then right brought him to a T-junction, with the city walls looming large ahead of him. Under the shadow of the walls dead ahead was the shop of Trekhos the Potter and Trader. The double doors of the popular shop were open to customers. Two tables sat outside with a small collection of the pots, urns, and vases on show. None of the expensive stuff that, as Trekhos had once told him over some Raki, he'd had imported from Kos.

Some customers were milling about outside, and three more ladies from rich villas were inside. The shop had a doorway, shrouded by long strings of beads, that led into a storeroom beyond. Another doorway to the left then led to the pottery, with a kiln inside and a larger one outside in a small open courtyard. The courtyard got the most sun during the day to help dry out the pots on high, lined racks around all three sides. The only other small room had wooden steps leading up to the first floor. The upstairs was Trekhos 's humble quarters, which he shared with Megas.

Two men were serving behind a long wooden counter. Of Trekhos and his ward there was no sign. The walls and floors were lined with pots, urns, vases, and bowls of every size, shape, and colour you could imagine. Some had come from as far as Sikelia in the west, Egypt in the south, Sidon in the east, and Kallatis to the North. Trekhos made his own pots, by potters he employed, and exported them to the far regions of the known world. In these pots he also transported olive oil, to double his profit margins in one swoop.

A large-hipped woman in front of Polydektos had just purchased a black vase the exact same shape as her body. As she left the shop, the general moved up to take her place at the counter.

"How can I be of service this fine morning, General Polydektos?" the man asked with a broad smile, rubbing his hands together.

Polydektos did not recognise the man, nor the other man standing next to him. "You know me, where I have never seen you before?"

"Who in Athens, nay Greece, does not know the name of the hero Polydektos? Our master Trekhos always speaks highly of you, General. Is there a particular pot or urn you are after this day? If not I can steer you in the direction of a certain type of pot that we keep under the counter for men of your stature." The shopkeeper leant over the counter and whispered to Polydektos, while eyeing the proximity of the two browsing lady shoppers. Polydektos did not like the way the man wet his lips each time before he spoke, nor the fishiness of his breath. "We have ones with undressed nymphs and heroes cavorting freely in a wooded glade if that so takes your fancy."

"I'm here to see your master, not bandy words with a piss-pot seller," Polydektos said, giving the shopkeeper his battle-stare. "Is Trekhos or Megas here?"

The man leant swiftly backwards and licked his wet lips in a nervous manner. "The master is not here, oh great Strategos, or Megas, before you ask." The man backed up a step from the counter.

"When will they be back?" Polydektos asked, looking from the shopkeeper to the door to the back of the shop.

"Many a month, General. He's taken young Megas to Krete to show him his birthplace, visit his aging mother, and bring back more pots than a Persian war galley could carry." Polydektos raised his eyebrows at the mention of Persian war galleys, but said nothing.

"His family requested his presence, as his mother was not long for this world," the other man behind the counter answered. Polydektos eyed the two men as his mind took in many things about the language of their bodies. They were nervous cravens, and were clearly a front; he doubted they knew much else then they had already told him. He tried to remember the details of the upstairs quarters he had visited on three occasions, usually the worse for some cheap Macedonian wine.

"I lent Trekhos a black and gold vase of Persian design I got on my travels. He was going to use it to try to copy its designs.

It is only the size of two hands but has a white horse chased by golden lions on it. You know the piece?" Polydektos had remembered it sitting on a high shelf in Trekhos 's andron. He just hoped it was still there and had not been moved months ago.

"Yes, General, a fine piece in the master's quarters upstairs. Shall I fetch it for you?"

"No," Polydektos said firmly, in his general's voice. "I would fear you dropping it. I shall fetch it myself." Without waiting for a reply, he strode around the counters and through the beaded doorway.

"Customers are not allowed in the back." The shopkeeper's lip-licking increased as he hurried through the beads after him.

"I am not a customer, though, am I? I am a friend of Trekhos of Krete, going to get my own vase I had long lent him." Polydektos turned and raised his neck, looking down at the cowering man. "Are you going to stop me, metic?"

The shopkeeper hastily scurried back through the beads into the shop, leaving Polydektos to look around the storeroom and the rest of the building unmolested.

The next room was an open affair with a large empty window whose shutter was fixed in the upright position to let the most light in. A firing kiln sat in one corner, and three wheels were set up inside. One open doorway led outside into a walled yard. It was fenced all around, just above Polydektos's head. Fixed to the wooden fence were shelves bedded with straw, where hundreds of pots of all shapes and sizes lay. The larger pots used for indoor planting just sat on the floor before them. Polydektos did not go outside, but went through the other inner door, which led to a shady, enclosed mezzanine stairwell. Under the stairs, covered by sacks, were pots and wooden boxes where the moist clay was kept. Polydektos, seeing nothing untoward, made his way up the steps to Trekhos's living quarters. He had a sudden feeling come over him that he was acting lower than a common thief. He shook the thought from his mind, concentrating on the mission to find the person or people who had killed his wife and daughter.

Trekhos's quarters were basic but homely enough. A large woven map of Krete was the main feature of the inner wall.

Polydektos moved through the living room into one of the bedrooms. It was small, with a single bed and badly made wall shelves decorated with carved and painted wooden soldiers. Apart from piles of dirty clothes draped over a chair, there was little else in what must be Megas's room.

Trekhos's bed and bedroom were a much larger and grander affair. With sheets of silk in reddish gold, the bed looked very opulent and inviting. Three chests sat on the inner wall across from the shuttered windows. Polydektos bent down to the first chest and stopped his hands only a hairsbreadth away from touching the lacquered wood. The feeling of guilt fell over him like a thick woollen blanket. This was not him, a thief going through others' possessions. Surely if Trekhos was involved in any witting or unwitting capacity, he would have no proof of his guilt in his home. Polydektos sat back against the bed—he needed to look into Trekhos's and Megas's eyes and read their reactions.

He stood up and exited the bedroom, not giving the black vase in the living quarters a second look as he walked past. He exited the shop as fast as his legs could carry him.

"Did you not find the vase, General?" the shopkeeper called after him, but he did not stop. He still had time before he had to meet Alkmaion and Talaemenes again, and even then they would wait for him to return. He walked briskly towards the Piraean Gate, needing to get to the port to make sure Trekhos and Megas had truly sailed to Krete. The Cretan merchant/potter had a warehouse there to store his incoming and outgoing pots: that was Polydektos's destination.

Talaemenes and Alkmaion had searched the rest of the villa as quickly as their consciences would allow. Talaemenes was young and still feared the spirits of the dead might linger there. It was also the place his sweet Kyra died. But they found nothing of interest. Alkmaion went off to fetch the alchemists, while Talaemenes was glad to get outside to search the grounds. It felt good to feel the intense heat of the sun on his neck and shoulders as he looked around the rear of the property. He searched the outer buildings and the livestock pens, wondering where the bloodletting could have happened. Talaemenes tried to put himself in the place of a lone murderer.

The poison fumes had done the job of killing everyone in the household quickly. A puzzling thought occurred to him: how had the murderer gotten the pots of poison in every room that mattered? They would have needed a pot for the slaves' room, one for the metics' quarters, and one each for Kephissa's and Kyra's bedchambers. How did they get them there unnoticed, and why didn't the fumes overcome the murderer? If the poison killed and then vanished into the air, why had Eretmenos's gardener succumbed to its effect in the morning? Had he disturbed a jar of the poison, or had the closed storeroom with no ventilation kept the fumes in? Perhaps they would discover the origins and potency of the killing draft when Polydektos and Alkmaion returned. How long would the killer have waited, even with their mouth and nose covered, to cut the metics' throats before going upstairs to dismember the ladies of the house? An hour to set off the fumes and wait for them to dissipate, he surmised. Then they would have had to take the bodies somewhere close by to drain their blood. It would have been dark outside, but on the hill away from any other neighbouring properties, a torch could go unseen at night. If it were that late, most would be in their beds anyway.

"You would not want to carry the bodies far, given they could only have a few hours at most to accomplish their goals," Talaemenes said aloud to the empty goat pen. Alkmaion had taken all the animals and fowl away, lest their meat be tainted by the deaths in the villa. To eat the livestock after such murders would be an affront to the gods. Alkmaion had taken them up to hills and sacrificed them all to Zeus, to lend his wisdom to the investigations.

Talaemenes rubbed at his bare, youthful chin. "Athene, forgive the terrible thoughts that I must now have," he said, looking up at the Akropolis on the hill behind the villa. "I have not one but two bodies to dismember and drain of blood and other bodily fluids. It is dark outside. I carry one at a time, over my shoulder, while carrying a torch, perhaps. Where do I go to accomplish this foul deed?"

Talaemenes looked at the stone walls of the small goat pen. It was a dirty, smelly place at the best of times, but today in the baking sun it reeked even more than usual. It had three waist-high stone walls and a wooden gate at the right-hand end. Two-thirds of it were open to the elements, while the walls of the left-hand side were built up a little further and had a basic wooden roof on top where the goats could shelter from the elements. The straw that was usually inside the sheltered area of the pen was scattered across the open area. Talaemenes ran back to the tool shed and fetched a hoe. Using it to flick the hay back into the covered area of the pen, he saw that the bottom layers of stray were baked with a reddish-brown, clay-like substance. He dug into the baked hard crust he found under the straw, and red pools of thick blood oozed out.

The sight and fetid smell of it made him stagger away, retching up his breakfast. He had found the place where the bodies had been dismembered, at least. He made for the nearby well on the property to drink the taste from his mouth. He sent down the bucket for the first time since the murders. His hands were sweaty, and he lost hold of the rope. The wooden pail dropped the last five feet, filled with well water, and sank to the bottom.

"By the dog!" Talaemenes cursed as he rubbed his hands in the dust around the well to get a better grip to pull up the pail. The pail had sunk right to the bottom of the well, and it took him longer to pull it from the deep water. His muscles were aching, and a sheen of sweat covered his torso and arms by the time he'd drawn it up. Two wooden ladles were hung on hooks on one of the wooden well uprights. He steadied the pail and plunged the ladle to the bottom to draw some water to his dry lips to drink. The water stopped just a hairsbreadth from his waiting lips. The water in the bucket was far from clear and refreshing, and there was a definite taint to its natural aroma. Talaemenes poured the water from the ladle back into the pail. It seemed to have a pink tinge that wasn't there before. Talaemenes unhooked the wooden pail and carried it over to the rear of the villa. Just inside and to the left was the curtained-off room where the household made their toilet.

There was a wide bowl set in the earth, which could easily

be lifted up and changed after use. Also resting on a wooden chest was a large white ceramic bowl to wash one's unclean self afterwards. Talaemenes kept the curtain pulled to let in the natural sunlight from outside, and poured the contents of the wooden pail into the white raised bowl.

The water showed up pinkish-red against the white backing of the bowl. He hurriedly put down the pail, his hand to his mouth. He rushed from the villa, back into the sunshine again, swallowing down the gorge that had risen in his throat. He moved away from the rear of the villa and the well towards the outbuildings there. He wanted to get away from this blood-filled, death-tainted house. He leant against a tall, thin structure with a stone base that rose into the chimney. It was the smoker, where they hung meats from the animals on the property they sometimes slaughtered.

A dire thought crossed the youth's already racing mind.

Talaemenes closed his eyes. He turned on the spot, facing the tall, thin wooden door on the front of the smoker. Nailed on one side was a footlong piece of wood, which lifted up to form the most basic of catches. Trying to stop his left hand trembling, he exhaled loudly three times and opened the smoker door. The smell of long-eaten smoked meats and charcoal entered his nostrils. But it was what he saw that made him retch again. The cold ash in the pit of the fire had been replaced with a brown, muddy, half-dried soup. Bloodstains covered the side of the smoker, and the hook on the iron bar at the top was covered with dried gore. Inside, on the natural shelf where the stones met the wooden three-quarters or the smoker, there lay a curved knife, its blade blackened by fire.

Talaemenes had seen enough. He shut the smoker door but did not put on the catch again. He headed past the outbuildings to the small olive grove on the boundaries of the villa and leant up against the stone boundary wall. He was trained to be lithe, strong of heart, and a swift runner. He would do well in the Greek army when it was his time, but he was not yet ready for such evil, deviously planned sights and thoughts as these. Hades must have a special place for a person or people who could do such acts of vileness and desecration to a corpse.

He let himself slide down the waist-high stone wall, ignoring the pain and scratches on his back. He sat in the dirt, getting a little shade from the wall and the olive branches above. He tried to think of lighter, more joyful occasions from his time living at the villa, but he couldn't. His mind was now tainted by the deaths and the blood that seemed to ooze from every corner of the property.

There he sat until Alkmaion found him an hour later, in the company of three bearded men in long robes following behind him.

Chapter 11

There was a chill in the air when Polydektos finally made it back to the villa. Grey clouds, borne on a brisk wind from the north, had covered the blue skies. Some of the clouds beyond the Akropolis looked dark with rain.

His mission to the port had been fruitless. Trekhos and Megas had left on yesterday's morning tide, according to a water rat he slipped a couple of drachma to for the information. The dockside beggar had only kind words for the pot and olive oil merchant from Krete. Polydektos hurried back to the city as fast as his sore legs would allow. In his tired mood, he forgot to collect the canaries on the way back home. He only remembered again, with an agitated click of his fingers, when he crested the top of the hill his villa sat upon, under the slopes of the Akropolis.

When he rounded the villa, he found Alkmaion arguing with three bearded gentlemen of a certain profession, all wanting their leave of the accursed place. Without blazing sunlight, the rear of the property was not the nicest place in Athens to be. The darker clouds would hasten the night, and not even Polydektos liked being at the villa after nightfall anymore.

"My learned friends, thank the gods you have remained here, showing both your courage and wisdom," Polydektos called out with open arms as he approached the group, which also included Talaemenes.

"We were just about to leave, Polydektos," said the alchemist with the longest and greyest beard.

"Then let me add a talent to each of your palms to excuse my lateness of return." Polydektos fished out three talents for the alchemists, which magically ceased their worries and grumbles.

"We have no livestock to try the poison out on," Alkmaion whispered as he went over to clasp his old general in welcome.

"I have an idea," Polydektos whispered back as they parted. He waved Talaemenes closer and the youth jogged over from behind the alchemists. "Talaemenes, I want you to run to Eretmenos's house and fetch him, Euneas, and two goats as fast as all your legs will carry you."

"What about Trekhos? Did you glean anything from him?"

"No, but we will take further counsel, us three together, when this experiment is over. Hasten now like Hermes, and do not come back without the father, son, and goats. Go, go!" Polydektos waved the reluctant youth off.

Loath to miss out anything, Talaemenes sprinted the short distance to Eretmenos's smaller villa, which had larger lands behind for crops and livestock.

It took a lot of explaining over the reluctant voices of Euneas and Dexamene to get Eretmenos to agree to come. He finally had to raise his voice to his wife, and his hand to his son, to shut them up. He alone in the household had believed Talaemenes and Polydektos innocent of the murders of Kyra and Kephissa. After the trial, they had to bow to his way of thinking or else. Eretmenos ordered Dexamene to her bed and Euneas outside to fetch the goats.

Twenty minutes later, Talaemenes returned, leading Eretmenos around the corner of the villa. Euneas came a few seconds later dragging one of the two goats, a rope around its white neck. Borilos, who had only just fully recovered from his half-poisoning, followed after, pulling a mottled brown goat. Both Euneas and Borilos looked less than pleased to be there.

"Welcome, learned men of Athens," Polydektos said. "Under the shadow of the mighty Akropolis, we will hope to discover how my entire household, including my beautiful wife and daughter, were murdered foully in their beds." He moved forwards in front of the small crowd of men, standing in the rear of her property.

"And how will you discover that, Polydektos? And why are

we, and my learned friends, here as witness?" spoke Mopsos, the most senior of the alchemists' present, having the longest beard.

"You have been very patient, and rewarded so with coin. Now you will be rewarded with the truth. Eretmenos, get Euneas to tether his goat at the farthest end of my lands. Alkmaion, Talaemenes, and Borilos, would you assist him please?" Polydektos asked with a polite bow. Far in the distance, a short rumble of thunder was heard in the heavens.

Alkmaion and the others took the white goat to the far end of the property, where Talaemenes drove the wooden post into the ground. Euneas, complaining this was slave's work, tied the goat to the post, giving it little leeway to pull away. With a rag tied around his mouth, Alkmaion brought one of the pots from the wheelbarrow stationed at the far left-hand boundary wall and placed it under the bleating goat. He then retreated with more haste than any time in the last ten years and rejoined the group.

A group that was missing Polydektos.

He came out of the rear entrance of the villa carrying a Corinthian bow he had picked up on his military travels. The group of men fanned out in a semi-circle, with Polydektos at the fore. He notched a white-feathered arrow from the quiver slung over his back and took aim. His first arrow fell a stride short of the sealed pot. He corrected for the wind that was against him. Worried he might skewer the goat, he waited with bow fully drawn for the wind to die down, then fired. His second arrow flew straight and true into the side of the pot, cracking it open into three large pieces.

Talaemenes, who had the keenest eyes, could see a bluish-purple powder inside the broken jar. The goat reared against its post, trying to get free, but was fixed fast. It continued bleating loudly, and after three minutes, Polydektos turned to face the other men present. Only Euneas had a smug, youthful arrogance thin smile on show. Talaemenes, Alkmaion, Eretmenos, and even Borilos looked nonplussed, while the three alchemists were talking in hushed whispers among themselves, probably glad of earning money for nothing more than a walk up to Polydektos's property.

Polydektos exchanged a frown with Alkmaion, who

shrugged back at him, just as the rain that had long threatened began to fall. Thunder rumbled over the very heavens above the Parthenon, like Zeus himself was mocking Polydektos's mortal arrogance. The grumbling alchemists had seen enough, and they were already turning to go. The coin they had received did not cover the inconvenience of getting soaked through.

Eretmenos, with his son and gardener behind him, looked to the dampening ground with embarrassment. Only Alkmaion and Talaemenes looked at him with any belief. Despondent, Polydektos walked towards his two companions, a craving for the wine he had renounced filling his downcast mind.

"Polydektos, look!" Talaemenes almost jumped forwards to grab the former general and spin him around. The youth's cry caused Eretmenos to look up from his wet toes and the alchemists to turn round.

A purple-blue vapour like some evil Persian desert spirit was rising from the broken remains of the jar. It spread out from the broken vessel in a rough circle, hugging the ground like some evil mist from the depths of Hades itself. The goat took one final, scared bleat, and its legs collapsed. It dangled, quite still, from where its neck was tightly tethered to the post, looking less alive than anything Talaemenes had seen in his life. The speed of its demise was shocking.

The alchemists moved up to where Polydektos and his friends stood. They looked on in awe at the deadly blue vapour that seemed to crawl on the ground, seeking out its next victim.

"We must get away from this place," Borilos cried in a scared voice, trying to drag Euneas back around the villa.

"Are we safe here, Polydektos?" Eretmenos said with a slight warble in his voice. He had seen first-hand the effects of this purple-blue haze. He had no desire for himself and his son to be its next victims.

"Do you know what this is? Should we retreat further?" Polydektos asked the three alchemists, who were whispering to each other in excitement.

"We have heard of this, but thought it only a myth," Mopsos, the speaker for the three alchemists, replied.

"What is it, where does it come from?" Polydektos urged,

his eyes flicking back to check that the poisonous gas was not spreading out too far.

"It is the Breath of Ahriman," said one of the other excited but cowering alchemists.

"Ahriman is the foulest of all Persian gods," Polydektos replied.

"Remember the siege of Sardis, General?" Alkmaion asked. "It is said that Ahriman's breath flowed like a dark fog into camp one night, killing an entire phalanx of men, without a single wound being found on their body." Alkmaion was a good but very superstitious soldier, Polydektos remembered. He had once refused to march under a blood-red moon, as it was an evil omen. It had brought him ten lashes of the whip, the General recalled.

"In its dry state it seems inert, and able to be dried and transported safely. Adding water to the mix seems to bring its deadly effects into life," Mopsos explained, pointing a shaking hand at the low blue mist.

The poisonous vapours rose no more than knee height off the ground and expanded outwards from the pot in all directions.

"Anything inside the vapours, breathing it in, would be dead instantly, so the legends say," said the tallest and youngest of the three alchemists.

"In a bedroom, with people sleeping low to the floor, this would easily have killed everyone in my household," Polydektos stated with sadness.

"Yes, a certain amount in the bottom of the chamber pot would let the murderer be many miles away from the scene of the crime when the vapour took hold," Mopsos suggested. "Look, it is dying away already."

The group of men looked on through the driving rain as the blue vapours melted away into the earth, like a mist broken by the bright warmth of the sun. The outer vapours disappeared until only a small cloud hovered over the broken jar. After fifteen minutes of getting soaked in the rain, even this dissipated into nothing.

"It comes and goes like a squall at sea, bringing death in its path and leaving only calm seas afterwards," Eretmenos said, wiping at the oil running from his hair and down his wet forehead.

Polydektos turned towards the alchemists. "Where could someone buy such a poison in Athens?"

"Nowhere, and possibly everywhere," Mopsos said with a shrug of his bony shoulders.

"You speak in riddles, alchemist?" Polydektos said, raising his voice.

Mopsos tried to expand on his earlier comment. "My fellow alchemists and I have only heard of this mist-like poison in legends from soldiers, sailors, and merchants who have returned from Persia. No Greek to our knowledge has the skill to make such a thing, nor has it ever been seen on our shores before. The ingredients to make such a thing could be held by any Athenian, but if we could examine it in its powdered state, we might be able to replicate it in time. Yet this could take many years of study."

Polydektos turned to his trusted companions and rubbed at his beard.

"It seems the finger of death points once more towards Persia and revenge, my General," Alkmaion said, putting a wet hand on Polydektos's damp shoulder.

"It would seem so." Polydektos frowned.

"What do we do now?" Talaemenes asked as the rains began to ease off.

Polydektos looked to Alkmaion. "Is the other jar safe and secure?"

"Yes, I hid it under an old dry water trough, turned upside down."

"Then when the rain has stopped, fetch it carefully to the alchemists to take away and examine at their own peril." Polydektos patted his old friend on the back.

Alkmaion headed off around the right-hand border of the property, keeping far away from the area once covered by the Breath of Ahriman. Polydektos turned once more to the three chatting alchemists.

"We will spread the words throughout the city of this new evidence," Mopsos said. "You were wrongly accused, and

sometimes the foul mud of murder sticks where it shouldn't."
He moved forwards to grasp Polydektos's arm in his.

"I have no cares about what the city thinks of me. If I fetch
you another jar of this evil poison in its powdered state, will
you keep it for me and try to divine its secrets? But at the price
of all three of you, silence on this matter and what you did witness here today. If there is some Persian agent abroad in the city
seeking revenge on me, then I do not wish them to be alerted
to this. Do you swear in the shadow of the temple of Athene to
this?" Polydektos eyed each man in turn.

"We swear on our souls, under the watchful eye of
Asklepios," said Mopsos, "that we alone will keep this secret
and report to you alone what findings we glean from the powder. How it is made and who might have the skill to make it," he
finished, followed by his two companions swearing the same
oath.

The rain had stopped and the thunder was gone by the time
Alkmaion returned, pushing the wheelbarrow holding the jar
covered with straw at arm's length.

"You can take the barrow," Polydektos kindly offered the
Alchemists.

There was an inner power struggle, which seniority won,
giving the youngest and darkest-bearded man the honour of
pushing the barrow before him. In the end, everyone left was
mightily relieved to see them leave with it.

"We will take your leave, Polydektos," Eretmenos said, offering out his arm, which the former general grasped. "May the
gods aid you in finding out the truth, my brother. Your strength
and persistence are like a mountain lion. You have done your
wife and daughter proud this day."

Polydektos felt a burning of emotion rising from his throat
and into his brain. "Get yourself home, Eretmenos, out of your
wet things, and take joy in the family around you."

The two groups of three men parted. Borilos and Euneas
followed Eretmenos like shrunken men, their wet clothes hanging heavy on their shoulders, tugging the lucky surviving goat
behind them.

"Did you discover anything here while I was away?"

Polydektos asked when they were alone.

"I have a few things to show you, Polydektos, but you might not want to see them," Talaemenes replied.

"Show me," Polydektos insisted.

Talaemenes nodded and led them over to the well first. After he had shown the older men the goat sty and the smoker, he felt sick to his stomach. All three men were sick of the place by now.

"My home, hot soup, and mulled wine beckon me, Polydektos," Alkmaion said, ready to depart. "You are more than welcome to join me."

Talaemenes looked hopefully at his older lover.

Polydektos nodded. "I can think of nothing better right now. We can talk on the way."

CHAPTER 12

Polydektos left just after dawn the next day, leaving Talaemenes and Gala naked and entwined in their bedsheets after a night of youthful passion. The air outside was fresh and cool. He dressed simply, wearing his blue wool himation over his chiton to keep out the morning chill and hide the short sword at his waist. He had a sack, tied at the top, slung over his shoulder as he made his way down the Hill of Nymphs. He saw only a few metics and slaves hurrying to start the day hours before their masters and employers woke. Polydektos knew that a slave could do the equivalent of a whole day's work of a wealthy Athenian before the latter had even taken their first morning piss. He made his way up the Panathenaic Way, walking on the newly relaid road. Perikles was always busy rebuilding, innovating and erecting new, beautiful works around Athens. Polydektos wasn't one for statues, temples, or buildings in general. He could hardly put up his own campaign tent of old if he were asked. He was more skilled in breaking things down, anyway.

He passed a few carts laden with goods for the Agora, which was nearly empty. It was very different to how the busy heart of the city would be later, under the burning hot sun. There were only a couple of slaves chatting away to each other. This was their only real time of freedom, to talk and relax without the worry of the whip. Polydektos walked on, glad that he had been born to an Athenian and not a lesser race of men. He would have made a bad slave and probably would have wound up dead within the first few days. Polydektos had never harmed his own slaves, and treated everyone under his roof as well as any man in Greece. He missed the hustle and bustle of his old home. He knew he would never get that back again. Silence seemed to be his only companion now. Apart from the four guards, the Dipylon Gate was clear, and he passed through with a wave from the soldiers there. He had been well known in the city—especially by the military—before his trial, but now everyone knew him. He could go nowhere in the city without being seen, such was his new notoriety.

At last he entered a place where there was no one to recognise him, no seeing eyes unless they were of the gods above. Polydektos strode through the cemetery to the graves where his family were buried side by side. He sat down on the cold, dewy earth and pulled the sack from his shoulder. Unknotting the rope at the top, he opened it and started taking the contents out. He crossed his legs as best he could manage, placing the wine, food, and perfumed oils before him. His wife's and daughter's graves were either side of him, his son Sokos's grave only one more along. He sat up on his knees and poured the scented oils over each of the graves on either side, using half a bottle of the flowery-smelling oil, as he prayed for Athene to look after them until the gods decided his time on Earth was up. He drank none of the wine, placing it on his wife's grave, then divided the food up between his dead children's final resting places. He ate and drank nothing himself. He would buy some fresh fruit juice at the gymnasium later. He had to get back into fighting shape again. The hot exercise would give him time to think of where his investigations would lead next.

There was a forced lull since the experiment with the lethal powder and goat yesterday. He could wait weeks for the alchemists to come to any conclusions, and even when they did, would it help in tracking down the person or persons who murdered his household? Then there were Trekhos and Megas. Both were on a boat to Krete and would not be returning for weeks or months. The trail of his family's killers was as cold as the earth he sat upon. Polydektos closed his eyes and wondered what to do next. He went through every detail he could recall, even though sitting next to his wife and daughter's graves brought pain to his heart. Yet like the cut-down tree away to his left; he was stumped. He opened his eyes to wipe away the tears that were brimming on the edge of his eyelids.

Something or someone caught his eye across the cemetery. He blinked and looked again, catching a flash of a vivid red cloak passing behind a tree and out of sight, close to the gate that led back into the city. Polydektos quickly got to his feet, peering over and through the statues, tombs, and gravestones for the flash of the red cloak again. He moved to his left, catching sight of the bare ankles of a woman, who hurried but did not run out of the cemetery.

Leaving the sack, he headed off after her. The cemetery was empty apart from the two of them. He wondered who she was and why it appeared that she was spying on him. A line of olive trees blocked his view of her as he ran as fast as he could onto the road leading back to the gate. He could see no sign of her anywhere. He ran back to the city, breathing hard and coughing, as he made it under the shade of the gates. The sun was warming up the city quickly already, and he had a sheen of sweat on his arms, legs, and forehead.

"Guard, did you see a red-cloaked woman pass through the gate a moment ago?"

The guard clicked to attention with his spear, seeing who was addressing him. He had been half-asleep dreaming of the barracks cot that he would soon fall asleep on. "No, General," he replied.

"Anyone else?" Polydektos asked, turning around to the other three soldiers. Two of them were behind a cart that had three broken spokes, and the other was above them on the wall. The gate was far busier now than when he had passed through an hour earlier.

"I saw no such red-cloaked woman," the guard above replied. The other two behind the broken cart just shrugged at him. Polydektos swore under his breath and headed off up the road and through the city. There were many more Athenians, metics, and slaves about their daily business. He spotted no women at all in anything like a red cloak. Polydektos rubbed at his beard and turned on the spot in the centre of the busy road. Seeing no signs of the mystery woman, he made his way to the gymnasium to exercise his mind and body.

From the corner of a bakery, she watched him pass, her beautiful, goddess-like face hidden from view under the shade of the straw awning. In her right hand, she held a green silk bag with a red cloak stuffed inside. In her left, and hidden from view behind her white dress, was a golden-handled dagger. The woman smiled wickedly, licking her red-painted lips, and headed back off to one of the hundreds of temples inside the city.

Polydektos trudged slowly to the gymnasium, wondering if he had really seen the woman at all. Had it been his own grief showing him a ghostly figure of his wife or daughter? Was one of the gods looking down on him? It took him half an hour of running and javelin-throwing to get the image of the woman in the red cloak from his mind. It was replaced by sweat and pain from his limbs begging for rest. He did not stop until he collapsed, after which he took to the baths to cool himself down. He talked to some old soldiers about campaigns they had been on, the woman in red pushed from his mind for the time being.

Talaemenes and Gala had woken late from their exhausted sleep. Talaemenes sensed straight away that Polydektos was not there. A quick wash and he was dressed and in his sandals in moments. A search of the rooms and the courtyard brought no sign of him.

"Come back to bed?" Gala called down from the doorway of the balcony off the rear of her bedroom; she was still completely naked.

Talaemenes was sorely tempted, rubbing at his groin area. But his worry about his mentor just about crowned his ardour for the beautiful, young (though older than he) hetaira girl. "I had better check that he is safe," he said, with an apologetic shrug.

"Where will you look?" Gala moved onto the balcony, her pale arms on the railing, showing off even more of her perfect female form.

"I will try at the gymnasium first," he said, waving to her.

She blew down a kiss to him, which he caught and moved

to his lips, then sent one back. Gala giggled at this and turned to give him a flash of her bare backside as she went back inside. Talaemenes took a minute to compose himself before heading out to the busy street. Across the street, a hooded figure in a tight alleyway watched, unnoticed by the youth as he headed off to try and find Polydektos. The figure waited for a minute after Talaemenes was gone from sight before pulling something from a bag on the ground. Keeping it out of sight, the hooded figure crossed the street into the rear courtyard of the House of Javelins.

CHAPTER 13

Polydektos strode past the Agora and into the hustle and bustle of the tighter outer streets, which were full of the sights, sounds, and smells of the large city-state. He had just turned into the Street of Nymphs when a half-dressed hetaira girl he knew by sight, but not by name, came running up to him and, on bended knee, clasped his hands in hers. "Come quickly, General!"

"Why girl, what needs such urgent attention?" Polydektos frowned and pulled his hands free from the now weeping, nearly hysterical girl.

"Murder and death have visited the House of Javelins! Hurry, you must come," she said, before turning on her bare feet and running off, back in that very direction.

"Gala," Polydektos said aloud, and ran after the girl.

Luckily for him, it was only two streets away. He unsheathed his short sword at the open entrance to the rear of the house and raced inside. The girl from the street was standing with her hands over her mouth, before a cloaked figure slumped before the fountain in the centre of the courtyard.

"Gala!" he cried, rushing to turn the body over. It was not she, but a man with a dagger sticking out from his heart, a man he recognised as Borilos the metic gardener, employed by Eretmenos. He who had been overcome by fumes in the very storeroom they had found the hidden tunnel in today.

"She is here," a voice called from across the courtyard. He looked up from the dead gardener to see two other girls pulling Gala to her feet, next to the bath. He rushed over to her and took her shaking body in his strong arms.

"Are you unhurt, Gala?" he asked, lifting her head. He could see that she was not. She had red marks around her left eye, and both her tender lips were split. She had scratches on her arms, and half of her tunic was ripped away to reveal scratches to her left breast. "What happened here?"

"I was upstairs when he burst into the bedroom." Gala began dabbing at her bloodied lips with two fingers. "He was saying that he was going to chop me up like the others that you loved."

"He mentioned my name?"

Gala nodded back at Polydektos. "He punched me and clawed at me, but I managed to grab the dagger from him and run down to the courtyard. He was too close behind to try for the street, so I ran to the fountain, turning around with the dagger as he leapt for me. The dagger went into him, and he died. Who was this man, Polydektos? Why did he want me dead? I've never seen him before in my life!"

"There, there, sweet Gala." Polydektos took the sobbing, trembling girl into his arms, cradling her to his chest. "His name is, or was, Borilos, a metic gardener employed in Eretmenos's household. He was there that morning at the villa when Kephissa and Kyra and the others were found. We went into the storeroom and were knocked out by the poisonous fumes." Polydektos stopped and looked at the stairs, lost in thought.

"Do you think he was involved with their deaths?" Gala asked, raising a soft palm to turn Polydektos's head towards her face.

"It would seem so," Polydektos nodded, and lowered his face to hers to kiss her split lips. "If he were involved, perhaps he went into the storeroom on purpose that morning to check that everything was hidden away, and the fumes that were still there knocked him out. I'm not sure if that was part of his plan or not, but why would Borilos want to hurt me? I cannot recall any ill I have caused him."

"But why did he come after me?"

"To hurt me again, to take away another person I care for. He saw yesterday that we were closing in on him, perhaps, in finding the blue powder that killed my household."

"But why not come after me sooner?" Gala asked through her puffy lips.

"He was unconscious and ill for a week or so after, so he had no opportunity to do so sooner. Maybe he thought the courts would do the rest of his work for him. When that failed, he wanted me to suffer more loss by hurting you." Polydektos leant down again and kissed her forehead. "I will never let anyone hurt you again. I promise, Gala. After all this is over you, Talaemenes and I will find a place to live far from the villa or the House of Javelins, I promise."

"That is all that a humble hetaira like me could ever hope for," she said, blushing and lowering her face.

"Are you well enough to stand?"

"With your help, I think I can."

Polydektos stood and reached down two hands for her. She grasped them and let him pull her nimble frame to a standing position. Standing up too fast got to her, and she wilted a little in Polydektos's arms. Putting his left arm under her legs, he hefted her up into his arms.

"Girl, seek out Talaemenes and fetch him here, where you will be rewarded," Polydektos said to the girl who had earlier sought him out in the streets.

"He said he was going to the gymnasium to look for you, Polydektos." Gala's voice was soft and weary-sounding.

The dark-haired girl nodded and raced out of the courtyard as fast as her legs could carry her. Polydektos hefted Gala in his arms, took her upstairs to her bed, and tended to her as if their roles were reversed. Polydektos had forgotten how it felt to hold her soft body in his arms and to kiss her soft, pliant lips. Then he left her in the care of two of the other girls from the house, and made his way down to the courtyard.

The flies were already buzzing around Borilos's corpse. Blood ran down the side of the fountain and into the dust on one side, while more of his blood tainted the water. Polydektos pulled his half-sodden top half from the water and laid it down in the bloody dust next to the fountain. He checked for signs of life, but there were none. He searched the body but found nothing on the man but a bag of coins at his belt. He looked like he was dressed for long travel, but had nothing on him—apart from the dagger now residing in his heart.

"Polydektos, are you unhurt?" Talaemenes cried as he ran through the arched gate and into the courtyard. The shock of seeing the dead man next to the fountain was instantly replaced with relief with seeing Polydektos alive.

"I am well, and was not here when this happened." Polydektos received the tight hug from his young ward. He stepped back, hands on Talaemenes' cheeks, and kissed him softly on the lips. "He attacked our sweet Gala, but she defended herself as stoutly as any veteran hoplite."

"Did he hurt her?" Talaemenes's face was full of youthful concern again.

"Only the odd bruise and cut, nothing to concern yourself about." Polydektos forced a smile to reassure the concerned youth. "She is being well cared for in her room."

Talaemenes looked from Polydektos's calm face to the corpse, then up at the steps leading to the balcony of Gala's quarters. He was trembling like a leaf and breathing hard. Polydektos had seen this all before with men in the aftermath of battles. Soldiers who had fought valiantly and slain many enemies during the fight, then afterwards had become quivering, vomiting wrecks.

"Let us examine our friend here and see if we can deduce any clues from his appearance," Polydektos said calmly, gripping the youth's shoulders.

Talaemenes nodded and looked down at the dead man, a dagger embedded in his heart. His hair was wet and hung lankly over his features, which Talaemenes suddenly recognised. "Is that Borilos, Eretmenos's gardener?"

"The one and the same," Polydektos nodded, bending down next to the corpse again. "It seems our little demonstration rattled him yesterday, and he thought we were getting closer to the truth. He came here to murder Gala and thus inflict more suffering to my heart."

Talaemenes warily knelt down on the other side of the dead metic gardener. He was trying to be calm and examine the body, not feel sick at the sight of the corpse before him. "Does this mean it's over, Polydektos, and that we have found our culprit? The man who murdered your wife, daughter, and household?"

"If he acted alone, then maybe." Polydektos drew in a long deep breath. "Yet we have yet to discover his motives, if he is our man. I hardly know Borilos. I can recall no slight I've lain upon him, or any connection he has to Persia."

"Maybe he is a spy?" Talaemenes wondered. "What city or island does he come from?"

"I have no idea, but Eretmenos would know."

"Do you think he or Euneas are connected to this mystery?"

"No, I don't think so. I have known Eretmenos many years, and he is a fair and just man. Dexamene has many faults, but she loved her sister very much and doted on my beloved Kyra. Yet they may have knowledge about where Borilos is from, and we should search his room at their home." Polydektos pulled at his beard and stood up. Talaemenes, eager to be away from the corpse, quickly followed.

"So what do we do with the body?"

"We take it back to Eretmenos," Polydektos said solemnly. He clapped Talaemenes on the shoulder and spun him away from the corpse. "Go see Gala. Kiss and hold her tight for a while. I'll send one of the girls to fetch Darios and his cart."

"And what will you do?"

"Guard the dead."

While Talaemenes comforted Gala, Polydektos paid the eight-year-old daughter of one of the hetaira women to buy him a fresh bowl of honey from a nearby shop. He put it two feet away from the corpse, in an attempt to keep the flies off the dead body as the day warmed up. Then he paid all of the hetairai for their silence on the matter. Borilos may have been a Greek, but he had no real rights within the walls of Athens. Yet Polydektos did not want the Rod Bearers involved until he could take the corpse back to Eretmenos.

Darios and the girl he sent to fetch him arrived half an hour later. The soldier formerly under Polydektos's command backed his cart into the courtyard. Talaemenes heard the noise and came down, reporting that Gala refused to leave her room until the dead man was gone. The three men wrapped the corpse in some old sacking Darios had brought for that purpose, then placed Borilos in the cart and covered him over with more sacking and two empty woven baskets.

Leaving Darios behind to guard the House of Javelins, Polydektos and Talaemenes drove the cart up through the busy streets of Athens. There were no clouds in the sky, and Polydektos wished for a hat and the simple comforts of the gymnasium. They passed many temples on the way, all with their different wares and hawkers outside, trying to sell relics of the gods to the unwise buyer. Polydektos wondered what gods Borilos had given offering to. Were they Greek ones at all?

He drove the cart past the Painted and Royal Stoas, and the Altar of the Twelve Gods to their right, as they rode up the Panathenaic Way. The road was lined with new statues that Perikles had ordered built. They were intersected with fig and olive trees that cast no shadows across the road at this middle part of the day. They rode in silence, wary of speaking about the dead man behind them in the cart. Not far past the Mint, they turned left and up the road that led to the hill and Polydektos's cursed house. They rode on past it with hardly a glance, making for Eretmenos's home.

Dexamene was outside on her knees, tending to a small memorial garden she had begun for her lost sister and niece. She tended it herself, not letting the house metics or slaves help her, except to bring her cool drinks. She wore a wide-brimmed straw hat and looked more like an old slave than a respected woman of Athens. She stood up and dusted off her hands as the cart pulled to a stop before their home.

"Welcome, Polydektos. Have you come to admire the memorial garden I have planted in Kyra and Kephissa's memory?"

Polydektos wasn't sure if this was a genuine or barbed greeting. He took it as generously as his heart could muster for the woman. She had been behind her son accusing Talaemenes and him of murder, yet he blamed grief at the loss of her beloved sister over any deeper plots against them.

"It is a fine tribute to their memory, Dexamene. Kephissa also shared your great love for pretty flowers," Polydektos said, before getting down off the cart. Talaemenes stayed on board, eyeing Dexamene with the suspicion of one who had been recently wronged. "Yet we are on grave business once more. Are Eretmenos and Euneas at home?"

"Yes, they are in the back with the slaves, trying to plant some crops. Borilos has taken off somewhere and can't be found. My husband is most displeased with his work lately, and will let him go, I fear, when he shows his face around here again." Dexamene took off her hat and shielded her eyes from the harsh glare of the noonday sun.

"Then we will take the cart around back, for we have found your wayward gardener."

"By the swift arm of Apollo's justice, I had no knowledge of this man and his apparent crimes, brother Polydektos." Eretmenos was beside himself with grief and remorse as he stood at the rear of the cart. Euneas was with him, looking pale at the sight of their former gardener lying in the uncovered sackings.

"Nor do I lay any blame on you or your family for harbouring such a malcontent. It is hard to deem the truth of a friend's heart, let alone a stranger's." Polydektos eyed Eretmenos and his son with a watchful stare all the same, looking for any telltale signs of lies or uncomfortable shifting in their bearings. Euneas, true to his nature, turned and threw up again, confirming what Polydektos already knew: that his nephew had no taste for death and no witting involvement in the murders of his family.

"You are more just than a suffering and scorned man should be, Polydektos. I swear to the gods that if I knew that we harboured such an evil man under our very roof, I would have slain the bastard myself."

Polydektos nodded. "I know."

"We will need to talk to every one of the household, from staff to slaves, about him, though," Talaemenes said, throwing the sacking back over the dead gardener's face.

"My home is your home, friends, to do with as you wish," Eretmenos replied, with his arms open wide and the gleam of watery tears in his eyes—not for the loss of Borilos, but for the shame the metic had brought on his household. "Who have you told about this?"

"Not a soul, apart from Darios and the girls present during and after the attack. This is a family matter and will go no further than this, Eretmenos." Polydektos glared at Euneas as he spoke. The youth wiped at his mouth with his tunic and cast his eyes ashamedly to the ground.

"I thank you once again, my brother by marriage. You do honour to this household, where there is none." Eretmenos bowed and opened his arms wide in supplication.

"Do you know much about Borilos?" Talaemenes asked. "What part of Greece did he come from?" He was eager to get started, and finished, so he could return to Gala by nightfall.

Eretmenos looked a little shocked by his apparent lack of knowledge of his gardener. "One of the islands far to the East, I think."

"Samos," Euneas replied, finally finding his voice.

"What else can you tell us about Borilos, Euneas? Anything would be useful. Do either of you recognise the dagger?" Polydektos waved Talaemenes up onto the cart to fetch the weapon.

Talaemenes pulled it from the corpse, which let out a sigh, it seemed, as he did so. The youth nearly fell backwards out of the cart, but Polydektos and Eretmenos scrambled to half grab him and lower him to the floor.

"He is one of the Shades of Thanatos," Euneas cried in a craven voice and retreated backwards ten paces from the cart.

"He lives still." Talaemenes tried to escape the older men's grips, but they had him fast.

Polydektos helped the youth gain his footing again. "He is dead, Talaemenes, and has been since Gala stabbed him in self-defence over an hour ago. The blade leaving his body just let some of his internal gases escape, that is all. I have seen much stranger sights and sounds than that after a battle. Let Eretmenos's slaves dispose of him, we need to find out all we can about this man. Show me to his quarters, Eretmenos?" Leaving the slaves to take care of the body, they ventured inside the house and out of the stifling midday heat.

Eretmenos had fewer metics and slaves than Polydektos once had in his household, so they could afford to give their small household larger rooms. Borilos's room was on the ground floor next to the exit, out into the gardens and fields he was in charge of tending. Small pots with tender plants lined the small room on shelves along each wall. The room was otherwise bare apart from his cot, a chest, a simple table, and a single chair. A jug and simple cup sat on the table. Talaemenes sniffed both vessels but smelt nothing untoward. Eretmenos had sent his son to the andron to get over his shock.

Polydektos made for the chest, while his host searched the cot. Eretmenos tipped the cot on its side, against the wall, to see if anything was underneath or tied to the bottom. There was nothing to be found. The search of the chest also found nothing to implicate Borilos any further than the attack on Gala had done. Talaemenes, meanwhile, was searching through each potted plant in turn. Polydektos thought it was unnecessary, but it gave the agitated youth something to do.

Polydektos pulled and then pushed the chest sidewards, searching for any clues that the hard earthen floor had been tampered with underneath. It appeared that it hadn't.

"This isn't helping us at all," Talaemenes suddenly wailed with frustration. He used his arm to knock down five clay pots from the nearest shelf to break on the hard bare floor. "What can we possibly learn from a dead man's meagre possessions?"

Polydektos grabbed the youth by the back of his neck and pulled him into a bear hug. Talaemenes's grief once again flowed from his eyes. He was a keen athlete, a fine Spearman, but maybe still too fragile for the cruelties of the world. Polydektos stepped on the dirt of a fallen pot of ivy. Something hard crunched slightly under his sandal.

"What is that?" Eretmenos hurried over to crouch at the other men's feet. Polydektos stepped back to give Eretmenos room to search through the large pot of soil. His fingers soon came up with an intricately carved figure, yet in pieces in each hand.

"What have you got there?" Polydektos knelt to pluck the figure from the other man's hands. At first, he thought he had broken the figure into pieces when he stepped upon it. But now he could see the wooden figure's arms, legs and head were fixed with tiny dowels and could be pulled or inserted back into the bare torso of the figurine. The male figure had a ring of ivy in his hair, and his penis was bold and erect.

Polydektos stiffly stood, putting the separated arm and leg back into the figurine. "Talaemenes, you'd better search the rest of the pots."

"Gladly," Talaemenes said with eager relish. He began throwing the remaining pots onto the floor to break them.

"What does it signify, Polydektos?" Eretmenos asked, staring at the figurine in the General's hands. The figure seemed familiar, but he could not place it.

Polydektos looked up and asked, "Did Borilos ever worship at the temple of Dionysos?"

They retreated to the andron to speak freely as men, as a female slave brought them water, wine, and something to eat. Euneas had already had more than enough wine to calm his nerves.

"Euneas, have you ever seen this figurine before?" Eretmenos asked his son, taking the image of the god to show his son.

"Yes, but not for many years. Borilos used to let me play with it when I was a child. I'd forgotten all about it. I've not seen it since before I was ten summers old."

"Did Borilos tell you anything about it?" Talaemenes asked.

Euneas shook his head and then blinked several times. "Wait, once when he had too much wine at the festival of Halona. He said that it wasn't just a figure of new life for the crops—that the figure had a more vengeful side, a side most people ignored at their peril."

"Did he say anything else?" Eretmenos urged.

"No father, not that I can recall. It was many years ago now. He never spoke like that around me again, and I never played with the figurine after that. I just grew up and forgot about it. Why, is it important?"

"Did Borilos pray at the temples, and if so, which ones?" Polydektos pressed.

"How should I know? I'm not his keeper," Euneas said back

haughtily. "Have you asked the slaves under him that tended the gardens and fields?" He grabbed another cup of full wine from the slave girl's tray.

Polydektos sat down, refusing an offer of wine from the slave and taking a cup of water instead.

"Girl, fetch all the slaves that work...worked with Borilos in the fields," Eretmenos ordered. The girl nodded, setting down her tray of drinks on a nearby table, before hurrying from the room. Polydektos watched the girl show them her bare feet, and she left the andron.

Three men, a woman, and a child slave soon entered the andron. All bowed their heads to the marble floor. The woman in particular looked troubled to be in the men's area of the house.

Eretmenos stood, arranging his tunic over his arms like he was going to speak to the Prytaneis council on some important state matter. "Now, do not be afraid. Speak freely and no harm will come to you."

Polydektos raised his eyebrows at Eretmenos's solemn words; it would not have been the way he would have started.

"You all have worked closely with Borilos, some for many years. I wish to know: did he ever speak to you about the gods he worshipped, or which temples he prayed at?"

The slaves looked as one toward the eldest man of the group. He was tall, with grey-black hair and beard, and was strong and sinewy from many long years' work in the fields.

"Borilos did not speak much at all to us, master. He gave us our tasks and let us get on with them. I twice saw him enter the temple of Dionysos while on errands in the city for you, master." The man spoke with accented Greek. His home, long forgotten, had been many weeks' travel to the west.

"He was a man of few words, father," Euneas said, feeling for the poor, worried slaves before him.

"Did he have any visitors, male or female?" Polydektos asked, putting down his water cup.

"No, none that I recall seeing. He kept himself to himself," the spokesman for the slaves replied.

"Then you can go. But if you remember anything—such as

seeing him with strange pots of dust, or digging in odd places around the fields—let me know at once," Eretmenos said, and waved them to leave.

"What do we do now?" Talaemenes asked after the slaves had left the room.

"You and I will visit the temple of Dionysos in the morning," Polydektos said. "Let us see where that leads us. But for now, we need to return to Gala and see how she is." He slapped his knees and stood up.

Eretmenos approached and held out his arm for the former general to clasp. "I am truly sorry for any part the members of this household had in the tragedy that befell your house, Polydektos, and for any further suffering we have caused since. Age has dulled my wits, so I can no longer see what is happening under my very nose, in my own house."

"We were all in the dark about this. Dark undercurrents run like riptides, even in the calmest-looking seas. Together we will delve to the bottom of the deepest sea to find out why this happened and who was responsible."

"Surely it is done now that we find Borilos is the murderer," said Euneas, from his seat.

"We have a killer, but what would be his motive? Was he planning and working alone on this? I fear there is much more we need to discover before any of this is laid to rest," Polydektos replied. "Now we will take your leave. If you discover anything else, let me know straight away.

"I will come myself as fast as these old legs can carry me," Eretmenos said, leading them to the door.

Much of the day had waned away. Polydektos was hot and tired by the time they made it back to the House of Javelins. They relieved Darios, who informed them nothing untoward had happened since they had left with Borilos's body. They took turns sleeping with the visibly upset Gala during the night, one holding her shaking body close on the bed, while the other kept watch from the open balcony doorway.

Now, in the dead of night, as most of the great city-state slept, Polydektos sat on a stool in the doorway. The death of

Borilos had left more questions unanswered in his mind. What would a gardener from Samos have against him and his family? What could compel him to commit such detailed, planned murders, something plotted for many months? Such thoughts could drive a man to despair and drink. He had decided that he had no time for either of these fates, until the truth was revealed to him.

He would need someone with a deeper knowledge of the cult of Dionysos.

Tomorrow, he would find such a man.

CHAPTER 14

When Gala and Talaemenes woke from their fitful slumbers, they were surprised to find the old soldier Alkmaion sitting on the stool guarding them, and not Polydektos.

"Where has he gone?" Talaemenes said to the old soldier, as he ran his fingers through his wild, curly locks.

Gala sat up naked behind him. Her breasts pressing against his bare back were an unwanted distraction at this time, but he could not simply push her away after yesterday's events.

Alkmaion gave an old man's thin smile behind his mainly white beard, recalling when he was as young as the two people he guarded. "He sent a runner to my farm just as dawn broke this morning. I pressed him on where he was going, but he would not tell me his destination. He said that I could leave once you were awake to guard Gala yourself. So I will take my leave of you both." Alkmaion rose with clicks of both his knees, draped his himation over his left arm, and moved onto the balcony.

"Wait, stay," Talaemenes bounded out of bed naked, stopping at the doorway as Alkmaion made his way down the steps of the balcony. The previous evening's chill still lay on the city, and the sun had not made it over the buildings opposite yet. "I need you to guard Gala, while I go after him. He might need my help."

"I would stay for him, but not for you, boy. Do as he has asked of you, as I have done what he has asked of me. I'm old. I need my morning meal and then my bed." With a wave, Alkmaion left the courtyard via the side street exit.

Two hetairai across the courtyard came out onto their

balconies at the noise. They looked at Talaemenes's nakedness and giggled among themselves, causing him to return to the bedroom and shut and lock the door behind him.

Gala was waiting for him inside. Sitting up on the bed she pulled back the covers to reveal her supple and toned body. "Come back to bed, Talaemenes."

Talaemenes looked at his clothes and sword on the chair by the bed, and then over to Gala's tempting naked body, her curves, and the roundness of her pert breasts. He did not know where Polydektos was, and he could not leave Gala unguarded. He might as well enjoy himself while he waiting for his mentor to return.

Polydektos had been at the gymnasium since Alkmaion had kindly taken over his watch for him. His naked body was covered in dust, oil, and sweat as he ran alone up and down the long dromas practice area attached to the side of the gymnasium like a long arm. He ran until he was sick, then ran some more, then headed for the baths to clean himself up. Then after a massage of his aching calves and an oil and scrape, he dressed, ready now for the important part of his morning mission.

He had to wait for the city to wake up around him. Getting to the gymnasium early meant fewer muscular youths were there to gawp and laugh at the lump of a man the once-great general had become. *The Man Who Lost Everything,* he was called now around the city. It did not bother him, for a man who has lost everything has nothing left to fear, so that others should fear him. His friend Sokrates had told him that once. Never did he think it would apply so aptly to him.

Polydektos picked his way through the vast city, mainly seeing slaves, merchants, metics, and wives out at such an early hour. He picked up some fruit and juice at the Agora to sate his grumbling stomach. He headed through lesser streets and more open ways to a slight hill, where three temples were situated like a mini-Parthenon. There was a closed olive shop that had fallen into disrepair on the corner, where the road split to encircle the slight rise. Polydektos hunkered down there in the cool shade of the building, hidden from view between two old olive trees. From there he could watch the comings and goings of the temple nearest to him. The temples were not large and served by one propylaeon gateway, leading into the shared temenos temple grounds. Here, three flagstone paths led up to each individual temple. Polydektos had never been inside this particular temenos before. It was out of the way from his old home, and the gods he favoured were not worshipped here.

There were no festivals or any religious significance to this working day, so the temples had few visitors so early. The temple he was interested in was of the hexastyle type, with eleven columns on each side and six across. It was the largest of the three, not due to the number of visitors it received, but because it was the starting and ending point of two large festivals during the religious calendar.

Polydektos watched for an hour, seeing who went in and who came out. It was difficult to see, once inside the temenos walls, which temples people visited. He had little choice but to cloak himself and enter to have a look around. He followed two priestesses leading a goat up the stone path, through the columns and the red-tiled, roofed gateway. They turned left onto the path to the temple he was interested in. He followed them up the sloped path under the columns. He stayed in the almost cold shade of the outer part of the temple as the two women parted. One priestess went inside, while the other, younger acolyte took the goat around the rear of the temple, where there was a holding pen.

There were two men and three women inside the cella, excluding the recently arrived priestess. A wooden lattice screen covered most of the entrance, apart from a single doorless opening. There were further smaller columns inside, leading up to a torch-lit, sitting figure of the god Dionysos.

"All are welcome inside, citizen," said a quiet, soft female voice behind Polydektos, making him jump a little.

"I've never prayed to Dionysos before, except when drunk at the festivals." Polydektos turned to find a very short priestess with oiled black hair in ringlets, gazing up at him with wide, sea-green eyes.

"It is never too late to start, citizen. Dionysos is the god of rebirth, after all." The tiny woman held an open palm towards the temple opening, and Polydektos had little choice but to enter the temple before her. The air seemed heavier as he stepped over the threshold. Was this the presence of the divine, or the heavily scented incense burning on the two braziers to either side of the large sculpture of the god before him? Polydektos turned to look at the woman trailing behind him, and she ushered him to a small marble altar, just in front of the depiction of Dionysos. It was twice the size of a mortal man, the dominant feature in the temple.

The sculpture had the god sitting nearly naked on a green chair. Only a loose tunic twined around his lap and lower legs. He had a full beard, with black curls of his hair running down to his hairless chest. In his left hand, he held out a bowl, and in his right some sort of long wooden stick, entwined with grape vines and topped with pine cones.

"He is the god of fertility in crops, wine, and the flesh," the woman said, moving around to stand beside Polydektos. "Of the harvest and rebirth; he is the bringer of life after death."

"He is a god, and gods always have darker sides," Polydektos said, wondering if he had pressed his point too soon.

"As do mortal men. You should know this more than anyone, Polydektos of Athens," she said, a smile floating across her thin lip briefly.

"Then you must know I am in more dire need of rebirth than anyone else in this city." He took off his hood and fixed her with his most honest look.

"That depends if you come seeking enlightenment for yourself, or answers for the tragic deaths of your family," she replied, her eyes, dark and unreadable, now fixed on his.

"What if one begets the other?" he simply replied.

"Then speak of what aches in your heart, Polydektos, son of Praxilios, before Dionysos, and see what answers or comforts he offers."

"Do I have to make a sacrifice?"

"I think you have sacrificed enough for many men. Blood lies on your hands and at your feet, Polydektos. You are the aggressor and the victim; to blame, but also innocent. Dionysos will see all of this and judge you accordingly."

"I want to know if a man called Borilos from Samos wor-shipped here at this temple. Did he speak to anyone? Did he have friends here? What was he like, and what did he pray for?" Polydektos hissed the words, trying to keep his simmering anger under control in the temple.

"That is not the question you truly seek," she said, and turned away from him.

"By the gods, woman, what do you mean?" His raised voice caused two men nearby to draw daggers from their robes and close in on him. The tiny woman priest waved them back as Polydektos lowered his voice to a dry whisper and said, "I am sick of this conundrum that encircles my life. I wish it gone. I wish to learn the truth and then join my family."

"You get nearer the truth of the matter," she said, turning to face him again with a wider smile. "What is it you really seek? Tell me and I will aid you with whatever knowledge Dionysos lends me to give." The priestess moved forward and took his large, rough hands in her tiny, smooth ones.

Tears formed and bobbed in the lids of his eyes. "I want to know if my wife and daughter's deaths were my fault."

The priestess closed her eyes, her lips moving without any sounds coming from her mouth. "Now that you come to the truth of your heart, Polydektos, it gives me leave to answer your questions. But not here. Meet me at sunset at the theatre of Dionysos. I will have your answers by then. Now, go. If Borilos did have friends here, if would be wise for you to leave quickly, and with all stealth."

"I give you thanks for this aid you give me, but why are you helping me?"

"It is what the gods decree; we have little say one way or the other in what the Fates lay before us. Now, go."

Polydektos cast his outer tunic over his head and left the temple before too many worshippers could see or recognise him.

The tiny priestess rubbed the smell from his body on her palms and down her face, then knelt at the altar, before her cho-sen deity.

Polydektos took his midday meal at one of the stalls in the centre of the now busy Agora. He had news to tell his closest friends and lovers, but he was reluctant to return to the House of Javelins for some reason. Instead, after a good draught of water, he headed up the Panathenaic Way to his old, empty home. A cooling breeze was heading down the road, ruffling his clothes. It blew his hood from his head.

"The will of the gods," he whispered. It seemed that he would head up the long road as Polydektos, without his identity hidden.

The walk was pleasant enough until he reached the foot of the rise that led up to his property. Slowly and with heavy steps, he made it up to face his old home. It looked untidy, with weeds already grown around the shadier corners of the building. There was no one left alive inside to tend it now. It seemed to him that Gaia, the goddess of the Earth, was trying to reclaim the tainted villa herself. Polydektos knew it had to be pulled down in time. Flattened. Razed to the ground so no brick or outline remained of the murderous memories inside. It was full of ghosts and death, but he was loath to tear it down, in case it held some further hidden clues. With more information about Borilos and his worship of Dionysos, he may need to search the house and grounds again. Like a broken pot one tries to glue, one odd-shaped piece might seem a mystery until the piece next to it is discovered.

Polydektos licked his lips but did not yet venture inside. Instead, he pulled the weeds and pissed on their roots. He circled the villa, avoiding the side that had the hidden hole into his storeroom, the passage Borilos had dug—or had he?

Polydektos stood by the side of his house, covered in its shade. He was glad to be out of the wind and the sun, as they led to burnt noses, ears, and shoulders. He stared at the bushes that hid the dark hole under his old home. Borilos could not have done this himself—surely one of his servants or metics would have heard or spotted him, unless one of his own had been culpable, too. Whether they knew his scheme or not, he could have paid a slave or metic to look the other way. He probably duped them with false words and the odd obol. They might have dug part of the tunnel themselves, not knowing they were sealing their own fate as well. Polydektos had seen the plays; the best way to keep a murder secret was to assassinate the assassin before he could be captured.

Polydektos circled the property. He stopped at his front entrance, but could not force himself to go inside again, not without due reason. It hurt his heavy heart too much. Too many memories flooded his mind at once. Of teaching Sokos to throw a wooden practice javelin in the pastas, until Kephissa chased them both outside with a broom for breaking her favourite Kretan urn. Of playing ball with a six-year-old Kyra. She had been beautiful even at that age. Of making love to his wife in every room of the villa one day, as he sent his entire household to watch the Thargelia harvest festival procession through the streets.

Tears flooded from his eyes as he turned and fled the hill, casting his hood over his face once more as the wind died away to a soft breeze. It took him until he reached the Agora to regain any kind of composure. He strolled into the courtyard of the House of Javelins in the middle of the afternoon, putting on a brave mask of a face, as his two young lovers ran eagerly towards him. Both Talaemenes and Gala hugged and kissed him, and their warmth of welcome forced a smile from his dry lips.

"Such a welcome I am not worthy of," he said, taking a step back from their embraces.

"Where have you been?" Talaemenes' youthful face looked saddened by his absence. Polydektos could see that going off alone had hurt the boy's feelings.

"We were worried," Gala said, smiling through the bruises on her face. It did not temper her beauty at all.

He kissed them both on their lips. "I'm parched," he said, then took them arm-in-arm and led them up to their private balcony. "And I will tell you all about my day."

They spent the rest of the afternoon and early evening in bed. Polydektos had joined in as much as polite effort would allow. Yet in the end, he let them exhaust each other. They fell asleep in each other's arms like young, spent lovers do. This gave

Polydektos the opportunity to slide off the bed and get dressed. Underneath his chiton and himation, he had on his breastplate and tunic of war, and his short sword, hidden beneath all the layers of clothing. He knew that there was a possibility that the tiny priestess was a comrade of Borilos and he was walking into an ambush. He left his young lovers behind once again and walked through the streets as the sun set on Athens.

Gala and Talaemenes stirred and woke in each other's arms just after sunset. They were dismayed to be abandoned by Polydektos for the second time in a single day. Talaemenes dressed and took his sword with him, begging Gala to arm herself with her dagger and secure the rooms behind him.

"I could come with you and help you look," she pleaded with him at the threshold.

"The dark of the city is no place for a woman—it could be dangerous." He kissed her and left the House of Javelins, Gala sadly watching him go as the day faded into the dark blue of first night. She closed the door and barred it behind him. Being alone, she went to fetch her weapon.

Polydektos found himself travelling up the Panathenaic Way for the second time that day. This time, he did not turn off up the left-hand road to his villa. Instead, he carried on around the side of the Akropolis to the theatre of Dionysos. The place was empty, and only a few torches were lit around the place. Perikles had ordered extensive renovations to be done to the prokenion part of the stage area. Polydektos entered through a side entrance as the sun faded from the edge of the horizon. He stared through the gloom up into the theatron. He could see no one sitting or standing amongst the rows of carved stone seats. Then movement from behind the altar of Dionysos in the orchestra made him look downwards. There in the fading dusk was the unmistakable figure of the short priestess. She stood alone, her right hand on the altar.

Polydektos took another look around the theatre to see if he could spot any hidden companions of the priestess. Either they were alone, or he was walking openly into an ambush.

Polydektos had little choice but to head over to where the priest-ess waited for him. No arrows thudded into his back as he crossed the round orchestra in front of the main stage to greet her.

"What do you know of Dionysos?" the woman asked with-out a greeting as Polydektos approached the altar.

"Wine," Polydektos said; it was the first thing that sprang to mind.

"Everyone says wine first," she said, giving almost a cackle of a laugh.

"Who are you, priestess? What is your name?"

"Names are not important here. This is the theatre of Dionysos, where the dreamers play out his myths and lies. What else do you know of Dionysos?" she asked, circling the altar to keep it between them.

"He has many festivals to welcome rebirth and harvest." Polydektos paused, feeling like a boy being schooled in the gods by his old teacher. "And… he was the son of Zeus and a mortal woman, and got sewn onto his father's thigh for some reason."

"All true." He could see her nodding, but her features were hidden by the night. "Anything else?"

"I thought you were meeting me here to give me informa-tion, not the other way around," Polydektos said grumpily. He hated being tested as though a boy; he was a soldier, not an ora-tor or academic. He wished he'd brought Sokrates along to help him; the philosopher's knowledge of the gods was unending.

"Dionysos was the son of Zeus and a mortal woman, Persephone. Hera, wife of Zeus, on hearing of this, sent Titans in a jealous rage to kill the child. They ripped Dionysos limb from limb until Zeus struck the Titans down with mighty wrathful thunderbolts. Zeus, in his grief, did not want his son to die, so he sewed the parts to his thigh, until Dionysos could be reborn for a second time."

"And this helps me, how?"

The priestess ignored his question and continued like he was not even there. "The female worshippers of Dionysos are named the Maenads. They are beautiful free spirits of the woods that flaunt and fornicate with any lucky man who happens to see them at one of their orgies. King Pentheos of Thebes thought that Dionysos's claim to be a demigod son of Zeus was a fabrication. So Dionysos, in the disguise of a beautiful woman, lured him into the woods at night. There, around a fire in a glade, the Maenads cavorted naked for Pentheos and addled his mind with lust and wine. Then Dionysos stood naked before him and revealed his true male form. Pentheus ran at Dionysos in a rage at being duped, but the Maenads fell upon the mortal man and tore him limb from limb."

"Tell me more," Polydektos pleaded, the story gaining interest now.

"When King Lykurgos of Thrace heard the twice-born demigod was in his kingdom, he grew fearful and imprisoned all his Maenad followers. Dionysos escaped the trap but sent a drought to Thrace, which turned the people there against their king. Dionysos, disguised as a serving girl, gave the king wine laced with crushed ivy. This sent King Lykurgos into an insane rage. He took up an axe and did battle with a harpy he thought was attacking him...only to discover when the wine wore off that he had killed and dismembered his own son. An oracle claimed that the land would stay dry and barren as long as the mad king lived, so his people had him drawn and quartered." The tiny priestess stopped and stared at Polydektos, her eyes flickering like those of an animal with night sight.

"So my family was killed by Maenads, the followers of Dionysos. Are you one, too? Did you bring me here to mock me with their deaths?" Polydektos raged, drawing his sword from beneath his robes.

"I am just a messenger from the temple of Dionysos, nothing more," the small priestess calmly replied.

"What is your name? Why do you tell me all these tales of death and dismemberment? Why were my family and household murdered?" Polydektos raised his sword and waved it across the altar at the priestess.

"My name is not important. My time on this world is short, like my stature. I have things to impart to you, Polydektos; now, listen." The priestess moved around the altar, letting the tip of Polydektos's sword press against her bare sternum. "I have nothing to fear from death, Polydektos, son of Praxilios. I am not the enemy you seek."

"Who are you then, and why are you aiding me?"

"Not all gods feed on death and despair. Men pervert the teachings and stories of the gods to bend like forged metal to their own ends, and to suit their own needs. Dionysos is not a god of death and dismemberment, but some pervert his divinity this way. I am the breeze through the trees on a summer's night that whispers the truth of all men's hearts."

Polydektos lowered his sword, knowing that threatening this fearless woman would do no good. "What is Borilos's connection to the murders, Dionysos, and the Maenads?"

"He came to the temple as often as his work allowed. Mainly he gave prayers to Dionysos alone. He wasn't an active member at the temple. He did not get involved in any of the festivals and brought no offering to burn. On three occasions he was spotted talking to a woman, her face covered with a dark veil and a hood covering the colour of her hair. She was a Maenad. I know this because other female metic members of the temple had been approached and tentatively asked if they wanted to know the real Dionysos by her, the stranger from another country that became a god."

"Did you find out her name?" Polydektos's lips and mouth suddenly became parched.

"I found out that they met in the woods outside the city on certain nights holy to our god. Their leader, this woman, was called Mel—" The priestess choked and stopped speaking in mid-word. She opened her mouth, but only dark liquid poured out. Polydektos had seen enough blood during the day and night to know what it was. The tiny woman slumped forwards and into his arms. Polydektos had to kneel to catch her, an arrow protruding from her back.

He looked to where the arrow could have come from. He saw the briefest movement of a small fleeing figure, high amongst the shadowy building works on the stage area, then only darkness. He wanted to pursue the assassin with the bow, but he did not want to leave the priestess to die alone, without giving up the answers he needed.

"I'll carry you to safety, I have a friend—"

"No need...my fate was sealed the moment I talked to you at the temple. The oracle told me seven years ago: A great leader of soldiers will seek answers from you that will lead to your death." She reached up and touched his beard. "Follow the stream that bears the name Eridanos up into the foothills near Lykabettos. There...there you might find your answers."

"What was the woman's name, the leader of the Maenads?"

But she was gone. He felt her muscles give way and her body slumped in his grip. He bent forwards, laying her on the stone beside the altar. Reaching round, he pulled and twisted the arrow from her back. He could see the feathers on the arrow were light, but not what colour in the darkness. Gripping the sword and arrow he ran off around the stage area to see if he could track which way the assassin fled. He had to go through the entrance, which was much longer that the direct route. The road and area around the theatre were empty, and he could see no fleeing figures in the darkness. Even he could not track someone in the night, with no moon above to help guide him. He waited for an arrow in the dark, but none came. The assassin would be far away by now, or just feet away, hiding with a notched arrow pointed at his chest. He could do nothing but give up the chase and climb the wooden scaffolding up to the remodelled stage area. The night revealed nothing to him, so he made his way down and around to the orchestra and over to the altar again.

Something was very wrong.

As he closed the gap between him and the altar, he could see that the body of the tiny priestess was no longer there. He knelt and touched the ground where he had laid her down. The ground was warm, but there was no blood to be found by his patting hands. Polydektos stood and looked around the theatre. Over the Parthenon, a shooting star arced across the sky and was gone, as swiftly as the blink of his eyes.

I am the breeze through the trees on a summer's night, that whispers the truth of all men's hearts.

Her words echoed through his mind. The body and the blood she had spilled were gone. Had the Maenads taken the body?

Had she even been a mortal woman at all, or some messenger from Olympos? The assassin had silenced the priestess before she could reveal the Maenad leader's full name. *Mel..,unless that is her name? Short for Melissa, perhaps?*

Polydektos knew a little more of the mystery that surrounded his family's deaths, but the more he found out, the less sense it made. Why were Maenads trying to kill everyone who loved him, and why was the priestess trying to help him? An attempt had already been made on Gala's life; Polydektos was scared that Talaemenes could be next. He could do nothing useful at the theatre until dawn, so he hurried off back to the House of Javelins to check on his two young lovers. Maybe this had been an orchestrated trap just to separate him from Gala and Talaemenes. He had to get back to them. Polydektos ran faster than he had in years.

CHAPTER 15

Polydektos ran up the balcony steps and crashed through the unlocked doorway to Gala's bedroom. A figure cast in shadows on the bed shrieked and pointed a dagger towards him, the lit torch on the balcony reflecting off the sharp blade.

"I'll kill you if you come any closer," snarled Gala, in a not very intimidating voice.

"It's me," Polydektos said, reaching behind him to grab the torch and light up the bedroom. Gala was alone and naked in the large bed. "Where's Talaemenes?"

"When we found you gone, he went out looking for you. I begged him to take me with him, but he said my place was here. I've been ever so frightened without you both here." Gala sounded close to tears.

"By the gods, the stupid, brave young fool." Polydektos lit an oil lamp and placed the torch back outside, then he closed and locked the door behind him. Putting the lamp on the bedside table, he knelt on the bed and took the sobbing young hetaira in his arms.

Polydektos wanted to go out into the city and search for Talaemenes, but he could not leave Gala here all alone. It had been Talaemenes's job to stay and guard her. Had this been part of the trap also, to divide them and pick them off one-by-one? Persian bandits had done the same to his men once in a campaign more than twenty years ago. Killing scouts, picking off stragglers or the men at the end of the line, dividing his main force into smaller, easier-to-attack units.

He just hoped Talaemenes had learnt something from their time together of how to defend himself and sneak about. He could not bear to lose anyone else he loved. All he could do was hold Gala's warm body to him and hope his young lover returned safely. The darkest part of the night was now covering the great city-state of Athens.

The first light of dawn woke Gala and Polydektos from their entwined sleep. Sometime during their nightly vigil, they had both succumbed to fatigue. Talaemenes, to their worry, had not yet returned to them.

Polydektos ate little of his morning meal with Gala. Before the city was fully awake, he sent the butcher's boy across the street to fetch Darios. He was one of the few men he trusted to look after Gala, lived much closer than Alkmaion on his farm, and was a good few years younger. Polydektos put on his battle-dress, fixed his sword, and covered it all with an old grey himation that disguised his intentions.

"Bring him back to us," Gala said, rising up on tip-toes to kiss his lips. He smiled down at her grimly, her intoxicating scent bringing back memories of happier shared times. Polydektos kissed her back and left her on the balcony with the grim-faced Darios.

As he strode along the city's streets with purpose, he wished he still lived at the villa, as it was much closer to the theatre than the House of Javelins. He worried over his young lover. Talaemenes was strong and quick of mind, but he had few years of life and tactics between his ears. Polydektos could just about recall the impetuous youth he had been. He reached down to tap the sword under his himation but stopped himself from that comfort. Yes, Talaemenes could look after himself all right, but why hadn't he come home when he found Polydektos was not at the theatre? Had he seen something Polydektos had missed in the darkness, or met the swift-of-foot assassin that had murdered the tiny priestess? No—Polydektos had to put such thoughts from his mind. He had lost so many people he had loved; he could not bear to lose Talaemenes as well.

He could do nothing, save quicken his pace until his calves began to ache and protest.

He reached the Theatre of Dionysos just as the slaves, metics, and architects turned up to begin the day's work rebuilding the main stage area. He could not just venture inside without permission. He instead searched the woods nearby to find any clues of the assassin or Talaemenes. He was only a few feet inside the woods when he was alerted that he was not alone. Someone was moving from the right, cloaked in grey like him.

Polydektos drew his sword and crept forwards, using all the military skills he had learnt over the years to move swiftly and silently in a wooded area. A blade appeared swiftly from behind a nearby tree, and Polydektos jumped back out of the way and raised his own sword to defend himself. Then the tension left his sword arm. He lowered it, seeing the white-bearded Alkmaion before him, dressed for stealth.

"Don't creep up on me like that," Polydektos exhaled. "What are you doing here?"

"Darios sent an exhausted and red-faced butcher's boy to my farm, telling me what has happened. I rode here to help you find the lad," Alkmaion said, putting away his own sword.

"You are an ally from the gods indeed, my old friend." Polydektos embraced the old soldier.

"Why are we searching the woods—do you think Talaemenes is here somewhere?"

Polydektos told Alkmaion the full story of what had gone on the previous night. He had been given only the briefest of messages from the butcher's boy.

"Then we need to know what is going on inside that theatre somehow, without raising any suspicion, just in case the priestess' body is hidden somewhere in the stage or seating area. We could walk up the side of the hill beside the theatron area and look down from above."

Polydektos nodded, for he could think of nothing better to do. He just hoped Talaemenes's body was not also hidden amongst the building site works.

They walked up the steep, sloping hill. The rising sun was on their backs, and the tettix were chirping loudly from all directions. They could see the workers below from their high vantage point. They seemed to be going about their work normally. There were no shouts of discovery or gathering of men to warrant the fear that any bodies had been discovered. With hands on their sweaty foreheads, the old soldiers peered down at the building site for over an hour.

Polydektos broke the silence. "Surely if there were bodies there, they would have been found by now?" His lips were dry, and he wished he had bought a waterskin with him.

"If there are any bodies to be found," Alkmaion said, leaning back against a tree trunk and enjoying the dappled shade if brought.

"Then where is Talaemenes?" Polydektos left the full sunshine and moved under the shade of the tree next to Alkmaion.

"I mean we have no proof that Talaemenes even came here last night, and the tiny priestess...well, she could have no body to find," Alkmaion said coyly.

"You mean the Menards took her body and cleaned up the blood?"

"I mean there might not have been a mortal body to take. This priestess could have been a messenger from the gods themselves, or one of the gods helping you to discover the mystery surrounding your wife and daughter's deaths."

"If the gods were so damned helpful, they would have saved my poor Kephissa and Kyra from their terrible deaths. Why punish them and not me?" Polydektos whispered.

"The gods have their own way of thinking, Polydektos, that we mere mortals are not here to fathom. So do we stay here and melt, or go and try to find Talaemenes somewhere else?"

"Let us go from this place and hope the gods point us in the right direction," Polydektos said, eyeing up the theatre one last time.

"Where shall we look?" Alkmaion asked as they trudged down the other side of the theatre seating. A low wall ran down the hillside, cut from the living rock.

"The only other place I can think of is the temple of Dionysos. Yet we are passing my old home, so we will take a look, but I don't think he will be there; too many ghosts." Polydektos's voice trailed off into a whisper. They went around the edge of the wood to fetch Alkmaion's horse.

Polydektos's old home was cool and empty, and they did not

linger longer than they needed to search the rooms. Graffiti had been scrawled on one outside wall, dubbing it *the house of death*. Even though the wall daubers had been outside, nothing inside had been touched. They were probably youths daring each other to go near the haunted murder house.

They continued on to the Agora, where they brought food and water to consume while they walked on to the temple of Dionysos on the outskirts of the city. Polydektos tugged Alkmaion's robe, instructing him to tie up his horse to a nearby tree, then acted as a guide leading him off the road and back around the closed shop he had spied from before. They were creeping around the last corner of the shop when Polydektos, in the lead, spotted someone hunkering down in his spot, under the two olive trees. The figure was knelt down, a large brown cloak hiding the face from behind. Polydektos drew his sword silently, as he had done on many occasions, and raised his hand to signal for Alkmaion to stay where he was. The old soldier nodded. Polydektos crept forward, glad the person was so intent on the comings and goings of the temples.

Polydektos, quick as a flash, pulled back the watcher's hood and put his sharp blade to their throat. The man gasped, but Polydektos recognised the hair and neck of his young lover Talaemenes at once. He lowered his sword and waved Alkmaion over.

"Polydektos, it's you! Thank the gods you are alive," Talaemenes said excitedly, rising to get to his feet.

Polydektos pushed him back down and then clipped him around the side of the head with his free hand. "Never leave your post. Never go against orders—and never, ever let an old man with a sword creep up behind you, you foolish youth."

Talaemenes rubbed his head and looked suitably embarrassed. Alkmaion smiled at the put-on angry face his former general was showing the boy.

"Is Gala safe?"

Polydektos cuffed him again.

"Ow."

"Why are you here?" Alkmaion asked, knowing that if Talaemenes said anything stupid and obvious again, Polydektos might punch him next time.

Talaemenes looked at his older lover, seeing if he was going to be hit again before he answered. Polydektos sat down behind the next tree and drank from the jug of stoppered water he had bought at the Agora. He did not look at the impetuous youth, for he was still angry with him for risking his life for nothing.

"The theatre was empty when I reached it. I stayed for a little while, then came here to see if I could catch a glimpse of any of evil murdering Dionysus followers connected to Borilos?" Talaemenes kept his gaze on the older soldier. His pride was wounded.

"And how would the hawk-eyed Talaemenes know an evil murdering follower of Dionysus if he saw one? Would they shine in the dark like a warning beacon, or perhaps they would carry a helpful wooden sign with an arrow pointing downwards?" Polydektos words were laden with heavy sarcasm.

"I wasn't sure. I suppose I was looking for women that looked out of the ordinary," Talaemenes said, in a soft, chastised voice.

"So is that woman an evil murderer?" Polydektos pointed across the road as a tall woman with dark hair entered the temple's grounds. "Or maybe that one? She has a sly look about her." Polydektos pointed to a shorter, prettier brown haired girl, feeling sudden heartbreak, for she reminded him of his beloved Kyra.

"I was foolish in my actions, General; I apologise." Talaemenes hung his head in shame.

"Do you really think a secret cult of women assassins of Dionysos would stand out or try and look any different to all the other women in Athens?" Polydektos kept on, annoyed at the stupid actions of the youth.

"Did you see anything?" Alkmaion said, trying to break the atmosphere between the two men.

"No," the youth replied in barely a whisper.

"Hmmm," Polydektos said, suddenly standing up. "Wait here." He cast his himation up over his head and left the shadows behind the shop and trees. His friends watched him stride across the road and through the entrance to the temples. He made for the temple of Dionysos. It was not busy, but there were a few men and women around and inside. He asked each and every one of them about the tiny priestess, but no one seemed to know her from the description he gave. He finally found a priest, but he assured Polydektos that there were no short priestesses like the one he described attached to the temple, or ever had been during his tenure.

Polydektos left the temple half an hour later and rejoined his colleagues hiding by the shop. He took a roundabout route so as not to be spotted by anyone following him.

"Find out anything?" Alkmaion said as he returned. Talaemenes looked up briefly, with the sulky face of a chastised child.

"Only more mysteries. Either they are all great liars, or no one has ever seen or knows anything of the tiny priestess I met yesterday."

"Then she could be a messenger from the gods to help you," Alkmaion said in hushed, reverent tones.

Polydektos ran a hand up through his beard and over his tired eyes. He picked up his jug of water and took a sip. If the gods were guiding him, he wished they could just show him the way, not make his head spin.

"We are no use staying here. Gala and Darios will be getting anxious. Come, we go." Polydektos stood and patted his young lover on the shoulder. It was time to forgive and forget. Polydektos was too tired to bear a grudge for long, nor did he want to lose anyone else he cared for. He smiled at Talaemenes, and the youth jumped to his feet and followed Alkmaion around the closed shop. Polydectos told Talaemenes of what had happened at the theatre and of the Maenads, as they walked home.

All of them felt quite weary by the time they made it back to the House of Javelins. Gala was ecstatic to see them both. She slapped Talaemenes's face lightly, then hugged him close and covered him with kisses. Polydektos she held long in her arms. Darios and Alkmaion got lesser hugs and kisses also, so not to feel left out. They retreated from the courtyard into Gala's rooms to talk. They sat round a small, rickety table in the room next to the bedroom. Gala fussed around them, serving roasted sparrows, cheese, bread, milk, wine, and honey cakes as the men spoke.

"So what is our next move?" Alkmaion asked, downing in his cup of wine, which Gala instantly refilled. "All this creeping around is not my style."

Darios put in his two drachmas' worth. "I agree with Alkmaion. Chasing these Maenads at their temple... it is impossible to know who is a devout wife and who is in this cult. I prefer an enemy I can see, dressed in armour and arrayed across the battlefield so I can choose who to slay."

"We should go to this place in the hills and slay them at the source tonight," Talaemenes said, bashing his fist into the table and making it rock a little.

"Begging your pardons, but would these Maenads be there tonight?" Gala said shyly, with her head bowed.

Alkmaion went to wave her from the room, but Polydektos stayed his hand. "Speak freely, Gala; all input is welcome around this table tonight. They tried to kill you also; your life depends on our next actions too."

"Well, these cult members must have lives also beyond being Maenads. Surely they would be missed by fathers, husbands, or lovers if they met every night. Would they not meet on certain special nights to do with Dionysos, like the festivals for harvest we have in the city every year?"

"She speaks wisely for a woman," Darios said, nodding his head in agreement.

"Then we need to find out what nights are holy to Dionysos," Alkmaion said. "But don't look at me; I leave all the reminders of holy days to my wife."

This brought laughter from the men around the table. Gala just smiled sweetly, like she had been taught since a young age.

"But your tiny priestess was killed, so who could we ask, Polydektos?" Darios turned to the former general, his wine cup half raised to his lips.

"We need a scholar," Talaemenes said, downing his wine.

"Then I think I know just the man," Polydektos said with a sly smile.

Sokrates stood alone, his staff leaning next to him on a flat stone block outside the Dipylon, on a hillock between the cemetery and the Academy where he liked to philosophise with his young students. The block was part of the remains of a temple destroyed by the Spartans many years ago. A fig tree had grown there amongst the blocks of stone and fallen columns, from a seed dropped by some passing bird, no doubt. The columns that still stood and the fig tree in their midst gave shade to the philosopher, while his students sat on and around the blocks, hanging on his every word.

Alkmaion, Talaemenes, and Polydektos had passed Sokrates' students as they had left the gate behind them. The scholar stood, his back against the fig, chewing the gum of the mastic tree. It helped him cogitate as his mind wandered over the things he had just spoken of to his students. He looked up as the three men approached, but did not move otherwise.

"Morning, my fellows. You three look a little long in the tooth to start learning anything from me," Sokrates said to them.

"We seek council and information," Alkmaion said, leading the three men to find places to sit before the philosopher.

"Nobody ever seeks me out for my 'A Thracian, a Persian, and a Spartan meet at a watering hole' joke." Sokrates smiled warmly at the old soldier. Talaemenes was taken aback, wondering if Alkmaion had insulted the great scholar, but Polydektos smiled back. He had heard the joke three times in so many years; it did not improve with age.

Polydektos got straight to the point as he sat down on the flat stone block where Sokrates's staff leant. He bent his right leg, his sandal on the block, and leaned on his knee, staring at his old friend. "What do you know of the Maenads and the cult of Dionysos?"

"Are you asking me to debate the roles of women in our religion, or the truth of the gods themselves...or just eyeing up one of their famed all-female orgies?" Sokrates bent his head to look through his bushy eyebrows at Polydektos.

"Never will I make the mistake of debating the roles of the gods with Sokrates, not without two wine jugs before and a full stomach," Polydektos laughed. It was a much-missed sound—so much so that Talaemenes gasped in hearing it again from his lover's mouth.

"Then you wish to know of the cult itself, or the god who comes in from outside?" Sokrates grabbed a waterskin hanging from the broken branch of the tree and took a long gulp before offering it around. Polydektos refused, and the other two men followed suit.

"What do you mean, the god who comes from outside?" Talaemenes interjected.

"Good question, young man," Sokrates said, replacing his waterskin on the branch. "Dionysos has a mysterious past. He was the last god to be accepted into Olympos. Some say he was always Greek, but other say he was born as a demigod in Thrace or even a more distant land we have no knowledge of, a land of blank boundaries on a map. Some say he is from the east of Kos; other texts and scholars think he comes from the fertile west, where grapes grow in every field." Sokrates chewed his gum and eyed each man in turned.

"Could he be a Persian god?" Alkmaion tried to fathom the connection in his simple soldier's way.

"No, no," Sokrates replied, raising a finger in the air. "He is not one of those devils. He is Greek, or has been assimilated into our culture to make him more palatable. We think of wine, crops, harvest, and rebirth, and sweep his darker side under the rug. The cult of which you speak revels more in this original side of him: female followers, orgies, death and dismemberment, his foreign side. You feel the Maenads and not the Persians are now connected to the deaths of your wife and daughter?"

Polydektos sucked at his teeth and nodded. "It has been suggested, yes."

"Then as wise as I am, I cannot see why they would want to kill your entire household...unless…" The philosopher trailed off.

"Unless what, Sokrates?" Polydektos cried back in an urgent voice.

"Unless we have been looking at the murders from the wrong corner of the room, so to speak. You thought first that the Persians had done this to get revenge on you, Polydektos. Now you think these Maenads want to punish you for some crime you cannot fathom. What if, in your hubris, you've been looking in the wrong direction? What if this was not about you,

Polydektos after all? What if either your wife or daughter were slain for something they knew, something they did, or a god they slighted?"

Polydektos was rocked back where he sat. He slipped his sandal off the block and stood, looking menacingly towards the philosopher, who stood his ground. Polydektos' two companions rose to try to intercept him, but the old general stopped dead in his tracks. He cast his eyes upon the dusty ground, then slowly raised his head to face Sokrates. "If you were any other man, I would slay you where you stand for suggesting it was their own fault they died!" Polydektos's hand hovered by the hilt of his sword, hidden beneath his outer robes.

"Do not slay the messenger, my old friend. Will you let me continue, so all possibilities and thoughts are aired?"

Polydektos nodded and sat back down, much to his companions' relief. They waited for a second and then seated themselves again.

"I just put these thoughts to the winds to see if they shed any sunlight on the subject. These are not my personal opinions, just my thoughts. What if you were not the target, Polydektos, as I said? What if your womenfolk were? For reasons we do not know. It could be that Kyra got caught up in this cult by youthful folly, and then, seeing the darker side of it, could not get out. The assassin or assassins waited until they knew you would be out of the house for many hours, until the late dark of night."

"But they could have done this to make Polydektos and me suffer," Talaemenes interrupted.

"And so they could, young man," Sokrates gave Talaemenes a stern look and spoke in the voice he used on noisy, disruptive students. "Let us run like the river with my trail of thought. The Maenads were not angry with you, Polydektos, but with your daughter or wife. They waited until the two men of the house were not present and killed all there. But only your wife and child did they defile in death with dismemberment, a known trait of this cult—laying Dionysos's vilest punishment on them alone, because they had slighted or betrayed the Maenads. Does any of this fit with the other facts you have discovered since last we met?"

"Borilos—" Talaemenes began, but Polydektos stopped him with a withering look.

"Borilos, a servant of Eretmenos, helped the killers plan and execute the attack on my home. He met with a woman named Mel, or whose name starts with those letters, at the temple of Dionysos. She is the leader of the cult of Maenads, but we know nothing of her or the way she looks. A priestess, who was murdered giving me this information, said they meet in the foothills of Lykabettos, but we do not know exactly where or how often." Polydektos raised an apologetic hand to his young ward, seeing the hurt on his smooth face.

"Melissa was a nymph torn to pieces by jealous women," Sokrates said absently.

"A coincidence, maybe?" Alkmaion said, but did not believe it.

Polydektos looked at the ground dejectedly and kicked a rock several feet away. "Just when the answers are in my grasp, new facts take them away again. What do I do now, my friends? Investigate my own wife and daughter and sully their memory in the afterlife?"

"I think you need to go to this meeting place in Lykabettos and find the answers there," Sokrates said, coming over to clasp his suffering friend on the shoulder.

"But when?" Talaemenes said. "We still don't have a clue when and how often they meet."

"I have a younger student who is interested in such things. Bright fellow, by the name of Aristaeos, big broad chap, and gleaner of knowledge. I'll get him to find out for you; he is from a wealthy family, and that always helps when you are buying knowledge."

"Tell him to be discreet and careful," said Alkmaion, rising.

"Oh I will, but he is a wilful young man. If anything can be found out, he will find a way." Sokrates patted Polydektos's shoulder and picked up his staff. "Will you accompany me back to the gate? We could have some wine and victuals together."

"We will walk back to the gate with you," Polydektos said, standing up, "but we need to get back to Darios and Gala. Seek us out at the House of Javelins, Sokrates, when you have any news?"

Sokrates pointed his staff at Talaemenes as he and Polydektos walked past the youth. "Fetch my waterskin, boy." Talaemenes frowned but fetched the skin, wondering if he would ever be treated like a grown man and not a slave.

Seeing the disheartened look on the youth's face, Alkmaion clapped him on the back in a hard but friendly way. They followed the other two men down the hillock to the road leading back to the city.

After they had left Sokrates at a suitable watering hole by the gate, the remaining three men walked through the busy city. Polydektos was deep in thought about his wife and daughter. So much so, he only grunted back at his companions after they tried to engage him in idle conversation. Polydektos sought to cast his mind back to the months before his wife's and daughter's murders. Had they seemed different in any way—furtive, or out late at night? The sad conclusion he came to was that he was not there enough to have noticed either way. He spent his days at the law courts or The Council of the Five Hundred, his nights fornicating and drinking. Apart from festivals and the odd passing meal, he realised he knew little about his wife and daughter, or what they had got up to when he was out carousing. He, the great general living off his past glories, had expected them to be dutifully waiting at home for him, running the household. And so they had, it had seemed to him. Yet now, Sokrates had put doubts into his mind. What if one or both of them had joined this cult of Dionysos? He often wondered if his wife had taken a young lover. He didn't think he would have minded, as he wasn't a possessive man. After Sokos had died, he had lost interest in family life, to his utter shame now. Maybe if he had been at home more, none of this unending tragedy would have occurred.

Darios and Gala were safe and sound, playing pebbles on the table on the balcony. Gala was pleased to see them and rushed down the outside steps to hug them all in turn. Polydektos let her hug him, for it felt good to have her young body against his; but it also brought guilt to the surface, reminding him of the wife and daughter he would never hug again. He dismissed Darios and Alkmaion back to their own lives, then went upstairs to Gala's rooms to think. A half-empty wine jug stood next to the pebbles board, which looked as though Gala (who always picked the grey pebbles) was winning. The smell of the sweet wine wafted up on a slight, cooling breeze. He knew only ruin lay in the bottom of that jug for him, so to save himself he picked it up and flung it at the side of the house, before stomping inside and shutting the balcony door behind him.

His companions had been shocked by the noise of the shattered jug. The red wine rained down the side of the House of Javelins like watered-down blood, staining the whitewashed brickwork. Talaemenes and Gala waved off the two old soldiers, who now wanted to remain and make sure their old general was all right. Gala kissed each of them on their bearded cheeks and led them from the courtyard. After a few moments, they grudgingly headed off to their homes, vowing to return the next morning to check on their old *strategos*.

Talaemenes waited for her to return before climbing the steps with her. They exchanged worried looks at the closed balcony door and took each other's hands for comfort. Opening the door, Gala led Talaemenes inside to find Polydektos lying on the bed with his back to the open doorway. Talaemenes closed and locked the door behind them, trapping in the heat of the day. Gala climbed onto the bed and silently spooned Polydektos's back. He did not make any movement or noise in response to her closeness. Talaemenes went to sit on a stool Gala used when oiling her legs and painting her delicate toes. But Gala waved him over and patted the end part of the bed behind her. Talaemenes, led by her slightly prior experience of Polydektos, joined them both on the creaking bed. The afternoon sun was high above the city, and Gala soon fell asleep. Talaemenes fought like a Trojan to keep his eyes open for over an hour before he closed his eyes and drifted off.

Polydektos, though, was wide awake. His unblinking eyes fixed on the cracks and crevices on the wall in front of him. He knew if he closed them he would be haunted by the death images of his beloved Kephissa and Kyra, and the guilt of letting them down.

CHAPTER 16

Gala turned over in her sleep and hit Talaemenes in the neck, causing him to sit bolt upright in shock. His jerky movements caused Gala to sit up also and look around in worry; Polydektos was no longer on the bed with them. They turned their heads in panic, only to see he was sitting outside on the balcony, sipping water. They jumped off the bed and hurried outside, to find three wooden plates on the table next to him, with grilled fish and steamed vegetables.

"I was just about to wake you two young sleepyheads," he said, nodding at the plates of food. "I've just cooked up dinner."

"Is it so late?" Talaemenes asked, his stomach rumbling as he sat in a vacant chair to Polydektos's left.

"After our usual time to eat," Polydektos replied, as Gala sat to his right and began to tuck into her fish.

"I didn't know you could cook," Talaemenes said around a mouthful of hot food.

"Never judge a cave by its mouth, young man. You never know what things lie hidden deep inside. Did I ever tell you of the time on my second campaign when I had to live off desert rats for two months when our supplies ran low?"

Both of his companions shook their heads, even though they had heard this tale, drunkenly told, several times. They did not want to spoil his good mood.

"Then I shall recall it all with detail. The sea voyage began badly when, only an hour out of port, the galley I was on began to sink and I had to be rescued by two other nearby vessels. To say the remainder of our sea voyage was cramped and miserable was an understatement. Poseidon was testing our mettle that day, and it only got worse from then on..."

Talaemenes and Gala were glad to hear the tale in full this time. When told before, they and Polydektos were drunk, so that the ending was commonly forgotten and the battle scenes embellished to legendary status. This time, they got the full, gritty hardship of war.

He told them how he lost half his men through watery back passage disease, rather than the actual fighting. He spoke of the stringy desert rats he himself cooked over campfires, to see that he would eat the same terrible food as his men, and how every wretched dark day ended an internecine victory.

Polydektos had won, but had not the army left to control the areas he had gained. With no ships laden with supplies or more men, he had to return to Athens. They lined the streets for his parade, but it was a hollow victory. His status as a famed general was secure, but half of his men and ships never returned to get funerals on Athenian soil.

It was nearly dusk by the time he had finished. The flies were buzzing over the long-finished fish bones on their plates. Gala cleared them away, leaving the two men to themselves for a time.

"Do you really think that Kyra or Kephissa could have been involved with the Maenads?" Talaemenes suddenly asked. "I've been wracking my brains, and I know the theory fits the facts, but I'm sure Kyra would never be part of something so odious."

"I've have been thinking along the same tracks, my young friend. I cannot see the woman I married or the daughter she bore having any knowledge of such things, let alone joining such a cult."

They sat in silence for a while, until Gala lit a lemony-smelling lamp and brought it outside to keep the flies away from them. She went to light some torches, but Polydektos stopped her. They sat together as dusk sank into night. When their bare arms began to goose-pimple, only then did they head inside and close out the night. The mood was sullen and reflective. Gala and Talaemenes played pebbles quietly in the corner, talking in soft, hushed tones as lovers do. Polydektos could not settle. He would spend only a little time sitting up in bed, his head against the wall, before rising, sword in hand, to check periodically that the windows and doors were all secure.

Polydektos finally settled into bed hours after his young lovers. Sleep did not come easily to him, though his mind and body were exhausted from lack of rest the night before. He tried to think of any times that his wife and daughter gave any clues to being involved in a cult, but he knew he had hardly been there to notice for the past couple of years.

The next thing he knew, he was in the clutches of a dark and misty-edged dream.

He was in the courtyard of his old home at the darkest hour of the night. He was not alone. Out of the black shadows came ten women, or so it seemed. Each was naked and shaved hairless, but their heads were those of the beasts of the field and the birds of the air. At first, he thought they wore masks, until they opened beaks and feral mouths to hiss at him. Goat, cow, lioness, hawk, and more, they formed an ever-enclosing ring around him. The half-women, half-creatures spun around and around him, as Polydektos tried to find a gap to escape through. There was no way. He found himself turning and turning, looking for a way out. Then, from nowhere, the half-women produced golden knives in each hand. The circle drew tighter and tighter around him until the tips of twenty blades pricked at his skin. In breathless fear and desperation, he grabbed at the head of the nearest she-beast: a goat-headed woman. He tried to pull at the face, but the goat head and slender neck of the female were as one.

He felt a stabbing sharpness in his groin; then his eyes flicked open from his nightmare to find a female face above his body. He stifled a cry as he saw it was Gala, and it was morning. Then he felt her slender weight upon him, his phallus rigid inside her as she sat astride him, riding his morning glory for all its worth. He had finished before he was fully aware of whether he was in the world of dreams still. Gala shuddered in ecstasy herself, joining in the pleasure, then collapsed upon his bare chest; her hair covering Polydektos's face.

"I love you with all my heart, lord, and master of my body," she whispered in his ear, before sucking on the lobe.

Polydektos did not know what to do. He had been in a

nightmare, then woke to find Gala making love to him, something he had not desired to happen; but now that it had, the warmth and comfort of her young body were most welcome. He put his strong arms around her and crushed her chest tight to his, revelling in the feel of her warm, loving body. Guilt flooded through him like never before when Kephissa was alive. He wasn't sure whether to fling Gala off him, but in the end, he held her breathlessly tight and cried into her lemon-scented, oiled hair.

Talaemenes, luckily, had not witnessed their coupling. Polydektos left the bed without a word to Gala and threw a himation around him as he headed down the balcony steps to soak away the night's terrors away, and the lust, in the shaded bath in the courtyard. He saw Talaemenes there, giving coins to a seven-year-old daughter of one of the other hetairai, bidding her to fetch fresh food and citrus juice for the early morning meal.

The water was cold and clean, just what Polydektos needed to cleanse his mind and body of the nightmare and his morning tryst with Gala. He had wanted neither, but in lust and in battle, the body sometimes took over and dimmed a man's free will.

Talaemenes waved the hetaira's daughter off, then came striding towards him. Polydektos sank lower until his head went under the cold water. The chill beat at his chest like the tiny fists of an infant, begging him to resurface. He saw Talaemenes's face above him, peering over the side, talking, but his water-clogged ears could not hear him. The handsome youth's face rippled through the water between them. Polydektos wonder if he should not order the young man away before his military service began, to keep him out of harm's way. Then he would have no one left apart from Gala and his friends; maybe it should be him that fled, to save all their mortal souls from a murderous end. Bubbles escaped his lips, and with great regret he sat up again, his head leaving the forgiving waters.

The young Talaemenes had a worried look upon his crease-less face. "I thought you meant to drown yourself!"

"I would not do the patrons of this house a disservice by drowning myself in a shared bath." His words had not erased the frown from the youth's countenance. "I just wanted to wash the sleep from my mind and clear my thoughts for the new day ahead."

This seemed to appease his young lover, and he forced a laugh and a smile. "What will this day bring?"

"Only the gods and oracles know that. We will have to live it to find out," Polydektos said, standing up naked from the bath. Talaemenes passed him his discarded himation. The general waved it away, stepping out into the first rays of sun that touched the corner of the courtyard. He heard the children of the other hetairai giggle at him, but he cared not. They had seen worse. He opened his arms wide and let the sunlight dry the water from his skin. He closed his eyes against the glare and wondered, like Talaemenes, what this new day would bring.

They did not have to wait long to find out.

Gala, Talaemenes, and Polydektos were just getting to the end of their morning meal when Mopsos, the white-bearded alchemist, arrived in the courtyard, accompanied by a tall brute of an Ethiopian slave as his bodyguard. Polydektos waved the pale, thin, bearded man up to where they ate on the balcony. The tall, muscular Ethiopian stood at the first step, making quite sure no one followed him up.

"I will clear away the dishes." Gala collected the wooden bowls, plates, and knives from around the balcony table.

The alchemist was puffing by the time he reached the top step to join them. Polydektos wondered if the man had ever seen the inside of the gymnasium in his life.

"Well met, my fellows," Mopsos said between his heavy breaths.

Talaemenes pulled out the chair Gala had vacated to let the hot and bothered old man collapse into it. "Juice or water?" he asked convivially, reaching for the jugs.

"You wouldn't happen to have wine to add to that water would you? I am so parched."

"I shall get Gala to fetch us some." Talaemenes was up and into the house and back before the two older men knew it.

"So what brings Mopsos to the House of Javelins at breakfast?

Do you have some news for us?" Talaemenes said, getting his question in before Polydektos as he sat down.

"I have news of the blue powder that you found at your villa," Mopsos began, eyeing up the honey cakes left behind. Polydektos saw this and pushed the wooden plate nearer the old alchemist. Mopsos shook his head at the former general. "We, I mean myself and my esteemed colleagues, have found out some, if not all of the facts of your mysterious powder that becomes a deadly gas when water is added."

Mopsos paused as Gala appeared with a clean cup and a small jug of wine. She poured the wine for the alchemist, letting him add as much water as he desired, which was hardly a trickle. He continued, as Gala cleared away the remainder of the breakfast things.

"One of the key ingredients seems to be the leaf of Atropos, not a Persian herb at all, but used widely around Greece for many purposes, including poison and sleeping draughts. Even used by certain cults like the Maenads to induce some sort of charnel-animal frenzy during their orgies, I've heard. And made into a pulp, it can cure gout. None of the ingredients making up this powder are from abroad at all. Everything can be found within the walls or the countryside of Athens, though the recipe is something none of our alchemists has seen before. Quite ingenious, in that it is harmless unless water is added." Mopsos sat back and drank his wine, looking pleased with himself.

Polydektos leant forwards in his chair. "So you are saying that anyone in Athens with the skill could get hold of these ingredients readily and mix it up?"

"Yes, if they knew what they were doing. Yet as I said before, whoever dreamed up this powder had knowledge beyond all the scholars and alchemists in the city. The knowledge may come from another land, but the ingredients that we can identify can all be found locally."

"Where would you find them?" Polydektos said, gripping the table with one hand.

"I'm sure I've got some in powdered or root form somewhere. From the port, from sellers at the Agora. If you want the actual plant, then it grows in the foothills surrounding the city."

"In the Eridanos foothills?" Polydektos pressed.

"Perhaps. My days trudging around the countryside looking for herbs and roots are long past," Mopsos said, downing more wine.

"Could we track down an individual who bought the ingredients?" Talaemenes asked the alchemist.

"I do not see how; you could pick nearly all of them up at the Agora, or even source them yourself from plants, roots, extracts if you were so inclined."

"Would you need the skills of a learned alchemist to whip up a batch of this?" Polydektos asked the alchemist.

Mopsos sucked at his teeth in contemplation for a while. "Sadly not. If you have all the core and secret ingredients, I think anyone with the recipe could make this within a day. It is very simple, but then all the best potions, powders, and poisons are. From the lowest slave to Perikles himself, anyone could make this deadly gas powder."

"Then we are no closer to finding the true murderer behind this than before," Talaemenes cried, an angry edge to his voice.

"No, but the facts sway like trees in a gale towards the Maenads being involved," Polydektos said. "There we must cast our net of suspicion next. All the facts point like a spear blade, up towards the sun, that they are behind the deaths of my wife and daughter. Now we have to figure out who they are and why they did it!" Polydektos slammed his fist down on the table hard, knocking over a jug of water.

The three men scrambled back and out of their chairs, before the water could pour through onto their legs. At the sound, Gala hurried out again.

"My apologies, my friends," Polydektos said, standing back and watching Gala clear up the mess he had made. He waited, trying to hold his simmering anger. He wanted to throw the table off the balcony and be done with it. He forced himself to say the alphabet in his head from alpha to omega. It was something one of his instructors at the academy had taught him, to counter the impetuous nature of his youth. Don't just rush in with your sword blazing in the sun; count the alphabet in your head if you have time. Take in your surroundings, weigh your options another moment, as another considered thought could turn the tide of a battle.

He waited for Gala to take the wet cloth and water jug inside before he followed two steps behind. He fetched Mopsos the reward he had promised him. At least the alchemist departed happy. Polydektos's mood was like a sizzling pan of oil, waiting for any moment to catch fire and burn. When Gala came back to pick up the last of the plates, she gently led Talaemenes inside with her. Even he could see that Polydektos needed time alone.

"I'm heading off to the gymnasium," he called through the open balcony door as he passed it, heading down the outside wooden steps. Gala and Talaemenes came back onto the balcony again to watch him depart. The youth went to follow him down the steps, but Gala lightly grabbed his arm and shook her head. He nodded at her as Polydektos headed through the archway and out of the courtyard.

Stripped naked and covered in dust, Polydektos had won the first and fourth race he had entered, against much younger opponents, on the dromos practice track. He had been badly beaten in his second and third races, but found renewed strength from the losses and the simmering anger he was feeling. He was sick and tired of the way his life was lost, like it was stuck in the labyrinth at Knossos. He would not let this defeat him; he had to find the answers for his womenfolk and his peace of mind. Someone had to suffer at the tip of his sword for the murders of his wife and daughter. He could not live with the guilt and pent-up anger inside him. He could not die without knowing the truth of this dark matter.

He ran two more races after that, even though his shins were aching and feet burning. He came third and then last, falling and eating dust on the final race, the anger dying within him as exhaustion wracked his middle-aged body. He got up and finished the race at a limping jog. He had bit his lip as he fell and must have looked a sight as he trudged along the dromos to the baths to clean himself up.

He was seated in the baths, head back, eyes closed, and arms stretchered out along the tile edges, when a familiar voice brought him out of his silent prayers. He had been calling on the strength of Artemis, goddess of the hunt, to help him track down his foes.

"Polydektos."

His eyes opened to see Sokrates and one of his students standing across the baths near the entrance. The young student was well dressed, and his hair was oiled and curled almost like a woman's, yet there the feminine finery of him ended. He was not tall, but big of chest, and had broad shoulders and muscles that Polydektos in his youth would have envied.

Polydektos stood up and waded across the baths to get out near them. A slave handed him a white towel. Polydektos dabbed himself dry and then fixed the towel around his waist.

"This is the lad Aristaeos, who I was telling you about," Sokrates said with pride, briefly putting his arm around the stocky youth.

Polydektos nodded at Aristaeos. "I will not be long. I will meet you both by the honey cake shop in the Agora in a quarter of an hour?"

"Very wise—even Athenian walls have elephant-sized ears," Sokrates said, turning the youth around with his arm and heading for the exit. "Don't expect there to be any honey cakes left by then," he called jovially over his shoulder as he left.

Polydektos suddenly found a smile from somewhere and left the baths to get oiled, scraped, and dressed as quickly as he could manage. Polydektos made it to the busy honey cake shop within the time he had said to Sokrates. The philosopher and the youth were sitting at a corner table that was already filled with wooden plates covered in cake crumbs. Polydektos grabbed the metic owner, whom he knew in passing, and ordered cakes and water for himself. The metic, a man originally from Andros, nodded and hurried off to fulfil the former general's order. Polydektos had come to the shop once a week for years when Sokos and Kyra had been younger. He felt a pang of loss as he sat down on one of the two spare chairs at the table. Sokrates leaned back on his chair, rubbing his belly. He was in the corner to Polydektos's left, and Aristaeos sat opposite his teacher.

"Have you found anything out, my friend?" Polydektos looked from Sokrates to his young pupil.

"We have, and we haven't. Ours was but a chance meeting, but a merry one at that, Polydektos," Sokrates said, and Polydektos felt his heart sink a little. He needed something positive to come from this day.

"So you have no information for me yet?" Polydektos asked as his water and honey cakes arrived.

"Soon, soon, my friend. Two more cakes for myself and the boy," Sokrates said to the metic, collecting the empty plates off the table.

"Worthless people live only to eat and drink: people of worth eat and drink to live," Polydektos stated as the server left.

"What fool said that?" Sokrates said, eyeing up Polydektos's cakes.

"You did, but you were drunk at the time. No wonder you don't remember saying it," Polydektos replied with a ghost of a smile on his lips. Then he tucked into his first sweet cake, loving the explosion of taste in his mouth after eating dust half the morning.

"Oh." Sokrates frowned, but his smile soon returned with his next plate of honey cake. "I am the wisest man alive, for I know one thing, and that is that I know nothing."

Polydektos and Aristaeos chuckled at this. They were Sokrates's words, and he used then frequently.

Sokrates waved at his young pupil as he tucked into another honey cake. "Aristaeos m'lad, tell him the tiny morsel you have found out."

Aristaeos looked around the shop, but no one seemed to be paying the three men any mind. "I have a cousin by marriage that has an aunt that once tried to cajole her into joining the cult of Dionysos. She, being a dutiful married woman of Athens, dismissed the aunt out of hand. She was far too busy running a household and having Athenian babies to worry about such distracting things. Now, that was two years ago, but I have spoken to said cousin to try and glean information from this widowed aunt, and to find out all they can about exactly where and when they meet." Aristaeos spoke quickly, and with deadly earnest.

"Is this all, Sokrates?" Polydektos asked of his friend, ignoring the youth out of hand.

"Trust the boy," Sokrates said, through a mouthful of cake.

"My cousin's aunt is...," Aristaeos began.

"And if my cousin's aunt had wheels, she would be a cart," Polydektos shot back, silencing the youth. "I need facts, dates, times, locations!"

Sokrates watched as the general banged his fist into his palm as he made every point. "And these things take time, my old friend." He grabbed Polydektos by the wrist to stop him banging his fist again.

"I apologise," Polydektos said, lowering his hand, his gaze finding the floor. He had felt so much anger and frustration this morning. Was it to do with his investigations getting nowhere fast, or that he had lain with Gala when he had sworn her off in memory of his murdered wife?

"You have no need ever to apologise for the ills that have befallen you and your late family, my friend. We will help you see this matter out and lay your family to rest in eternal peace. The deaths of your wife and daughter are bitter and fresh, but we must look away from emotion and find the core of this evil deed."

"And what is that, my old friend?" Polydektos said, looking up at Sokrates. The scholar and philosopher had honey cake crumbs in his beard.

"From the deepest desires often come the deadliest hate. For someone to do such an evil act to your womenfolk after death shows that the murderers had not just revenge on their minds. They had a passion and fervour that took them beyond what even a callous soldier might do. Anyone can kill, by accident, in war, or as a choice. But to do what they did to your poor wife and daughter after they had died has some hidden meaning in it. This was planned for many months, maybe even years. Who suffers from this barbaric act, and who gains?"

Polydektos scratched his head as he shook it. "This is what I have been trying to think of every waking second, and every night that sleep does not come to me. Wracking my brains: who, why, and for what purpose?"

"Maybe these Maenads will have the answers you seek?" Aristaeos ventured, just to get into the conversation again. "And I will try my hardest to find the information you seek, Polydektos."

Polydektos looked at the broad-shouldered youth. Maybe he had underestimated him, just because of his age. "I hope you can," he simply replied.

Polydektos made it back to the House of Javelins in the middle of the afternoon. Talaemenes and Gala had been going out of their minds with worry over him, but he waved them away, saying he was fine. He went inside, where it was only a little cooler, but out of the harsh rays of the sun. He disrobed, then sat naked on the edge of the bed. Gala brought him some water, which he drank down swiftly. *They hang around me like flies on a carcass, waiting for scraps of information.* Polydektos regretted his barbed thoughts as soon as he had them. Without his two young lovers, he would have taken a blade to his own throat ages ago.

"I am well, and no, we have no news as yet from Sokrates and his pupil." Polydektos wiped the water from the bristles on his chin over the rest of his hot face.

He saw Gala nudge Talaemenes with a delicate elbow, and they left him alone in the bedroom. Polydektos rubbed at his tanned belly. It was decreasing in size. The combination of manic exercise and cutting down on food and wine was becoming evident now. He hoped to get fighting fit again, but he was not sure he had any wars or campaigns left in him. There was little for him to do but wait for news from Aristaeos. As a general, he did not like to be reactive, but rather proactive with scouts, spies, and outriders.

"You have little choice but to wait, son of Praxilios," he muttered to himself, as he lay down on the bed for an afternoon nap.

CHAPTER 17

Gala woke him with a honey-scented kiss to the lips, while one hand caressed other parts of him, bringing him to full consciousness almost immediately.

"How may I serve you, great general?" she purred, almost like a kitten. Her hand gripped him hard, and he almost let himself fall back onto the bed and let her have her fun with him.

"Where is Talaemenes?" he managed to say in a raspy voice. He looked around the bedroom. The door to the balcony was open halfway to let in the breeze. The hot sun was lower, but nowhere near night yet.

"In the courtyard, playing hoops with Talia's daughter." Gala kissed his neck, while her hand kept up its slow rhythmic tugging. "I think he enjoys it more than she."

Polydektos lightly gripped her slender wrist to stop the movements that were causing him distraction. "You do not have to do that anymore. When this is done and Talaemenes in the academy, I will find us a new home far from here, and you can take care of me in my elder years."

"I am yours, Polydektos, but I am also a hetaira trained in pleasure. Just lie back and let me do a little of what I am good at, please. It would make me happy, my beloved general." Her eyes were wide and near to tears. He exhaled through his nose, let go of her wrist, and lay back down again. Gala smiled wickedly. Her hand was followed by lips, and then other parts. Polydektos drank in her perfume, letting her hair fall down and cover his face as they both finished. He had abstained for the memory of his dead wife, but now he resumed keeping his loyal hetaira happy. He held her tightly afterwards, but could not keep the thoughts of his dead wife and child away for long. Gala washed him and dressed him before he could do it himself, and he let her, knowing she liked to take care of him. She probably loved him in a way, and he probably loved her back as much as a citizen could love a hetaira girl.

Talaemenes looked red and out of breath when he returned. He gulped down the watered wine that Gala gave him. They sat on the balcony, now that the shade had come round the back of the House of Javelins. They drank together, saying nothing—Gala and Talaemenes drinking watered wine, Polydektos sticking to water. Wine was a far easier thing to give up than the curves of Gala's young body. They ate olives and dried fig snacks, silently enjoying their time together. Talaemenes would soon be of age to serve in the army; Polydektos hoped the situation with the murders would be resolved soon. He had promised Gala a new life far from here, but he wasn't sure it was a promise he or the gods would keep. Even if they lived through this nightmare, would Polydektos want to go on with all his family dead?

At dusk, Alkmaion and Darios turned up with more wine and food, and their merry gathering swelled to five. As the sun set, the children of the hetairai went to their beds. The cries of children playing were replaced by different, deeper cries from the other apartments around the courtyard. They stayed up late, talking into the night about deeds of arms the old soldiers had done. Gala had sat on Talaemenes's lap to listen and had fallen asleep with her face snuggled into his neck. Polydektos looked at them and smiled; his duty now was to protect them both.

Talaemenes carrying Gala inside to bed brought the pleasant proceedings to an end. Alkmaion headed home to his wife and family, while Darios, who was younger and unmarried, took the short walk across the courtyard with a bag of coins in his left hand.

Polydektos fetched his sword and laid it across his lap. He let the torches flicker and die. Sitting in the dark, he protected Talaemenes and Gala from the evils of the night.

Polydektos woke his companions early, and for their safety, he took Gala and Talaemenes with him to the gymnasium. Darios, who had stayed the night across the courtyard, went with them. He sang Gala songs of love as they headed for the Agora to eat and shop. Gala, being a woman and a slave, could not enter the gymnasium.

Polydektos stripped bare and they began with javelin training in the palaestra. While Talaemenes did the long and high jumps, Polydektos watched from a stone bench inside the cool covered areas around the central open space. He hoped either Sokrates or Aristaeos might wander up and sit next to him, but they didn't appear to be there today. When he deemed Talaemenes suitably puffed out from his jumping, he challenged him to a race along the entire length of the dromas. Polydektos took an early lead, but by halfway the youth was catching him. In the last third of the race, Talaemenes powered past, winning in the end by two horses' length or more. They ran five more races, with Polydektos's times getting progressively worse. He had to concede that this forty-six-year-old body would never be a match for a sprightly, seventeen-year-old boy. He took the defeats in a good manner, knowing that his fitness was slowly coming back to him. It would take many months, not weeks, to get it anything like he wanted. Yet it was a goal, at least, to focus on—one he could at least try to control, where the rest of his life seemed to be thrown to the winds on the whims of the gods. They bathed, oiled, and scraped each other clean before dressing, then joined Gala and Darios in the honey cake shop. The former soldier was still singing songs of love, making Gala giggle and blush. He was annoying the male patrons while getting the lustful eye of their wives, mothers, and daughters.

Talaemenes and Polydektos ate well and drank many cups of fruit juice. Darios was laughing heartily, and Gala was smiling away at the men on her table. Talaemenes looked fresh and handsome, a vision of male Athenian youth. Even Polydektos couldn't help but smile at his former soldier's antics. They wandered in the Agora for a while, listening to the orators and watching a man juggle with lit torches. Before they returned to the House of Javelins, Gala brought some fresh fish to grill them later for lunch. The sun was out but had many white clouds to hide its full, burning strength. After an hour, Darios headed home for some well-earned rest.

Polydektos had not had a better day since his wife and daughter were murdered. Guilt made him head off to his villa on his own after lunch. A muscle in his left thigh felt tight from the morning exercise, but he hoped his trek up the hill would work it out. The villa was closed and untouched, and he did not linger there long. It was a house of death still. The smell of poison and blood might have gone, but vile memories haunted every room. He resisted the urge to drop by the house of Eretmenos. It would only remind him of their servant Borilos and the part he had played in killing every member of his family and household.

Instead, he headed up the hill to the Parthenon, to pray to Athene to watch over this polis for the next millennium to come. He bought a good jug of wine from one of the vendors at the bottom of the hill, and gave it up as an offering to the goddess. He did not need wine, so it was an easy thing to give up. When he left the vast high temple and its golden statue, the pain in his thigh had vanished. He walked down the hill again, feeling lighter and sprightlier than he had in a long time. He bought flowers for Gala and the scented oil that Talaemenes had a fondness for as he cut through the Agora to the street leading through to his temporary home.

His lovers were pleased to have him safely back, and glad of the thoughtful gifts he had brought them. They talked and laughed; even Polydektos forgot his woes and heavy heart for a time.

It wasn't until Sokrates and Aristaeos arrived at his door two hours later that the gravity of his life came weighing down upon him, as though Atlas had handed him the heavens to hold. Talaemenes led them to the room inside, away from prying eyes and twitching ears. Gala served them drinks before Polydektos bid her to leave so the four men could talk freely. He saw a glimmer of hurt in her eyes as he dismissed her, but she kept her smile as she left the room.

"What news, Aristaeos?" Talaemenes jumped in before Polydektos could open his mouth to ask the same question.

Sokrates smiled broadly and patted his student on the back. "Tell them, young Aristaeos."

"Well, my relative reliably informs me, via one of her contacts still in the Maenads, that there will be a gathering under the full moon two nights hence in the secret grove they use."

"How will we find this place? It is no good us stumbling around in the dark and alerting them to our presence," Talaemenes said.

"There, my pupil has surpassed himself. Show them, Aristaeos." Sokrates urged his smile even wider than before. He held his wine cup halfway to his lips, waiting in eager anticipation of what Aristaeos drew from a leather bag on the floor by his feet.

"I have a map," Aristaeos said with a smile, laying it on the table. It was a hastily drawn affair but seemed detailed enough for an old soldier like Polydektos to follow. He roughly knew the area but hadn't been that way for over a decade, he estimated. The map was passed around the table for everyone to study.

"What do you intend to do, my old friend?" Sokrates said before drinking of his wine. His eyes fixed upon Polydektos.

"I intend to get there first, and set a trap. I need to capture or kill as many of these Maenads as I possibly can. I must look into each of their eyes and find out the truth. I need to know the reasons why my womenfolk and household had to die."

"Best we take Darios and Alkmaion to scout the place out during the hours of daylight," Talaemenes suggested.

"Four men blundering about their sacred grove might alert them," Aristaeos countered.

"And what do you suggest, that we go up there blind, and try and catch them like fish with nets?" Talaemenes said, raising his voice. "This is not your concern."

"I will surely come," Aristaeos said, raising his hackles also. "I have risked much being drawn into this, and surely I should come, too."

"Quiet," Polydektos commanded. "Darios is one of the best trackers I know. I will send him there tomorrow. He has a cousin who farms goats on those hills; two goat herders will be less conspicuous than Polydektos and Sokrates wandering around the hillside together. Now, Aristaeos, do you know if there is much preparation for such meetings? Will there be Maenads waiting there guarding the place during the day, or do they just turn up at night?"

"Some are wives and daughters, so I've heard, so most cannot get there until an hour before the rituals begin. Whether this is true of all the cultists, I cannot say."

"Then sending Darios will be our plan. He can scout the area and find us a suitable hiding place. We will get there in the early afternoon of the ritual night and hide ourselves nearby. Only when all the Maenads are there, and they are occupied, will we close our net around them. None must escape, as we need them to talk." Polydektos said, with a dark look on his face.

"Then I have an idea that will exact the proper revenge on these witches," Talaemenes said, with an excited, almost girlish squeal to his voice.

"Then tell us," Sokrates urged.

And he did, and Polydektos could not have felt any prouder of Talaemenes if he were his own son.

Polydektos was restless after Sokrates and Aristaeos left. He left Talaemenes to guard Gala and went to visit Alkmaion and Darios in turn. The sun was scorching overhead, and he wished he had brought his straw hat. The pain in his leg had returned, as well as a mild headache. The tension in his neck and lower back, all of which had gone earlier at the temple of Athene, was building up again. He just wanted the night of the Maenads' ritual meeting to hurry up and arrive. He hoped he would get the answers he needed to move on from his grief.

He went out on the long walk to Alkmaion's farm. The soldier's old wife was not pleased to see him, and spat on the ground at his feet before going to fetch her husband.

"You must forgive my wife; she thinks you are death itself, and that soon I will be the next person to die for being close to you," Alkmaion explained as they left the farm and headed to Darios's house.

"Then I both forgive her and do not blame her, my old friend. She only speaks the truth of the matter."

"She speaks too much on many issues; do not worry on that point." Alkmaion laughed, and Polydektos could not help but join in. They found Darios in his shed at the end of his dry, dusty, flowerless garden. He had a small kiln there and made pots with his hands. Each would depict great battles in which he fought, or images of the gods at play. He was stripped to the waist, his hands and forearms caked in clay, like a layer of extra skin.

"I was wondering when I would see you two next," he said, getting up off his stool to plunge his arms into a bucket of cloudy brown water. "Do we have a plan of action, my general?"

"Yes." Polydektos nodded and entered the humid shed to look at the pots on the high shelves above Darios's potter's wheel and kiln. Polydektos loved the artistry of the pots lined up together. He did not know his friend was so talented. Polydektos's artistic skills had never progressed past stick men with large phalluses. "These are very good. You should have a stall at the Agora."

"I could, but then I would have to part with them; I just like making, painting and looking at them all. They are the story of my life in pots, here to live on beyond my mortal life after I die."

"Do not speak of dying, my friend. I have lost too many I care for already." Polydektos turned to see Darios drying his wet arms on a large stained cloth.

"If Zeus himself wishes to make me immortal, I would not complain, but until he does, these pots will have to be my legacy. No time I had for wives and children; only whoring and warring."

All three old soldiers laughed aloud at that.

"I have honey mead inside. Let us partake, and you can tell me what my mission is, general." Darios walked past them towards his meagre home.

Alkmaion and Polydektos exchanged a concerned look before grinning at each other. Darios was the best scout Polydektos had ever had in his army, because he seemed to have a sixth sense of danger before it happened. Polydektos often joked that

Darios had been blessed by Athene and her mother Metis with all the cunning he had. Darios would only wink back, tap his nose, and say, "Do not jinx it, for what gifts the gods hand over, they can quickly take back."

Darios sat down after giving honey-mead to Alkmaion and Polydektos. "So, what do you want me to do?"

Polydektos took a copy of the map Aristaeos had given him from a pouch on his sword belt and handed it across the table. Gala, who was more skilled than he, had copied the original. "Here is a map of the Maenads' meeting place on the slopes of Lykabettos. We know you have a cousin who keeps goats near there. We thought you could join him and scout the place out, and not look out of place at all."

"Epikrates owes me a favour." Darios nodded as he studied the map. "When do you want me to go?"

"We have two nights before the Maenads gather there, so on the morrow, my friend. We need to know the lie of the land and a good place close-by to observe unnoticed, and to hide five to six men."

Darios studied the map carefully for a few more moments, a curt nod his only reply. Then he walked outside and threw the map into the fireplace of his kiln. Alkmaion and Polydektos were unconcerned, for they had seen their friend do this many times before. His memory of maps and terrain was beyond the skills of any other scout they had known. Once he had locked it in, there it would remain in his mind to be recalled at any given moment. Polydektos was unsure if Darios had been blessed by the gods, but they were blessed to have him in their ranks.

They waited for Darios to check his drying pots, while Alkmaion poured himself some more mead. Polydektos raised his left hand and refused any more. He needed to keep a clear head for the next few days. He hoped at the end of it, his quest to catch and punish his wife's and daughter's killers would be over.

The three soldiers and friends parted at Darios's front door. They would meet again at the House of Javelins tomorrow, after night had fallen, to discuss their battle plans. Darios went back to his pottery shed, Alkmaion back to his farm, and Polydektos back to Talaemenes and Gala. He refused to talk any more about the Maenads and the plan of action. He, or the men that followed him, could easily die two nights hence. These women were fanatical followers of the Dionysos cult. They had shown in the past how ruthless and bloodthirsty they could be—not just killing his wife and daughter and leaving their mutilated bodies in such a terrible dismembered state, but also murdering his entire household for no reason. Surely they could have used a sleeping draught and not the blue powder, for there had been no need to murder all the metics and slaves. The killer, or killers, had wanted to push forward their point. Polydektos would make their suffering slow and lingering, until they begged for the release of death.

But now he would spend his time with his young lovers. They ate a light lunch and then retired to their bed. If these were the last few days of his life, he would give the people he loved happy memories of him. He enjoyed himself and his young lovers with carefree abandonment. Only after they were asleep in each arm did he stare at the ceiling and weep for his lost family one last time. He kissed Gala and the Talaemenes on the lips as they slept, then went back to his seat on the dark balcony, alone with his thoughts of revenge and torture.

CHAPTER 18

The next day, Polydektos tried to smile and laugh, while hiding the tension of the situation behind his cheekbones until they ached. He and his young lovers ate out and went to a small local theatre.

He tried his hardest to be happy and gay in their presence, but as dusk rolled around, his old war wounds ached and reminded him that battle, blood, and death were coming. By sunset, he was pacing the balcony of the apartment in the House of Javelins. He was dressed in his battle gear, hidden under a grey himation. His sword felt good against his thigh once more.

Alkmaion was stationed at the archway entrance to the rear of the courtyard. Acroneos, another former soldier who had helped guard Polydektos during his court appearance, was stationed down at the streetside doorway. An hour after dark, torches and braziers lit the rooms and courtyard, but still there was no sign of Darios. Sokrates and Aristaeos joined them just before sunset.

Fear, like icy sweat, coated the back of the general's neck, running down his spine every now and again to remind him of the situation. He had no fear of death in battle, only fear of losing more people he cared for, and fear that the killers of his wife and daughter might escape his wrath.

It was nearly three hours after sunset when he heard the signal whistle from Alkmaion at the arched gateway to the rear courtyard. Polydektos and Talaemenes flew down the wooden balcony steps as Alkmaion, and a tired-looking Darios, came around the corner.

"I was getting worried about you, old friend," Polydektos

said, clasping Darios's forearms before pulling him into a bear hug.

"We had no trouble in the hills; it's just that, with age, walking back here takes onger than I used to remember." Darios gave a dry, quick laugh.

"Come, let us go upstairs and discuss things behind closed doors. Talaemenes, fetch Darios some water to quench his thirst before he speaks." Polydektos clapped the tall, thin youth on the shoulder.

"Make that wine and I will talk with more ease," Darios said with another grunting laugh as they all headed upstairs.

"So you and your cousin found the place we seek; this is good," Alkmaion said, passing around the wine jug to the men seated at the table. Only Gala and Acroneos were not present of the group—Gala as she was not going on the mission, and Acroneos as he was on guard. He would be staying behind on the night to protect Gala from any reprisal attacks, anyway.

"Yes, my cousin Epikrates and I pushed his goats as close to the sacred meeting grove of these Maenads as we dared. We passed it once during the afternoon, and it was clean and clear of people, and then again at dusk. It was only then I spotted someone hidden in the shadows behind the trees. A thin, cloaked figure, most likely a woman, armed with a bow."

At this, Polydektos's eyebrows rose and then met in a V shape on his furrowed forehead. A cloaked female with a bow? Could this be the same assassin who slew the tiny priestess at the theatre of Dionysos? She was added to his list of reasons for revenge on this female cult and its members.

"Did she see you?" Talaemenes asked, without thinking before he spoke.

"Of course she saw us, but I made sure I did not give away that I spotted her. The grove is hidden in a small dell, with the banking tree-covered hillside shielding any torch lights from the prying eyes of the city and farms below. The hills around it are rocky and out of the way, that only a goat herder might wander past. Earlier, my cousin showed me a small cave nearby where he once sheltered from a hailstorm. It is a little way up the slope of the hill, hidden from view of the grove by trees and line of sight, but it has space enough for all of us to hunker down until nightfall."

"You have exceeded your mission tenfold once again, my friend," Polydektos said. "If I were still your general, I would promote you and give you the pick of the best whores."

"You can keep the promotion, my general—now tell me more about these choice whores."

This brought bawdy laughter from around the small table.

"Where is your cousin now?" Aristaeos asked after the laughter had died down.

"He keeps his herd further down the hillside, so he can watch any comings and goings on the nearby road. He will wait there for us tomorrow."

"Talaemenes, I want you and Aristaeos to visit Mopsos early in the morning, to follow up on your good idea," Polydektos said. Sokrates, I think you should stay here with Acroneos and Gala tomorrow, as you can hardly keep your eyes open, my friend." The philosopher had been silent most of the night and dozing for the last few minutes.

"I am just conserving my energy for the fight, Polydektos," Sokrates replied grumpily, forcing his eyes wide open. "Your army has only two spring chickens anyway. You need guile and wisdom on this sort of a venture, and I am still not too shabby with a bow from a distance, don't you worry. Stay behind with the women? Not on Poseidon's fishy loins, I won't."

Everyone around the table except Aristaeos grinned at this. He feared for his teacher's safety but did not voice his concerns. He did not want to show his mentor up in front of his friends.

"Then, we are nearly ready," Polydektos said, raising his cup of water above the table. He looked at the face of each of his companions in turn. "We will wait in the cave until darkness, and when the Maenads gather, we will encircle them and spring our trap. Aim for legs and arms; I want to bring them down and speak to as many as I can. Kill them only as a last resort, if your life feels threatened."

"By a bunch of girls?" Aristaeos said with a dismissive shrug.

"That slaughtered my entire household in silence without

taking casualties. Do not take any foe lightly. I give you that advice for free, young Aristaeos," Polydektos warned him.

"The immortality of youth, eh?" Sokrates raised his cup to his wounded-looking pupil.

"May the gods look down on our venture and grant us total victory and revenge for the fallen innocents." Polydektos raised his cup and drank down the rest of his water. It tasted tepid and oily, and he hoped it wasn't an ill omen for the events to come.

The men stayed at the House of Javelins that night. Only Darios sampled the delights of his favoured hetaira. Polydektos let him rest, as he was up early with the dawn. He left Talaemenes and Gala entwined in their bed and sat on the balcony in the cool morning breeze in his short battle dress. He wished for his spear and hoplon shield, but they would be too bulky for a fight under the trees. He would wear his armour over his short battle chiton, and under his longer outer himation. He would bring his xiphos short sword and a dagger, just in case. He was still pondering whether to bring his helmet in a sack when Gala came outside to join him. She was completely naked and shaved bare, except for the light brown, almost golden hair on her head. She looked at him like a shy virgin on her wedding night, and he thought she was a gift of beauty and pleasure sent from Aphrodite herself.

Naked, she silently stepped close and sat down on his lap. She kissed his lips softly once and then buried her neck into his. He hesitated, and then held her tightly to him.

"Don't worry, my little jewel from the west. I will come back to you, and only death may part us." Polydektos spoke to reassure her, in truth not knowing if he would make it back. Even if he did, and the debt of vengeance were paid upon the Maenads that murdered his wife and daughter, would life still be worth living, with no heir or family around him?

Then Talaemenes stepped outside, rubbing at a dry sleepy eye. He too was naked, lean and thin, and with a stomach that went in like a shallow cave, and not out resembling a boulder, like his. Polydektos waved his hither and hugged them both. Maybe he had love, life, and a family to live for after all.

Gala served all the men a hearty breakfast and gave them each individual packs of food and waterskins to get them through the long day. Talaemenes and Aristaeos were dispatched early to visit Mopsos the alchemist, while the older men finished off their early meal. They were to meet the rest of the group at the eastern gates of the city, so Gala kissed them both in turn, the longest and wettest kiss reserved for young Talaemenes. Afterwards, they dressed for war, hidden beneath their outer clothing. Only Sokrates refused any offers of boiled leather breastplate. He would take only his short bow and quiver of black feathered arrows, trusting in the gods to protect his head and body.

When it came time to go, Gala lost all her womanly reserve and flung herself upon Polydektos's chest, not caring the pain his hidden armour caused her. Her tears flowed, and she covered him with kisses and begged him to return safely to her arms again. He gave her a little time to sob in his neck, then delicately pulled her arms from around his shoulders and held her hands tightly.

"I will return if the gods will it, Gala, and if I do, it will be back into your arms once more," he said kindly to her, knowing that the other men were close by and watching him. Then he kissed her forehead and let go of her long, delicate fingers. She wiped away her tears and stepped back, her chin raised proudly. Then she turned and kissed Darios, Alkmaion, and Sokrates in turn, before fleeing back up the stairs to her rooms.

Acroneos stepped before Polydektos and clasped his arm. "I will protect her with my life."

"I know, my friend." Polydektos patted the man's shoulder and turned to his companions. "It is time for us to depart."

"Good hunting, General," Acroneos said.

The other three men nodded. They waved and bade Acroneos fond farewells. He watched them leave the courtyard, then went up the rear steps to check that the front door was barred and then check on Gala. He left her sobbing into her pillow in her bedroom and took his vigil outside on the balcony. He was in for a long day and night, but as a former soldier, he was well used to that.

The four older men met the two younger bucks just outside the Diochares Gate. They were both fidgety and eager for battle. Polydektos, as a veteran, could see the mix of fear and excitement in their eyes. He had to temper that, or they might get themselves killed. A long walk in the morning sun should fatigue some of that away.

"You have it?" Polydektos asked as they approached the youths sitting in the shadows of a wall.

"Yes," Talaemenes replied. He reached back over the wall to carefully pick up a white sack, which had a rope tied to each corner to form an X, making it easy to carry on one's back.

"Good. Let us hope it does not rain," Polydektos said, with a grave face.

Talaemenes instantly looked up to the skies, but could see not a cloud in the blue heavens. He looked back down to see Polydektos smirking at him, trying to put him at ease with a joke. He patted the youth's arm, and they set off down the road that led to the east. It was not their destination, as they had to double back on the road to head north, over a bridge, to follow the river Eridanos up to the foothills to meet with Epikrates. This part of the journey was strangely pleasant. It was a stroll in the countryside with good friends and companions of war. Sokrates regaled them with heroic tales of his youth and army service. Alkmaion and Darios piped up with tales of their own, but Polydektos did not want to talk of old battles. They sipped watered wine, passed around in a skin as they walked. Around noon they met up with Darios's cousin and his herd of goats. On a low round hillside overlooking Athens, they ate together in good humour. It was only once they had to get up to leave that they found smiles and frivolous war tales harder.

As they moved higher into the limestone hills towards the forest-covered Mount Lykabettos, they walked in silence. A few birds flapped about in the trees as they passed below them, but apart from the noisy insects, the forest was silent. Epikrates stayed with his goats in a small valley that had some shaded grass for his herd to eat. He wished them all well as Darios led the men up a rocky incline towards a crevice in the hillside. They had to use the low trees to help them scramble up. Talaemenes and Aristaeos fell back to help the less athletic Sokrates to the top, where they moved into the cool shades of the forest proper.

Darios led them on a long back way up to the cave they would use to hide until nightfall. Even the younger men felt aches in their calves as they sat down on the cool floor of the cave to rest. The wineskin was passed around the group once more.

Once rested, Darios and Polydektos alone went out to scout the area where the Maenads' midnight ceremony would take place. Both Talaemenes and Aristaeos wanted to accompany them, but Polydektos gave them a firm no. If the Maenads' guard caught wind of a group of men roaming the hillside, they would cancel the ceremony and the trip would have been for naught. The men needed the scope of the ceremonial dell, but in the smallest possible numbers, giving less chance of being spotted.

The two youths had to agree with the general's logic. They sat back down and checked over their weapons, mostly for something to do. Polydektos took the heavy roped sack from Talaemenes and carried it with him.

Darios led Polydektos through the trees to a rocky outcrop high behind the dell. The sacred grove was hard to see through the trees, but they could see no movement of female figures far below. They watched for fifteen minutes or so, but still saw nobody present.

"Cover me," Polydektos said to Darios, with a pat on his back. The former soldier readied his short bow, scanning the trees as his former general crept closer to the dell. Polydektos made his way to a large, thick old tree that leant over the sacred dell like a doting grandfather. Pulling the bag tight on his back, he climbed up the tree. Darios had a nervous wait for Polydektos, and it took the general nearly half an hour to return from his tree-climbing exploits. When he did, the roped bag on his back and its secret contents were gone.

"Let us go," Polydektos whispered. Darios, like a good soldier, did not ask what his former general had been doing for so long, as they crept slowly back to their hiding place. The rest of their companions were glad to see their safe return. They covered the entrance of the cave with fallen branches and bracken and hunkered down to wait for nightfall.

CHAPTER 19

The six men lit no fire and ate only cold food. Talaemenes ate very sparingly, and Aristaeos could stomach nothing at all but water. Slowly the sunlight moved across the covered entrance of the cave and disappeared from sight. They spoke little and in whispers. Polydektos talked to each man in turn about their positions during the night assault.

Day turned to dusk and then night. The churning in Talaemenes's stomach was so loud he thought others could hear it. He had a dreadful urge to pee but did not want to stink out the small cave they all hid in. He could do nothing but grip the spear he had brought along, and close his eyes against the rising fear in his core.

Even though it was dark now, they still had hours to wait before they made their way into their positions around the dell. To Polydektos and the older former soldiers, it was time to reflect on their plan. To the two youths, it was torture of the soul.

Gala had popped her head round the door half an hour earlier, asking if Acroneos wanted any more food or drink. He waved her back inside quickly and bade her to shut and lock the door behind her. He had little time for the girl, but his former general held her in high favour, so that was good enough for him to risk his life.

He exhaled and stood up from the chair from which he watched the rear courtyard. There was noise and light across the way and to the left, but he sat in utter darkness. He had made Gala promise not to light any torches, fires, or burners inside her apartment. Let everyone think the place was empty tonight. Movement caught his eye under the stairs of one of the other apartments. He drew his short sword and leant over the balcony for a better look. A giggle and a heavy slap of hand on flesh brought a hetaira girl and her erstwhile lover running from the shadows into the door of a ground floor room. Acroneos scoured the courtyard, fountains, and shadows, but he could see nothing untoward, so he sat down again. He laid this cold blade across his bare knees; it was the second-to-last sensation he ever felt. The last was an arrow just through the top of his ear and into his startled brain. He slumped to the side in his chair, and died without even a murmur.

It seemed to the two youngest men of the group that they had been cooped up in the cave for most of the night, and they were sure they had missed the Maenads' ceremony. Then, the exotic sound of a flute drifting over the hillside was their signal to move at last. Polydektos and Alkmaion moved the brushes and branches away from the cave entrance as quietly as they could, and the six men poured out into the darkness, their outer clothes discarded; except for Sokrates in his himation, they were dressed for battle. Their weapons and breastplates they dulled with soot that Darios had brought with him from their lunchtime campfire. They decided on stealth, so they had no helmets or shields to protect them, only the cover of night.

Darios took the point position, followed by Alkmaion and Polydektos, with Talaemenes, Aristaeos, and Sokrates bringing up the rear. In a wedge formation, they slowly made their way through the forest, carefully picking where to tread, and trying not to rush and give themselves away. Darios had his bow ready, with an arrow notched. Polydektos had his sword and dagger still in their sheaths. Alkmaion had a bow also, and a sword at his side. Sokrates was the last of the bowmen in the group. Talaemenes had his spear and Aristaeos carried three throwing javelins with him.

They moved to the rocky outcrop over the dell. Darios and Polydektos looked on to see what the fast, high-ranging flute music was encouraging below. It took a while for Polydektos's eyes to adjust to the fire in the centre of the dell. Behind the high flames was a single tree, and tied to it was a young slave boy of about fourteen years. He counted fourteen women, mostly naked, or wearing belts of ivy around their heads or waists. They danced around the fire and the tree, where the gagged, frightened boy was tied. Wine flowed and pipes played wild, hedonistic tunes. One woman with a bull mask had a rigid leather phallus strapped over her groin. She moved around the group entering any woman at will, and making love roughly to them, like a man. This seemed to bring shrill grunts of ecstasy from her female lovers.

Polydektos managed to look away from the Maenad ceremonial orgy, to point to each of his companions to take up their positions surrounding the sacred grove. He had to focus on the appalling deaths and mutilations played out on his wife and daughter, to get into a war frame of mind. He could see the two youths were wide-eyed with desire at the scene below. Polydektos had taken this into account in his battle plans. They would stay near the top of the ridge flanking Sokrates and his bow. Darios the scout, their quietest man, would move around directly across from Sokrates to cut off the Maenads' escape. He and Alkmaion would position themselves across the dell from each other, hidden in the tree line.

Each man crept slowly down and out of sight into their designated positions for the attack. As they did, they set out tripping traps of black cord at ankle height at the base of the trees they passed, spinning it out on a wooden spool. Polydektos was trying not to leave anything to chance. They had only one stab at this, and if they failed and the Maenads escaped, he was sure they would never get the opportunity again.

Finally, with their trip cord traps set, Polydektos stepped over them and moved in as close as the cover would safely allow. He needn't have worried. The naked Maenads, like woodland nymphs, were fully occupied with the ceremony to Dionysos going on in the centre of the dell. The pipes had ceased. The women of all shapes and sizes were in a circle around the youth tied to the tree. The one with the bull mask was standing next to another tanned young woman, who had a snake mask on, and a great snake coiled around her right arm, the back of its head held in her closed fist. Bull Mask went around the circle of women holding hands, and from a bowl she held, she popped an ivy leaf into every willing open mouth as she passed.

"Dionysos, hear our cries, take our sacrifice, let the Omophagia begin," the Snake Woman cried up into the night. She pressed the head of the snake to the youth's neck before Polydektos could even blink. He screamed into his rag in his mouth once, and then his head went limp as the snake's venom did its work.

"Omophagia," the rest of the women chanted as one, and then in an act shocking to even Polydektos's veteran eyes, rushed at the dazed youth and began tearing him apart with their bare hands. The frenzy and bloodlust of the attack were beyond anything he had seen on the battlefield. The Maenads tore into the boy's soft flesh with their teeth and nails. They seemed to revel in the hot blood covering them. Lust, and fanatical worship of their god, gave them strength and power they would never experience in their day-to-day, subservient lives. Bones were cracked, flesh bitten off and consumed. Polydektos saw the remains of an arm torn from a bloody socket and could take no more. He hooted like an owl and waited for his plan to spring into action.

He pulled a scarf up over his mouth and waited. He was about to hoot the signal again when the trap was sprung. Up on the rise of the hill, with Sokrates' urging, Talaemenes cut a strong, thin rope hidden in the vines of the tree that towered over the sacred grove. Down from the boughs of the trees, a large earthenware pot fell between the Maenads and the fire. It shattered into many pieces. Inside was a blue ground dust. On top of the large urn had been two sealed jugs of water, which also smashed on impact. Hardly any of the Maenads even noticed it fall, so intent were they on tearing the boy limb from limb and feasting on his warm flesh.

The bull- and snake-masked women, and two others close by, did notice. They moved to examine the pot just as a vaporous cloud of blue belched forth and enveloped them. The snake woman and the two nearest Maenads fell to the floor in an instant stupor.

"Run for your lives!" the bull-masked woman managed to cry out, before the blue mist took her down.

The Maenads, seeing the blue mist and the fall of their priestesses, screamed and ran in all directions. The blue mist spread fast, and Polydektos stood up, worried it might spread too far and affect his men. Only six escaped the deadly blue mist. The rest were overtaken as they feasted on the dead boy. Two ran towards Alkmaion, one towards Darios, but three headed Polydektos's way.

One ran blindly into Polydektos's path, letting him step sideways and bring the hilt of his sword crashing down upon the back of her head. She fell like a stone. A faster one to the left was caught by the swift running of Talaemenes. The other, lean and spry, was past Polydektos in a flash, yet his cord trap did its job. He heard a scream and a crash in the undergrowth. He found the naked Maenad trying to rise, wincing at the pain in her ankle. He dived upon her, winding all escape from her, and tied her hands with ivy vines ripped from around her waist.

The operation had happened so quickly and went so well, Polydektos could not believe it. They quickly dragged, led, or carried their prisoners up and away from the now-tainted dell, back to the safety of their cave camp. The one Alkmaion had caught never woke from the blue gas. That left five Maenads to question. Out of the five, only two were conscious and able to speak. Both were wide-eyed in the fire that Darios lit, still suffering the effects of the ivy leaves they had consumed. Both of them had chins, bodies, and hands covered in the boy's blood. That ensured they got little sympathy from the older men.

Alkmaion and Talaemenes were sent to check on the blue mist, to see if it had dissipated in the slight breeze or was heading their way. Aristaeos, with his young eyes, kept watch on the camp, while Darios guarded the unconscious and secured Maenads in the cave mouth. Sokrates and Polydektos gave the two dazed but conscious Maenads water to drink, and washed away as much of the blood on their faces as they could.

The one Sokrates questioned looked up at him with dazed eyes and just said, "Omophagia," over and over again.

The one with the sprained ankle seemed to be more lucid,

perhaps due to the pain clearing her mind more quickly than the other's.

"Who are you and whom do you serve?" Polydektos said, grabbing her throat lightly in his right hand and holding her in a sitting position, with his other hand gripping her right arm tightly.

"I am one with Dionysos, I serve only him," she replied.

"Your leaders are dead and your cult broken. What was the name of your leader who died tonight?"

"Our leader is Melissa, but she can never die, for she is one with Dionysos. She led us from oppressive lives as men's slaves and showed us another path."

"I assure you Melissa is very dead; killed by the same blue mist that took my household. Why did you kill my wife and daughter? What had I ever done to you, to warrant them being killed and mutilated so?" Polydektos said with rage, shaking the young woman.

The young woman laughed wildly at him. "You can't kill someone who lives in the shadows, and is like a wraith of our god." Polydektos tried to swallow down his rising rage. He could see bits of the boy's flesh in her teeth, smell the taint on her breath.

"Why did Melissa want my daughter and wife dead?"

The woman continued to laugh.

Polydektos let go of her throat and drew his sword, pointing the tip in the soft flesh under her chin. "Tell me why they had to die! Why did this Melissa order their deaths, to punish them or me? Speak and I will let you and your companions live."

"Our bodies may die, but the cult lives on in Melissa," the Maenad girl said, smiling at him.

"Is that so?" Polydektos took his sword and, with a swift, arching cut, beheaded the girl Sokrates was holding nearby. Her head rolled into the darkness and was lost from sight.

The girl and Aristaeos cried out in shock. Even Sokrates was taken aback and pushed the blood-spurting body away from him. Darios looked at the other two of Polydektos's shocked companions but said nothing. This cult had slain Polydektos's family and household in one night. They would get what was coming to them.

"Speak, or I will cut off the heads of each of your companions and make you watch. If that does not loosen your tongue, I will take a foot or hand, then maybe an arm, but keep your alive to face the wrath of Zeus, just bits of the woman you once were," he snarled into her worried face.

"Melissa will get her revenge for this," the girl said, in a less confident voice.

"Was the snake mask or the bull mask women Melissa? As both are dead, I assure you."

"Melissa is still alive, she ordered the killing of your household. She ordered the death of your wife and daughter. And do you know why?"

"Tell me?"

"For one—" Her words were ended by an arrow to the throat. She gargled and spat blood, then fell dead out of Polydektos's arms. Polydektos looked up angrily, expecting to see one of his companions holding a bow. But none were, and they were as shocked as he was.

Another arrow thudded into the head of one of the unconscious prisoners. It seemed to come from nowhere. Polydektos and his companions stood up. The rest retreated inside the cave as another arrow thudded into another prisoner's chest. Polydektos still stood his ground. Another arrow came out of the darkness from an elevated angle into the eye of the next prisoner. Someone was trying to stop them talking to him. Melissa was still alive after all.

Polydektos could not lose the last of the Maenad prisoners. He had to interrogate them and find out the reason, once and for all, why his family had to die. In a last throw of the dice, he stood over the remaining prisoners, his legs apart, defying an arrow to strike him down. The archer assassin had orders to silence the captured Maenads from talking. Was it another of their cult, or the fabled Melissa herself? He was banking on the fact that they could have killed him any time since the first attack on his villa. For some reason he could not fathom, they had wanted him alive, and he hoped that this was still the case.

There was a movement high up in a tree, a dark shadow against the trunk. He saw the archer.

"Sokrates, your bow?" Polydektos reached with his right arm towards the cave, where his companions were taking shelter. Yet it was too late. A dark-fletched arrow whistled through his legs and into the eye of the last Maenad captive. She gave a grunt and then was dead. Polydektos felt the bow and three arrows being pushed into his hand, his eye never leaving the shadow archer in the tree as they began to scramble to escape. Polydektos drew the bow and took aim. Waiting for the right moment, just before the assassin found the dark safety of the lower canopy of the tree, he let fly.

There was a cry of pain, and the assassin disappeared, falling or jumping down from sight.

"Everyone, grab a torch and fan out to search for this archer. Be on your guard, I may only have clipped the fiend's wings." Polydektos grabbed a nearby torch Darios had brought and hurried off into the night before the rest of his companions could even draw breath. He vaguely heard them calling out his name as they gathered their weapons and torches to join the pursuit. Polydektos was focusing only on the tree the assassin had fallen from, and nothing more. He ran as directly for the tree as the woods would allow. He had the flaming brand swishing this way and that before him as he ran. The bow and two remaining arrows were in his right hand. If the archer was waiting for him near the tree, he would not be able to drop the torch and notch an arrow in time. He had to hope the archer was not too wounded to live to answer his questions, but enough not to be free to shoot an arrow in his face as he approached. He had no fear of death anymore, and ran through two bushes into a small clearing and under the tree where the assassin had hidden to fire down on their camp.

There was no sign of the archer anywhere.

He searched around the tree but saw no bodies, heard no movement, could see no figures fleeing into the night. A blow to the back of his head caused him to stagger and then fall to his knees. He dropped the torch as a figure limped towards him in the darkness. A foot in a black sandal came into his vision, and the assassin was ready to strike again. Polydektos used all the strength his dazed mind had left and rammed the heads of the two arrows into the assassin's left foot. He heard a shriek of high-pitched pain before another blow to the head brought the dark of night into his mind.

CHAPTER 20

"Do not worry, Talaemenes—he has a head made from mountain stone, this one."

Polydektos recognised the speaker as Sokrates as he slowly regained consciousness. Blinding morning sunshine sent daggers of pain into his already throbbing head. Tears welled in his eyes as he forced them into slits. Slowly, the dazzling, blinding white and blue light formed figures and movement all around him. He was laid out flat, being carried on a stretcher hastily made of branches and leaves from the forest.

Polydektos turned his head. They were no longer in or near the forest or foothills; they were approaching a gate back into the city. Aristaeos, Darios, Alkmaion, and Sokrates were carrying him.

"Where is Talaemenes?" he croaked.

"By all the gods, he lives," Darios cried aloud as he looked down upon his former general.

Sokrates turned and smiled back at him. "Talaemenes is slightly wounded, but here, my old friend. We all are." Polydektos tried to raise his head, but it felt like a landslide of rocks had suddenly come crashing down on his skull. He turned his eyes to see Talaemenes limp into view before crushing him in a tight embrace. Polydektos though he might have survived the assassin's attack, only to be suffocated by his young lover.

"Give him some air, boy," he heard Alkmaion say.

Talaemenes kissed his cheek and lips and then retreated to walk with a definite limp nearer to the stretcher.

"What ails you, Talaemenes?"

"I heard your cry and saw the assassin knock you to the

ground before escaping. I tried to give chase, but the archer turned and shot me in the foot as they fled. With my wound, I could not keep up the chase. I'm sorry I failed you, Polydektos. The assassin fled into the night." The boy began to sob now.

"No need for tears." Polydektos flopped out his left arm and Talaemenes took his hand to kiss and hold tight. "Did the archer seem wounded to you, Talaemenes?"

"Not that I could see, but I could see very little in the dark, and the archer shot me early on in my pursuit, sadly. I am sorry again for letting you down."

"Worry not, Talaemenes, for if anyone failed it was I. I greatly underestimated our enemy and the lengths to which this Melissa will go to cover her tracks. Carry me to the House of Javelins, I need to see Gala again and rest before..."

"Polydektos," Talaemenes cried in worry as his lover's words died away.

"Leave him be, boy, he still lives. His head just needs rest and time to recover," Alkmaion said to the weeping youth as they entered the city once more, carrying their unconscious leader.

When Polydektos awoke again, he found himself in Gala's large bed. The sun had crossed half the sky, and he was not alone. Gala lay next to him, curled in the crook of his left armpit, her arm across his bare chest. He saw that her arm was bandaged around the forearm, and a patch of dried blood had seeped through.

He sat up a little, and his head swam. When his vision returned to normal, he saw all his companions were standing around the room, still armed for war.

"What happened here?" He pushed himself into a sitting position. Gala's pained eyed flickered open and with a beaming smile of relief she kissed his lips, face, and neck until he gently made her stop.

"I am so glad to see you alive, my general," she said, relieved.

"Acroneos is slain, by an arrow," Alkmaion said, bluntly.

"How, when did this happen?" Polydektos said, as more grief stabbed at his punctured heart. How many more losses could one mortal man have to bear in one life?

"I came out on the balcony in the dead of night to see if he required more refreshment, and found him slain," Gala said, her eyes full of quivering tears. "Then a dark figure pounced on me from the roof above, slashing at me and wounding me slightly. I managed to push the fiend down the stairs, more by accident than any act of bravery. The lone man fled, limping away like he was badly injured."

"How did you know it was a man?" Sokrates pressed.

"I know the feel and shape of a man's body on top of me, above all others." Gala looked downwards at the bed, slightly ashamed.

"Then are we seeking two assassins now?" Talaemenes said from his seated position in a chair. His bandaged foot was resting on a low table.

"Or one that can be in two places at once?" Darios said.

"Or has the swift turn of foot that would put Hermes to shame," Aristaeos suggested.

"This was no act of the gods; this has been a bloody plot from beginning to end, which only a man or woman could have devised," Sokrates proclaimed.

"I think we all need to rest and take time to digest last night's events, and maybe later form a better council for Polydektos," Alkmaion advised. "We take turns in twos to guard the wounded, while the others rest. We must be prepared for another attack, in reprisal for the events at the sacred dell and what followed after. Our friends, and ourselves by association, are still targets, and maybe one or two or more assassins are still at large. We must be on our guard." The weary group nodded their agreement.

Sokrates and Darios took to the spare room to sleep, while Alkmaion and Aristaeos kept watch like hawks outside.

"I will fetch you and the others refreshment," Gala said, pulling down the covers to her waist, making to leave the bed.

"No, no, no," Polydektos said, laying a gentle hand on her wounded arm. "They can fetch their own vittles, Gala. You and Talaemenes should take the bed and rest up. My head is made of hard wood anyway. You two have suffered just for your affection towards me. Maybe I should take a lone boat to Lesbos and take the danger with me." Polydektos struggled out of bed, as Talaemenes hobbled over to him.

"We are in this together to the very end, Polydektos," Talaemenes said earnestly, as he sat on the bed next to the former general.

Polydektos felt Gala press her body against his back and kiss his shoulder. "We would live and die at your command, such is our love for you."

Polydektos patted her hand as it rested on his arm, and smiled thinly across at Talaemenes.

"Such love and loyalty—no mortal man could ask for more," Polydektos said, and stood on slightly unsteady feet. "I need some air; you two rest."

He left his two lovers on the bed and walked outside, closing the balcony door after him. Aristaeos was standing guard with his javelins ready by the fountain, in the centre of the courtyard below. Alkmaion was sitting on one of the seats at the small outside table, splashing water onto his weary face to keep the sleep away. The table had been scrubbed, but parts of the floor were still stained with Acroneos's blood.

"You look like my head feels," Polydektos said, slumping down on a chair next to his old war comrade.

"That bad, eh?" Alkmaion managed a dry laugh.

Polydektos poured himself a cup of water and drank of it deeply.

"So, after last night, does the mystery deepen or unfold, General?"

"We have no captives to interrogate. This Melissa remains elusive as an eel, and I lose more close friends and family every day, it seems. I deem we are worse off than ever before."

"I was thinking, General, that Borilos was a man, a male follower of Dionysos. Gala said a man attacked her and killed Acroneos. Maybe the greatest disguise this Melissa could have is to have everyone think she is a woman when she was, in fact, a man."

"Like that Spartan warrior we once slew, only to find out he was a bearded she." Polydektos nodded and sipped some more water. Something one of the Maenad captives had said before she died came to mind. Dark thoughts started spinning around his mind so quickly he felt like his heart had frozen.

"The little priestess," he whispered to himself.

"What?" Alkmaion heard him say something, but was not sure of his former general's words.

"When I met the tiny priestess at the theatre of Dionysos, she told me about the lore of Dionysos. Dionysos disguised himself as a beautiful woman and lured an enemy King Pentheos into the woods for his followers to dismember. When King Lycurgus of Thrace imprisoned the Maenads, Dionysos disguised himself as a serving girl. Maybe she was trying to impart something important to me; that Melissa, like you said, could be a man, disguised as a woman for his followers."

"It would be a perfect way to throw us off the scent. If we are chasing a woman, this man posing as Melissa could walk past us now and we would not suspect him," Alkmaion said, sitting straight up in his seat.

"Maybe he walks past us every day," Polydektos said gravely, turning to face his old comrade. "When you and Talaemenes went to check the dead, were you together at all times?"

"At first, yes, but when we searched the sacred dell, we each took a side of the woods to check the area. I did not see him again until we all found you unconscious by the tree."

"Who found me first?"

"Talaemenes did, but he was not there when I came across you. The others found us soon after. Talaemenes came limping back with his arrow wound a little while later, saying he had lost Melissa because of his wounded foot."

"I wounded Melissa in the foot with my arrows before the assassin knocked me unconscious," Polydektos stated.

"Surely you cannot suspect Talaemenes! The lad is devoted to you!" Alkmaion said in a hushed voice.

"Love does strange things to people."

"He loves you. Why would he kill your family and hurt you?"

"To have me all for himself. With my wife and daughter out of the way, he would have no rival for his affections."

"Except Gala, perhaps," Alkmaion said.

"Twice her life has been threatened, and only by sheer luck has she survived," Polydektos pointed out.

"I thought he was with you when your villa was attacked?"

"Yes, but he had time when I slept in such a drunken state to creep out at night, do the vile deed, and come back before Gala or I awoke. He knew Borilos and the lie of my house." Polydektos put his hands over his face and exhaled. "I've been chasing nightmares, phantoms, and Persians, when I should have been looking closer to home, all this time."

"You have facts that fit, but no proof," Alkmaion whispered.

"Then I will wring it out of his neck." Polydektos rose. "Wait here; let no one inside."

"Are you sure about this, Polydektos?" Alkmaion warned.

"I'm not sure of anything in life anymore, my friend. But this ends today, one way or the other." Polydektos returned to the bedchamber and closed the balcony door behind him, then walked over to the interior door and shut that. The noise woke Gala and Talaemenes from their snoozing. Polydektos went over to his armour and drew his sword and approached the bed.

"Are you well, my sweet Polydektos?" Gala asked sleepily as she sat up in bed. Talaemenes, rubbing his tired eyes, sat up with a yawn.

"Do you both love me with all your hearts?" Polydektos said.

His young lovers exchanged bemused glances and nodded.

"Then you must let me speak and do not cry out or speak without permission. Do you understand?"

They nodded, looking once again at each other and then back to their older lover.

Polydektos turned his short sword to face inwards in his grip and pressed it under his left breast, wherein his heart beat. "I will push this blade deep into my broken heart if you do not confess to me that you killed my family, and have been working against me all this time in some twisted act of love!"

"Polydektos, no," Talaemenes almost squeaked in shock at what his older lover was doing.

"No lies now—this ends today. Either you tell me you did

it and why, or I will kill myself and rid you of this evil malady that has turned your heart to murder."

"I do not know what you mean!" Talaemenes squealed louder in fright.

"I will end this now," Polydektos raged, pressing the tip of his blade through his skin. Blood trickled down in two lines from the small wound. "The next lie and denial from your lips will bring my death, so choose your words well, Talaemenes!"

Gala in a panic leapt out of the bed and prostrated herself before Polydektos, just as Sokrates and Darios burst through the inner door, woken by all the commotion.

"Get out the way, Gala, my mind is made up! Either he confesses, or I die!"

"He cannot confess, nor can he save you, my love, for I am Melissa, and I killed your wife and daughter."

Only then did Polydektos look down and see the blood-stained bandage around her left foot. Polydektos let his sword slip from his grasp to drop on the floor. It spun three times before coming to rest, pointing directly at Gala.

CHAPTER 21

"Gala, no, it cannot be you, it cannot," Talaemenes wailed from the bed, beginning to cry.

"What do you want us to do?" Darios asked, reaching down to collect the sword and putting it back in Polydektos's right hand.

"Take the boy outside to the courtyard, and wait for me there," Polydektos said in a voice drained of all emotions but hate.

"No, what are you going to do? Gala, why?" Talaemenes sobbed as the other men dragged him from the bedchamber. Only when the door was shut and the sounds of the sobbing youth diminished did Polydektos speak.

"Why?"

"Because I love you will all my heart, Polydektos, and knew, just being a simple foreign hetaira, that you, as a citizen of Athens, could never marry me, never lie with me as husband and wife until I rid you of the distractions of your family. With them gone, I had a chance of a life and love with you. I knew that you would rely on me forever until your dying day." Gala looked up at him with streaming eyes.

"Distractions? They were my life, my blood, my soul. You killed them and dismembered them and murdered all the people in my villa so I would come to rely only on your love!" Polydektos waved his sword at her, looking at Gala through his own hurt tears of utter betrayal. "How did you do this thing? How did you weave such a plan to murder my family?"

"Just because I am not an Athenian woman does not mean I do not love, or have thoughts or wants of my very own."

She paused. "Months it took for my plans to come to fruition. Borilos was easy to corrupt. He was known to visit the temple of Dionysos. He had a man's thoughts, and they are easy to seduce. He dug the tunnel under your villa in secret, and he put the pots of blue death into your storeroom, ready for that night. All I had to do was drug the wine you and Talaemenes were drinking, and it gave me hours to do the rest. The vapours of death do their work quickly, and within an hour they are gone. I scaled the very tree and wall that you always told me you used if you got home too late after the doors were shut. Everyone died in their sleep, and my followers and I set about my work." Gala said, pride in her words.

"Work!" Polydektos's raged. "You cut the metics' throats and then took my wife and daughter outside and cut them to pieces like they were butcher's carcasses. Why did everyone have to die?"

"So you would only love and rely on me, Polydektos. Only I can love you forever and pleasure you into your old age. I am sorry you had to suffer so, but I am here now, and we can be together for all eternity, you, me, and Talaemenes."

"Talaemenes, tell me he had nothing to do with this?" Polydektos pointed the tip of his blade just in front of her nose.

"He is innocent. I love him also, and we were to be a happy little family of three, just us. That's why I could not let him marry Kyra. We are enough for you, Polydektos. Look at you now: you are fitter and leaner than you have been in years. You have a fire in your belly again. I know you love me and desire me," Gala opened her nightshift to reveal her milky white breasts and pert nipples.

"So you killed my family and household, then pretended to be attacked. What did Borilos want of you when he came here?"

"What all frightened men wanted, but I killed him because he was like a loose seam of a hem ready to unravel. It was easy to make out it was he who attacked me. Sadly, my Maenad sisters had to be sacrificed to keep them from possibly exposing me like the priestess of the temple of Dionysos. I did it all for you, Polydektos, to make you the man and warrior you once were. You are a better man than before they died, you are my man, and I love you with all my heart." Gala raised her arms to him, but he just took a step backwards from her.

"Your love for Dionysos and me has driven you mad, Gala. What you have done has closed my heart forever. I will never love again after you join my wife and daughter in death." Polydektos raised his sword high to strike her down, in revenge for all those who had died because of her twisted love for him and Talaemenes.

"Let me at least speak the last words that may come from these lips that made you happy for so long," Gala pleaded.

"Let them be quick, for the souls of the slain wait in Hades to tear the flesh from your bones and feed the scraps to Kerberos."

Gala pulled her thin night clothes from her body, and put her hands to her bare belly. "I am with child, Polydektos. The soothsayer says it is a boy, your son."

"You lie, just to save your own skin."

"I have not bled for two months. See the swell...here." Gala rubbed at a little bump that showed in her thin frame.

"Then you condemn another innocent to death," Polydektos said, and brought down his sword.

Sokrates and Aristaeos held the struggling Talaemenes in a tight grip as above them Gala screamed in pain, and then fell silent. Alkmaion and Darios rushed up the wooden steps just as Polydektos came out onto the balcony holding his sword down at his side. Blood dripped from the blade down onto the balcony.

Talaemenes fainted away in Sokrates's and Aristaeos's arms at the sight of the bloody blade. Polydektos saw Alkmaion and Darios slow their climb up the steps to join him.

"I need your help," Polydektos said, then moved closer to whisper to his friends.

Sokrates watched as Alkmaion and Darios went inside and Polydektos came down to the courtyard. He dropped his blade as he walked over to help carry Talaemenes from the House of Javelins for the last time.

"Where are we taking him?" Aristaeos asked as they passed under the arch and entered the busy streets of Athens.

"Home," Polydektos replied as they headed through the city towards his villa in the shadow of the Akropolis.

EPILOGUE

Hermione tried her best to hurry, while also trying to keep the boiled water from slipping over the sides of the bowl to burn her arms, which would cause her to drop it. She could hear the cries of pain from up in the temple of Demeter as she hurried down the hill to the meagre dwelling where the priestess ate and slept at night. She could see the blue waters of the Aegean Sea hitting the rocks far below. She always loved the simple beauty of the view on the track down from the high temple on the small island of Ios. Yet today, she had no time to take in the view.

The cries suddenly ended as she burst through the door and set the bowl of water down on a table near the blood-stained bed. The high priestess and the four other members of their small temple were around the figure, lying on the bed.

"It's a boy," the High Priestess said, washing the squalling infant in clean, hot water before swaddling it. She handed it over to the woman that had been their guest for the last six months. Hermione let out a small gasp of shock at the woman's appearance. It was the first time she had seen her without her headscarf and veil. The High Priestess gave her a withering look, as she handed the baby into the mutilated hands of the woman who had just given birth.

Even though she was missing all four fingers of her left hand, and the first two fingers of her right, she gathered the baby boy to her naked breast to suckle. She smiled down at the beautiful boy, but with her nose missing it made her look even more grotesque.

She was forbidden to leave this island, on pain of death. She would never hold a bow again or ever be a thing of beauty to a man's eyes, but she had her son and would devote herself to loving him for the rest of her mortal life…hoping that one day, his father would come to claim him as his heir.

ABOUT THE AUTHOR

A lexander Arrowsmith has had a lifelong fascination with Ancient Greece; its myths and its culture. It is a country he loves and has visited on many occasions. He has had eight books published in other genres, but this the first in his series of historical crime novels set in those times.

He lives in Surrey, with his family and two cats.

Alexander is also the author of The Medousa Murders

Curious about other Crossroad Press books?
Stop by our site:
http://store.crossroadpress.com
We offer quality writing
in digital, audio, and print formats.

Enter the code FIRSTBOOK
to get 20% off your first order from our store!
Stop by today!

www.ingramcontent.com/pod-product-compliance
Lightning Source LLC
Chambersburg PA
CBHW060433180626
46817CB00007B/2789